JASON'S FORBIDDEN WOMAN

RAWLINS BOOK 2

DEBORAH WALLACE

Jason's Forbidden Woman: Rawlins Book 2

Published by Deborah Wallace

4/22

ISBN 978-1-951457-02-0

Cover Art by Raymond and Deborah Wallace
Rawlins town by Raymond Wallace

Chapter 1

Jason Ballard couldn't take his eyes off the woman dancing to the tempo of the loud music in the center of the floor under the only spotlight in the club, as if she owned the stage. Just over half the tables were occupied, early enough that the floor wasn't crawling with other dancers.

His eyes returned to her. Never before had he felt so drawn to a woman. Every sway of her hips got his heart pounding. He wanted to run his hands through her long brown hair. The soft glow around her head warned him that she was off limits. Still, he couldn't tear his gaze away. She spun and her dress flared out. It wasn't as short as some of the other women's, but it showed off her long legs and perfect curves.

Mark nudged him. "She's going back to the table with her girlfriend. Go ask her to dance." It figured Mark would notice.

"I can't. She's a—distraction." Oh, man. He almost said she was a virgin. Mark didn't need to know about this particular ability. He'd used his infrared vision a few times on missions with Mark. At least it was useful. But how could he explain a virgin detector?

"She's dancing like she's begging for sex."

"And I have a job to do, so can it." Even if he hadn't come here to meet the woman he was hired to protect, he wouldn't dance with a virgin. And that one was way too tempting.

Mark glanced at his watch. "We still have fifteen minutes left. There's time to get in a couple dances."

Jason glared at him, tamping down his revulsion. Mark had no idea of the risk to Jason. He stared at the entrance, willing his new client to walk through the door, except he didn't know what she looked like. Mark had a picture of Jack's daughter, who would bring her.

In high school, he had needed to talk to his father about his apparent new ability. He still felt the embarrassment thinking about it.

"Um, Dad. There's something really strange happening." This was more embarrassing than the birds and the bees talk, but his father was the only one who could help him.

"What is it, son?"

He glanced at his mother across the room. "Can we talk where Mom can't hear?"

"Kat, Jason and I are going for a walk."

His mother nodded without looking at them, as she flipped a page in her book.

As soon as the front door closed, Reese asked, "So, what's going on, Jason?"

The sun was low in the sky as they hit the sidewalk. They always went to the park, a block away, when Jason needed to talk. Unfortunately, they had to pass the house he'd lived in until he was four. Two families had owned it since then, but he still got a creepy feeling when he looked at it, even though the evil ended with the deaths of his birth parents.

Jason was relieved that the street was empty. "I, um. Can we talk once we get there?" Maybe by then it would be easier.

Reese pointed to their usual park bench and they sat down. "Now, tell me what's bothering you," Reese said.

Jason leaned forward with his elbows on his legs and clenched his hands. "This weird thing is happening. I think it's a new ability. Can we get rid of abilities?" He glanced at his father and back to his hands.

"Except for the dreams, we can choose not to use them."

"Well, so far that's not working. I'm flooded with it!" He hoped his face wasn't as red as it felt. Any normal fifteen year old wouldn't have to deal with this.

"I'm sure we can do something. What is it?"

"Um." He couldn't look at his dad when he said it. He'd known it would be hard to talk about, but it was so much worse than he imagined. His mouth went dry, and he spoke in a hoarse voice. "I can tell if a girl is a virgin. She sort of has this glow around her head and I can feel it in here." He touched his chest, and looked at his father. "And guys, too. Why would anyone need to do that?"

Reese squeezed his shoulder. "I never knew how your biological father chose his...girlfriends, but this must have been it. I don't want to further tarnish your impression of him by explaining his use of that ability."

"No, I think I need to know, so tarnish away." Jason couldn't look at his adopted father as he heard yet another evil thing his own father had done, especially since it was about an ability Jason had inherited. The more he found out about Nathan Proctor, the more he hated the man. He never thought of him as his father. Who would want a murderer's blood running through him?

"Nathan had a new girlfriend every few weeks in high school. While he dated them, each girl acted a little different. I think he had an ability to influence them somehow. Anyway, years later, I found out that each time he took a virgin, he increased his power."

Would Jason be able to influence people? He didn't want to find out. He had inherited his ability to create lightning from Nathan's father. He only knew that because

Reese had told him that's how his mother's mother and brother died. He didn't know which parent he got the infrared vision from. It didn't matter.

Jason stared at his hands. "I'm so glad you're my father and not Nathan. How can anyone be so...evil?"

"He came from a long line of evil men."

That was his biological family. Was some part of the evil in Jason? He didn't feel it, but would he know? He tried extra hard to be good, because he was afraid that if he did anything he wasn't supposed to, it might let the evil take over.

Jason threw his arm around his father and Reese gripped his shoulder. "I'm glad you're my father." Jason leaned back against the bench. "I'm never having sex with a virgin, ever. I don't want to increase my power and risk becoming evil."

Reese put his hand on his son's shoulder and gazed into his eyes. "Jason, I don't think that would happen. You're nothing like Nathan."

Jason turned away. "Just the same, I'm not taking any chances."

Jason shook his head. He hadn't thought about that conversation in years. He automatically chose experienced women. Not that there'd been many.

***

Shauna Meyers sidestepped an exuberant couple with eyes only for each other and bumped into another couple before she reached the table. She sat next to Kristy and took a long drink of her soda. Dancing had been a fun distraction, but it hadn't totally kept her mind off her concern about Nick. She'd run to Kristy when she'd found out the danger she'd placed herself in. She shivered and pushed thoughts of murder away. "That was so much fun. I haven't let myself go like that since dance class in my teens. You should have joined me." She brushed her hair back.

Kristy's short, blonde waves were still perfect. She laughed. "I dropped out of dance class, remember? And I've only gotten passably good at slow dancing, since it's a good way to pick up guys. You had an audience, especially from that table across the floor."

Shauna started to turn and Kristy grabbed her arm. "Don't look!"

Shauna rolled her eyes. "You sound like a teenager." She turned and glanced across the room. "How can you tell? It's too dark over there."

Kristy chuckled. "I'm trained in scoping out attraction."

Shauna shook her head. "You do way too much of this."

"Probably. And you don't do it at all. Maybe we need a happy medium."

Kristy had gone to frat parties while Shauna stayed in their dorm to study or watch movies. If Shauna and Kristy had met on campus, they probably wouldn't have become friends, but they'd been like family since kindergarten.

Kristy checked her phone. "It's almost time I look for our contact." She pulled a paper out of her purse. "Don't you just love this spy stuff?"

Fun for Kristy. It wasn't her life. Shauna couldn't fault her. Kristy found fun in nearly everything. When they were young, they'd made up the wildest stories about Kristy's father and his spy missions. He probably wasn't a spy, but he taught Kristy to shoot when she was ten, and they completed the weirdest puzzles together.

Kristy spun around in her seat, checking faces against her picture. The room was too dark to see features farther than the few tables around them. "Nobody nearby matches. I think we'll have to go for a little walk for a closer look."

Shauna glanced around. The club had gotten crowded since she stopped dancing. “Shouldn’t we wait for them to find us?”

“Nope. I told Dad I’d find them.” She meandered through the crowd, scanning faces as Shauna followed.

Kristy had pushed her father, Mr. Collins, for them to meet in the club. Shauna never did clubs, but Kristy had wanted to try this one out for a while. Shauna was always amazed at how often Kristy got what she wanted. The club was more than an hour from her house, so likely not on Nick’s radar, and he’d never taken her to clubs.

They’d searched half the room when Kristy paused. She glanced up and back to the picture a couple of times. “Found my contact.”

Both women stared across the room. “You’re sure?” That area was still too shadowy.

“Only one way to find out.” Now that she had a target, Kristy picked up speed.

Three more steps and Shauna grabbed her friend’s arm. “Kristy!”

Her eyes were glued to the man with dark curly hair. He smiled at her. She knew that smile, that perfect, straight nose. It was too dark to see his eye color, but she knew they were the darkest blue. His cheeks would have a sexy stubble and his lips could drive her crazy. He was real.

Kristy turned around. “What’s wrong? You look like you’ve seen a ghost.”

She bit her lip. “You know that dream I keep having? The one that seemed like more than a dream?”

Kristy’s eyes lit up. “Yeah. The hot one with your dream man, Jason. I wish I had dreams like that.”

“The guy is sitting at the table you pointed out.” Her eyes flicked over Kristy’s shoulder.

“You mean my contact looks like your dream man?”

She shook her head. "No. The other man. It's him. Not just looks like him. I can't go over there."

She hadn't told Kristy everything about her dreams—how she'd run her hands through his dark curls, got lost in those deep blue eyes, felt that hard body against her. Each dream had been more like a memory than a dream, and she ended up making love with Jason. Oh, yeah, she knew his name. She screamed it as he brought her unimaginable pleasure. Her cheeks flamed at the thought of all the different ways they'd made love. They didn't come from her subconscious. It was no fuzzy dream, and every detail had been seared into her memory.

"You have to, Shauna. He's supposed to protect you. Besides, he won't know what you dreamed about." Kristy tugged free and then seized Shauna's arm. "Come on. We have to do this."

***

Jason watched two women approach the table. No. The virgin he found so attractive couldn't ask him to dance. He'd say yes in a heartbeat to the blonde just so he could get away from the forbidden woman. Or he could honestly say he was working.

The virgin stopped her friend and they had a short conversation. He thought she'd changed her mind, but her friend grabbed her arm and dragged her toward them. Not good.

The women stopped at their table and the blonde studied his friend. "Mark Simmons?"

She was the woman in the photo Mark had shown him, Jack's daughter and friend of his new client. The virgin. Dread filled him. He had to spend nearly every waking hour with a woman he was attracted to who might send him to the dark side.

"That's me."

"I'm Kristy Collins. This is my friend, Shauna Meyers."

Mark straightened and smoothly transitioned from pleasure to business. "You don't look like your father. This is my friend, Jason Ballard, who I've enlisted to help us."

Kristy sucked in a breath and whipped her wide-eyed expression around to Shauna. Shauna shrugged, clenched her hands on the back of a chair, eyes downcast. Then Kristy squinted at him. Something strange was going on.

Mark cleared his throat. "Have a seat, ladies."

Mark sat across from Jason at the round table, so Kristy worked her way to the other side and sat between them. Jason noticed how Shauna scooted her chair closer to his friend.

Mark leaned in. "I pulled Jason in because he's not on the team anymore. I thought it would make it harder for anyone to track Shauna." He glanced at Kristy. "He knows everything your father told me. I've let Jason plan how to hide her. I figured, the less we know, the safer Shauna will be."

This was his first job on his own, without the team. He was done being a civilian dropped behind enemy lines, not able to share with his family what he did for work and who he worked for. The last job had gotten so totally screwed up with misinformation that one team member had died, and Jason had barely made it out. Fortunately for him, Mark had gotten wind of it and rescued the rest of them.

"There's no way I can contact her once she's in hiding?" asked Kristy. "How will I know she's okay?"

Mark nodded toward Jason. "Jason will email me weekly reports. I'll pass on what he has to say to your father. If Jason feels they've been compromised, we've got an emergency safe house set up."

Shauna dropped her shoulders. "All this for me, and I don't even know enough to testify."

Kristy clasped Shauna's hand. "Yeah, but you know enough to get yourself killed, unless you want to marry him."

Shauna shivered. "No, thanks. I can't believe Nick fooled me."

Jason didn't have the whole story, except that Shauna had been engaged to and working for some sleaze who had probably killed someone. At least she'd found out before she married him.

Jason glanced at his watch. "We have a long trip ahead of us. We really have to get on the road."

Shauna flinched, knocking over Mark's glass. His chair fell over as he jumped up and out of the way with a chuckle. Jason would have laughed at Mark's quick response, but he was more concerned with how nervous Shauna seemed about going with him.

"Oh, Mark. I'm so sorry." Shauna covered her mouth, her eyes wide.

"It's fine, not a drop got on me." He waved down his pants. "I think it's time we all got out of here anyway. Let's pair off."

He stepped to Kristy's side and took her hand. She held it willingly. Jason stepped closer to Shauna, but she retreated a step.

"Shauna," Kristy stage whispered, "we're trying not to look suspicious."

Shauna muttered. "Not like spilling a drink didn't draw attention." She held her hand out to Jason.

He took her trembling hand. He hoped she'd be comfortable with him soon, considering they'd be spending a lot of time together.

They stepped into the night. A couple brushed past as

Jason scanned the parking lot. It would have been a whole lot better if they'd met up in a parking lot somewhere else instead of in a crowded club. Jack had given in to his spoiled daughter's wishes. The men transferred Shauna's two suitcases to the back of Jason's SUV, which happened to be parked three cars down from Kristy's car.

Kristy closed her trunk and Shauna threw her arms around her friend. "Thank you for helping me. I wish I wasn't so nervous about Jason."

Jason was sure he wasn't meant to hear that. He had no clue why Shauna would be nervous. Sure, she was about to drive off with a stranger, but he was her bodyguard, approved by her friend's father. It seemed like there was more to it. He'd have to work to make her at ease. He opened the passenger door, trying to subtly hurry them along.

Kristy gave Shauna a quick squeeze. "My father trusts Mark wholeheartedly, so if Mark trusts Jason, then you can trust him."

"Maybe I don't trust myself. Look how wrong I was about Nick."

"I think you should pretend you're in those dreams and see where it leads you." She leaned back and smiled impishly.

"Kristy!"

Kristy chuckled as Shauna walked toward Jason.

What had Kristy meant about pretending to be in a dream? Jason cleared his throat, feigning he hadn't heard every word. "You ready?"

She took a deep breath and nodded. Giving him a wide berth, she slipped into the seat. Had the guy she'd been engaged to hurt her?

Jason was a bit nervous himself. Hopefully, Shauna wasn't more temptation than he could handle.

He held out his hand. "Give me your cell phone."

She glanced at his hand, then at his face. "I left it at my house when I ran. I remembered something about people being able to track you by your phone."

"Good. You haven't had it for a few days." He closed her door.

She stared out the side window as he got into the driver's seat. He looked past her and saw that her friend and Mark were heading back into the club. He shook his head. Mark could pick up girls in any situation.

He reached in front of her and Shauna shrank into her seat as he opened the glove compartment and withdrew his gun, tucking it into the holster under his jacket. The gun seemed to frighten her.

"Wouldn't you expect your bodyguard to have a weapon?"

She shrugged. "I hadn't thought about it." She turned her face to the window.

They'd traveled in silence for over an hour, leaving city lights well behind them. There was a steady, light stream of cars on the highway, easy enough to see if they had a tail.

Shauna startled him when she broke the silence. "Where are we going?"

Jason glanced at her and back to the road. "We're stopping in Charlotte for the night. We should get there a little after midnight." It was an incomplete answer, and he knew that wasn't what she was asking. He was surprised when she didn't rephrase her question.

Shauna pulled off her jacket, rolled it into ball and tucked it under her head against the door. It wasn't long before she relaxed into sleep. Relieved, he reviewed his plans for the trip to Rawlins, but his thoughts returned to Shauna.

She looked so young and vulnerable as she slept. They

hadn't said more than a few sentences to each other, but even without looking at her, he could feel her near him. Something about her reached out to him, starting when he saw her on the dance floor. In a way, he was almost as afraid of her as she was of him. At least, what being attracted to her could do to him. He'd have to behave very professionally with her, keep his distance. In only a few weeks, she'd be out of his life. He could handle that.

***

Jason pulled into the hotel's parking lot and found a space a short distance from the door. He breathed out a sigh of relief. He hated hours of night driving.

He spoke just above a whisper. "Shauna. We're here." She didn't stir. He repeated it louder. The third time, he touched her shoulder. She jerked and gasped.

"Sorry. You weren't waking up."

She nodded. "All this worry about Nick has exhausted me." She rubbed her eyes and yawned. She must have trusted him enough to keep her safe from Nick, enough that she could fall asleep beside him.

She slipped her jacket on, and picked up her purse, then met him at the back of the car.

"You should have waited for me to get your door. Given me a chance to make sure it was safe."

Her eyes widened. "Oh. Sorry. I didn't think of that." Sleep was gone from her face now as her gaze darted around the parking lot.

He opened the hatch. "Can we bring in only one of your bags?"

"Yes, the smaller bag is fine."

She stepped forward, reaching for it at the same time he did and they brushed hands. She jumped back. Did she feel the surge of warmth he felt? Even through her jacket, her heat touched him. It was like her core wanted to entwine with his. Closing his eyes for a few seconds, he worked to regain control. What was it about this woman?

He pulled out her bag and his duffle, closed the trunk and stalked toward the building. Bushes bordered the walk leading to the double glass doors. Shauna's footsteps echoed in the quiet behind him as they entered the lobby. She stood several feet away while he registered, then followed him into the elevator. They stepped out on the fourth floor and strolled down the hall. He unlocked her door, flipped the light on and twisted the lock on her side of the connecting door between their rooms. He set her bag on the low dresser and had to drag his eyes away from the king size bed.

Once in his own room, a mirror to hers, he dropped his duffle on the dresser, turned the second lock on the shared door, and opened it, peeking into her room. "We'll leave the door ajar so I can make sure you're safe."

She nodded. "Good night," she said, and headed to the bathroom with her night clothes.

Jason had never met a woman who talked as little as she did. He used the bathroom in his room then settled into bed. Minutes later, bedding rustled in the other room. Hopefully she'd be more at ease after a good night's sleep.

He started to drift off when a noise at the door brought him fully awake. He bolted up and grabbed his gun from under the pillow.

A man in the hallway laughed. "Charlie, you've got the wrong door," a woman said. The voices faded down the hallway.

He fell back on the bed, shoved his gun back under the pillow and willed himself to relax. His last thoughts were of watching Shauna on the dance floor at the club.

Chapter 2

Shauna settled under the covers. Since she'd already gotten some sleep, she wasn't tired enough now. She flipped onto her side, facing the connecting door. Bedding rustled in the other room.

She hadn't pushed Jason about their final destination, and now wished she had. Sort of. She wanted to know, but that would have meant looking at him and hearing his voice, reminding her of those embarrassing dreams. She couldn't think about them with the object of her passion sitting next to her.

For the umpteenth time, she reminded herself that Kristy's dad trusted Jason, so she was safe with him. It had taken a while for Kristy's father to convince Shauna to disappear with a stranger. It wasn't safe to be anywhere near her ex-fiancé, and she'd planned to take off on her own to hide. He'd hinted that there were questionable activities happening around Nick and convinced her that he had shady resources she couldn't fight. She needed a professional to protect her. He couldn't give names, but said this guy protected politicians and heads of industry. She was still a little nervous about it, but he must be one of the best if Mr. Collins, some kind of ex-government agent, trusted him.

Jason had gotten them separate rooms tonight. He could have gotten one and easily convinced her that they needed to share a room to keep her safe. He seemed like a professional she could trust. A professional who worked out. A professional with confidence who she remembered kissing and...No! Just a dream.

Change of topic. Better yet, blank her mind and go to sleep. She punched her pillow and dropped her head back down.

All this running and hiding because of Nick. How could she have gotten herself into so much trouble? He probably didn't realize why she'd run. She hoped he'd forget about her. She'd left that giant engagement ring sitting on her office desk. He wouldn't have to come after her for that. He could move on with his life. Like she was doing. Sort of.

She couldn't believe that she'd even agreed to marry him. He'd been kind to her and helped her through so much, but she didn't love him. Looking back at his proposal, she remembered her surprise. She'd only said yes because she was grateful for everything he'd done. She couldn't base a marriage on that. And she certainly couldn't get married to a man after having steamy sex in her dreams with another man. It was almost like being unfaithful.

Even without that, she probably would have left Nick eventually. Initially, he was so nice to her, but later, she saw how badly he treated other people. He must have grown more certain of her and let his real personality show. Or he got tired of hiding it. He snapped at waitresses over the littlest things. Nick's receptionist, Missy, had seemed timid, but after witnessing his screaming fit over a minor error, she realized that Missy was probably afraid of him. Shauna couldn't imagine working for someone who treated her like that. It bothered her and when she'd discovered the mistake the other accountant had made, she wanted to fix it before Nick found out. So, in saving the accountant, she'd saved herself. How long would it have been before he started yelling at her or worse? This line of thought wasn't going to help her sleep, but when she let her mind drift, it settled on the man in the bed next door. All alone, like she was, just steps away.

She flipped over again and let out a long breath and then another, willing herself to relax. She brought up a memory about a vacation she'd taken with her father and smiled, finally unwound enough to sleep.

***

Jason walked into the bedroom and stopped breathing. She'd come to him, ready for the next step. Shauna opened her golden-brown eyes and smiled up at him. He hadn't expected to find her here. He closed the door and slowly walked toward the bed, untied his robe and let it slide off his shoulders. She licked her lips. He needed to taste them. She threw back the covers and his eyes traveled down her body as she scooted over to make room for him. Her breath quickened and her nipples stiffened under her nightshirt. He leaned over and kissed her before sliding in beside her.

Jason was going to make this special for her. She trusted him, and he wouldn't let her down. He pulled her close as his lips found hers again, and skimmed his hand down her side. He'd never wanted a woman as much as he wanted and needed her. He buried his face in her neck as a light flower fragrance tantalized him. His hand slipped under her shirt and her smooth skin excited him more. He pulled at her plain white panties, she lifted and he slid them off, then trailed his hand up her smooth leg.

She trembled.

Unsure if it was excitement or a bit of fear, he'd have to take it slow. With gentle movements, he slid his hand over her slim hip, dipped at her waist and over her warm ribs. He cupped his target, and she gasped, but she didn't stop him, so he flicked his thumb over her hardened nipple, eliciting a moan. It was clear she wasn't afraid. With one thought, they pulled her shirt over her head. Her naked breasts pressed against his chest— the best aphrodisiac.

He brushed his hand lower, knowing her shiver was anticipation. Nothing mattered as much as her pleasure. His fingers found her moist heat and she moaned, moving against him.

A bang against the wall beside Jason's head startled him awake. His hand automatically snaked under the pillow, gripping his gun. A curse next door let him know it was a noisy neighbor. He relaxed, and stifled a groan, as the vision of a naked Shauna came to him. Reality flooded back. Shauna wasn't in his bed, but on the other side of a partially open door at the hotel. That was the most intense sex he'd never had. It had seemed so real. His body was satiated but ached to have her again. He knew how she tasted, how smooth her skin was, how she'd surrounded him with her warmth. This time he couldn't stop a groan.

"Jason, are you okay?" Her voice was deeper, sexier, as if from just awakening. The sheets rustled in the other room as if Shauna had pulled back the covers to invite him into bed. His frustration kept him silent.

"Jason?" Her voice was just on the other side of the door.

"I'm all right." If she came in now, as he was fresh from a dream where he learned so many ways to please her, and his body craved to hold her again, he'd probably scare her half to death. She'd need a bodyguard from her bodyguard. He closed his eyes and shook his head before reading the bedside clock. Five in the morning. Much earlier than he usually got up. "Since we're both awake, why don't we get on the road?" He knew he wouldn't get back to sleep.

"Um, okay."

"Can you be ready in twenty?" Fifteen minutes of cold shower and five to get dressed.

"Yes."

Jason smiled. Beautiful without primping. "Call out when you're ready."

The water had no time to warm before he stepped into the tub. Images from his dream overwhelmed him, and he could almost feel Shauna stepping into the shower behind him. If she did, he'd pull her close and kiss her. His soap lathered hands would slide down her body, paying special attention to the swell of her breasts. He pushed the thoughts away and took deep breaths, leaned his head against the wall and talked himself down.

He'd take it as a warning dream, like the couple of times he'd had dreams that felt real before a mission. Those had saved his life. Maybe this would save his life as he knew it. There was no way it was going to happen. Besides her being a virgin, they were headed to his parents' house, and he wouldn't be able to get into Shauna's bed anyway. And, maybe it wasn't a precognitive dream. It could have just been his imagination taking flight because he'd watched Shauna dance. What normal man wouldn't have fantasies about that?

Shower finished, he quickly dried and dressed.

Shauna called out, "Are you ready?"

At least she wasn't standing next to the door this time.

"Give me another minute." He stuffed clothes in his bag and ran his hand through his still damp hair. He slipped his shoes on and with a sigh, headed for the connecting door.

***

Shauna leaned back against the headboard, her packed bag beside her. Although she'd gotten only four hours of sleep at the hotel and two in the car, she felt more refreshed than most mornings. She'd slept surprisingly well, considering the object of a few sexy dreams was on the other side of a partially open door. She'd expected dream overload, but was pleasantly surprised to waken with no remembrance of one. Hopefully, now that they'd met, she wouldn't have any more.

She had the first dream two nights after she'd gotten engaged to Nick. She'd found it more confusing than anything. Then a few nights later, she'd had another. It was like her subconscious was telling her that Nick wasn't the man for her.

Shauna still couldn't figure out how the man in her dreams, a man she'd never met, was real. They had done things she'd never imagined doing, not in real life. She'd never known that people did some of those things. Didn't dreams come from a person's own experiences?

The door swung open, and Jason stepped into the room, the strap of his bag slung over his shoulder. His wet hair was a little darker brown and less curly. His dark blue eyes weren't quite the same as in the dreams. They'd almost glowed with happiness, but now, the muscles around them were a little pinched, maybe worried

He approached and she straightened away from the headboard, not totally comfortable sitting on a bed with him so near. She'd been there, done that in a dream. Shauna looked down at her hands as she twined them in her lap.

Jason stepped so close, she could feel his heat through their jeans as he picked up her bag. For a second, she thought he was going to kiss her. Her heart kicked up. He smelled like in her dreams. She knew how he would taste.

"You ready?"

Ready for what? A kiss? She looked up at him. No, that wasn't it. She held her breath and willed her heart to slow.

She nodded but couldn't stand because he was too close. They might make physical contact. Maybe that was what he wanted. His closeness and scent made her crave his touch, but her overwhelming lust scared her. Officially, they met nine hours ago, but her body knew every inch of his.

He took a step away from her, and she pushed off the bed, following him out the door.

***

An hour down the road, after Jason made sure they weren't followed, they stopped at *Mel and Harriet's Diner*. He chose a seat where he could watch the door, which put Shauna's back to most of the room.

The bustling waitress poured coffee before he'd asked, then was back with their pancakes and sausages in a few minutes. Shauna poured syrup over her pancakes, looked up at him and frowned. She must have felt his eyes on her. He hoped she couldn't read his mind since she'd catch him wondering if she really had a tiny mole just above her left breast. In his dream, he kissed it. He glanced toward the window, scanning people coming in, checking cars for anyone still sitting in them.

Jason took a sip of his black coffee. "You don't talk much."

Shauna shrugged. "I'm an accountant. I'm used to working alone."

"We're not working."

Her eyebrows rose. "You are."

"You know what I mean." He should let it go. It was best if she was just a job and they didn't talk. He didn't want them to become friends because it risked becoming more.

She sighed. "I don't get out much. Kristy moved two hours away from me, so I don't see her often. The last few years before my father died, he worked too much. Sometimes, it was days before I saw him. I got used to doing things by myself."

"Okay. Just so long as it's not me. I'm here to protect you. I don't want you to be afraid of me."

"I'm not exactly afraid of you." She ducked her head and took a bite of the pancake that she'd been shredding.

Topic closed. What did "exactly" mean? Jason didn't find it reassuring.

***

Jason stopped for gas and got back on the highway after they ate. Still no tail. For a short time, he tried to make conversation, but it was hard when the only responses were one or two syllables. The quiet was getting to him, so he turned on the radio. He didn't recognize the soft voice of the woman who sang.

Moments later, Shauna's hand shot out and silenced the song. Jason's eyebrows shot up. She was as nervous as a chipmunk who'd come across a snake. He wished he hadn't thought of that, because it reminded him of the serpent in the Garden of Eden, which reminded him of evil, which reminded him that he could become that evil serpent because of the woman beside him.

"You don't like music?"

She bit her lip. "Um. Maybe just that song." She stared out the window, which didn't hide the dark pink in her cheek.

The lyrics played through his head. *Dreams, you're in my dreams*. She'd been in his dream which made him think that she had a similar one. He'd forgotten until now that her friend had said something about following through on a dream. He got hot just thinking about her having the same sexy dream as him. That could be scary for a virgin. No wonder she was so nervous around him. Maybe he full of himself thinking she'd dreamed about him. She could have had nightmares about her ex-fiancé. Except Kristy wouldn't tell her to follow through with that.

"Do you have a problem with dreams or nightmares?"

"I'd rather not talk about it."

Yeah, it was a dream about him. He smiled a little, but it disappeared a second later when he reminded himself that he couldn't have her. Now he needed to take both their minds off those dreams.

"So, tell me how you got involved with your ex."

The silence lasted so long that Jason was sure she wouldn't talk about it.

Shauna shifted in her seat. He tipped his head to hear her low voice better. "I'd seen Nick a few times over the years. My father had been his accountant for five or six years before Dad died in a car accident a little over a year ago. Suddenly, Nick was always there to help me. He arranged Dad's funeral, he checked up on me, he made sure I had everything I needed." Her hands twisted together and she rubbed her ring finger. "A few months after Dad's death, Nick asked me out. I felt obligated after everything he'd done for me. And then about six months ago, the company I worked for made job cuts and let me go. Nick asked if I wanted to be a junior accountant for him. The guy he'd hired to replace Dad wasn't as efficient, and the books were falling behind. I agreed."

"And then you got engaged," Jason added to keep her talking. He'd only heard through Mark that the guy was a sleaze. He wanted a fuller picture of how badly this guy wanted Shauna.

"Yeah, well, we were only engaged for about a week."

"What happened to make you run?" He'd been filled in on it, but wanted to hear it from her. He felt her eyes on him and glanced her way, catching the fear in her eyes. "You're safe with me."

She bit her lip.

"So, what happened?" he prompted.

"I stayed late one night to fix something the accountant messed up. Nick must not have realized I was still there. Both our doors were open, so I could hear when someone walked into his office. Nick said, 'Did you take care of him like I asked?' And the guy said, 'He won't be a problem.' Nick asked, 'What did you do with it?' And the guy said, 'Dumped it in the river.' At the time, I thought the guy dumped an object in the river, like a gun or cell phone. Two days later, the body of Terrence Fredrick was found floating in the river. They estimated it had been there for two days." She shivered. "It clicked. I had no doubt he was the 'it' dumped in the river. That's when I ran. I couldn't look at Nick again without giving away that I knew something."

Without thinking, Jason touched her arm. She must have been too distracted to flinch. He wanted to draw her in and kiss her, but instead, moved his hand back to the steering wheel. "I'm sorry you had to go through that."

"Thanks. I hope it's over. He might not even know why I ran."

"How did all this happen?" He waved between them. What she knew was only a guess. The police wouldn't listen to her. Her fiancé wouldn't have suspected anything since they never said anything really incriminating. Maybe she knew more than she told him.

"This elaborate escape thing?" At his nod, she continued. "I guess I know the right people. Kristy and I met our first day of kindergarten. We've been best friends ever since. Her father was, I don't know, in some kind of government security. When he'd go away for weeks at a time, Kristy and I used to make up these fantastic stories about spy missions he was on. Anyway, I packed my bags and ran to Kristy. She called her dad. He did some checking and said Nick was being investigated and I wasn't safe anywhere near him."

There must have been a whole hell of a lot more that Jack hadn't told Shauna. He'd have to get it out of Mark.

She continued. "He called Mark, who he said owed him. They worked this out. Why are you the one Mark chose?"

He smiled. "Same reason. Mark owed Jack Collins for saving his life. I owed Mark for saving mine."

Her eyes widened. "You mean like, you'd be dead if it wasn't for Mark?"

"Yeah. He's a good guy to have at your back."

"What happened?"

"Things got screwed up that shouldn't have." It wasn't something he wanted to think about right now. Almost dying at twenty-five gave him a new perspective on mortality and how important family was.

"Where are we going?"

"To a little town called Rawlins, Massachusetts."

"Why there?"

"It's my hometown. Because of…that little thing that happened that I owe Mark for, I quit the team and I'm moving back to Rawlins to open a security company there." His mother had been ecstatic when he'd told her he was moving back to town. She'd been surprised that he'd already accepted his first job and was bringing Shauna with him. She didn't mind that they would pretend that he and Shauna were a couple. He just had to find a way to tell his skittish client about the ploy.

"My sister, Jamie, is at school in Boston, but my brother, Tony, and sister, Abby, are at home. He's nineteen and she's sixteen. We're going to let them think that you're my girlfriend, but my parents know the truth."

Her eyes widened. "Girlfriend?"

He nodded. "The fewer people who know the real reason you're there, the better."

She bit her lip and let out a breath. "All right. I guess I understand."

"And we need to change your name."

"I thought of that already. Can I keep Shauna? I can use my grandmother's maiden name for my last name. It's Williams."

"Williams is good. It's fairly common. But Shauna has to go."

Her eyebrows squinched. "But I like my name. I'll feel like I'm not me without it."

Jason laughed. "Choose another name."

"Marie? It's my middle name and also my grandmother's name."

"Nick may know your middle name."

She pursed her lips. "No. Only Kristy knows it."

"It would be easy enough for him to find out. How about Rachel?"

She sighed. "All right."

He grinned. Nice to meet you Rachel Williams." Something niggled about Marie Williams, but they hadn't chosen it, so it didn't matter.

Chapter 3

Shauna's gaze swept from one side of the street to the other, as they drove slowly down a street with stately old homes on the left and a park opposite. Jason pulled into the circular drive of a huge colonial-style house, light gray with darker gray shutters.

"This is your parent's house?" Shauna had expected a modest two-story and they'd have to park on the street. The porch spanned the full length of the front with stately white columns and railings. It must have a lot of rooms. She fell in love with it. The only times she'd been in a house like this was when she paid admission. Now she got to stay in one.

"Eight generations of Rawlinses have lived here," he said, pride in his voice.

Shauna gave him a puzzled look. "But your last name is Ballard."

"Well, my mom is a Rawlins. So, I guess, technically, it's seven generations of Rawlinses and one of Ballards. The land it sits on has been in the Rawlins family since 1693."

"Wow. To trace your family back that far is amazing. I don't know anything beyond my grandparents." She narrowed her eyes. "Wait. Your mom is a Rawlins, like the town?"

His smile showed his pride. "Yes. Her family was among the founders. Her ancestor planned his family's escape from Salem."

"Escape? They fled because they were accused of being witches?" Running from those accusations would have been worse than her having to run from Nick. Maybe not, since in both cases they could end up dead.

"No. They left after the hysteria. They were afraid it would start again." His door opened. "Are you ready to go in?"

He was changing the subject. He seemed to know more Salem history than most people, but he was holding something back.

"It didn't start again," she said. "Why would they think that?"

"It was tough times back then. Any little thing could have set it off again. You ready?"

She put her hand over her stomach. "Why do I have butterflies like I'm meeting a guy's parents?"

Jason laughed. "Because you're meeting a guy's parents?"

"You know what I mean."

"You're supposed to be pretending you're my girlfriend. It's good you're really getting into the part. Come on. Let's go in." They retrieved their bags and climbed the steps. Jason opened the door, adorned with a beautiful stained glass peacock for a window, and allowed Shauna to enter first. He set the bags down, and a small, attractive, older woman ran toward them.

"Jason!" Her arms flew around him.

"Mom." He laughed and lifted her off the floor. "You act like you haven't seen me in years. It's only been two months."

"I know. But you're back for good now." After she kissed his cheek, she released him and stepped back, tipping her head at Shauna. "And this is Shauna."

The woman gave her a quick hug. "I'm Kathleen. It's nice to meet you."

Something felt off, as if Shauna really was meeting her

boyfriend's parents for the first time. She raised a brow at Jason. He told her he'd already talked to his mother about this. His mom and dad knew he was hired to protect her, but the rest of his family would think she was a friend, probably a girlfriend.

"Mom, we're going to call Shauna 'Rachel' to help hide her."

Shauna hoped that put things in perspective.

"Since I'm not used to you being Shauna yet, I'm sure I won't have a problem with it."

"It's nice meeting you, Kathleen. Thank you for letting me stay here."

"You're very welcome." Kathleen gave her son another hug. "Jason, why don't you show Rachel to Jamie's room? Dinner should be ready in a half hour."

Kathleen headed back to the kitchen. Shauna took a deep breath and the aroma of pot roast made her stomach growl.

Jason picked up the bags. "Follow me."

"This is a beautiful railing." She ran her hand along the banister as they ascended. There were two alternating styles of balusters, one twisted, and the other with vertical cuts down the length. At the top of the stairs, the rail curved to the left. If this was anything to go by, the rest of the house would be spectacular. It was so much better than a museum house tour.

He stopped beside the first door on the left. "This is my room." He dropped his bag in front of the door. "Across the hall is my brother, Tony's room." Pointing to the end of the hall, he said, "My parents' room and the last door on the right is the bathroom." He took a few steps to the room next to his and faced the door on the opposite side of the hall. "That's Abby's room, which used to be mine. I traded with her when I went to college so she could have the private bath."

He tapped his knuckle on the door behind him. "And this is Jamie's room. She's away at college." He pushed the door open and allowed her to step in ahead of him.

Two steps into the room, she stopped. It was much larger than it appeared in her dream. Her eyes darted around, taking in all the familiar antique furniture, decor and objects. The carved doors on the wardrobe matched the carving on the headboard and the drawers in the dresser. Even the heart-shaped wooden box on the dresser had been in her dream.

She trembled. It was scary enough that the man in her dreams was real. The place was real, too. Images of naked bodies flashed through her head like a video set to fast forward.

"Oh. My. God." She turned to flee and ran into Jason. His warm hands grabbed her upper arms. "Let me pass. I can't stay in this room." Even to her own ears, there was unreasonable panic in her voice.

He wrinkled his brow. "Are you all right?"

She shook her head and tugged away from his hold, her chest heaving.

"Let's go down to the library."

"Let's go." Fine by her. She'd only been in the house five minutes and needed to get away. Shauna followed Jason down the stairs, and paused when he turned away from the front door. "The library?"

Jason pointed to the back of the house. "It's back there."

She followed him to what could only be called a library with walls of built-in bookcases.

He sat her on a couch in front of the fireplace. "I'll get you a drink." He headed somewhere behind her and was back in seconds, handing her a glass. "Here, drink this."

She tipped it up to her lips and took several swallows. It burned a path down her throat and wound around in her stomach. "What is it?"

"Brandy."

The brandy or maybe being away from that room had an effect. She calmed, but fear still nipped her gut. She gazed up at him. "I don't know what's happening."

"I know. Let me go talk to my mom, and then I'll try to help you figure it out."

She leaned back and frowned. "You know what?" He couldn't know about her dream.

He shook his head. "I'll be back in a couple minutes."

Shauna grabbed his arm. "No. What do you know?"

He patted her hand and removed it from his arm. "We'll talk in a few minutes."

After he left, she couldn't stay seated and paced from one end of the long room to the other. Dark shelves covered most of the walls. She ran her hand along one shelf. Some of the books looked so ancient she was afraid to touch them. She smiled at a bottom shelf with paperback romance novels, and wondered if they belonged to Kathleen or one of her daughters.

A large table surrounded by chairs sat at the far end as if it was in a public library. She paused at a window. In the slanting light of late day, the trees at the back of the large yard threw long shadows. She touched the squishy window seat cushion. Maybe she'd have a chance to curl up there during her short stay. Overstuffed chairs were artfully arranged throughout the room.

She glanced toward the door. Jason hadn't returned yet. If she'd met him without the dream, she might be attracted to him, although she'd never been interested enough in any guy to go out. The dream seemed to foster an attraction that was more than she could handle. It would have been better to meet at a coffee shop or party. Instead, the first man she was attracted to, she had first got to know his gorgeous body and then meet him.

She stopped in front of a huge framed family tree. No, seven family trees. The heading read *Rawlins Founders*. Scanning across the bottom, she found Kathleen Rawlins joined with Reese Ballard. Apparently, he was descended from one of the original Rawlins families, too. Many of their ancestors had married people without family connections. Under their names was listed their children, Anthony and Abigail. That couldn't be right. Where were Jason and Jamie? Looking further, she found Jason Proctor (Ballard) and Jamie Proctor (Ballard). Their parents' date of death would have made Jason about four at the time. How sad. Since Jason called Kathleen, Mom, they must have adopted the children. He was so fortunate to have found a loving home.

She continued to check more family trees and froze when she found 'Marie Williams.' It couldn't be, but the date of birth was her grandmother's. It didn't show a date of death, but they wouldn't have known when she died since her grandmother had cut off all ties with her family. Shauna had given up on getting information out of her grandmother about her parents.

Shauna's knees trembled. She was part of this town. Somehow, she had ended up here and found out within an hour of arriving that her grandmother grew up in Rawlins. Maybe that explained the dreams about Jason. She stared at her grandmother's name, everything a jumble in her head. She touched a finger to the glass. It was cooler than she expected. The chill traveled up her arm as the room grew dim and her thoughts twisted and turned. Blackness overtook her.

***

"Mom, there's something strange going on with Sh–Rachel."

Kathleen shoved plates at him which he automatically took.

"I think she had a dream about me before we met. She seemed really nervous around me. Then last night I had a dream about her. Of course, it could have been because we met, but I think she had the same dream."

She lifted an eyebrow. "Why don't you ask her? That seems simple enough."

"No, it's not simple. It's not like the dream you and Dad shared. Yours was, um, sweet. If hers was like mine, it was x-rated. I don't think she'll want to talk about that to the man she barely met who—participated."

One corner of her mouth tipped up for a moment. "I see your point. Well, don't talk to her about it until she's more comfortable with you."

"I have to. I took her up to Jamie's room, and she practically had a nervous breakdown. I hadn't noticed during my dream that it was the room we…" He looked down at the plates in his hands. He wouldn't have said anything about this to his mother if it had been real. It was embarrassing enough being a dream.

"Switch rooms with her."

He smiled. It might not help long-term, but that should ease Shauna's fears. "Why didn't I think of that? Thanks, Mom."

"Because you're too tied in knots to think. Now let's get the table set. Your Dad and Tony should be home soon."

Picking up a tray with glasses, silverware and napkins, she followed him. After setting the second plate on the table in front of a chair, Jason heard a thud. He looked at his mother and set down the stack of plates with a clatter and raced to the library.

He scanned the room and found Shauna crumpled in a heap. He was by her side in seconds and lifted her up, carried her to the couch and gently laid her down. He lightly rubbed the back of his fingers repeatedly down her cheek.

"Shauna, wake up. Shauna. Shauna."

Her eyes opened and she blinked a few times. She focused on him and frowned. When she reached up and touched his cheek, he realized that he was still touching hers and pulled his hand away.

"What happened?" Her voice was barely above a whisper.

"I was going to ask you that. Don't you remember? You passed out."

Her eyes closed.

"Shauna!" What could have happened to her? Some kind of protector he was.

"Jason, I'm Rachel." Her eyes flicked behind him, where he felt his mother's presence.

It would be horrible if she really believed that was her name and not Shauna? No. He saw her confusion clearing.

He held her hand. "I remember. Do you know why you fainted?"

She tried to sit up, but he pressed a hand to her shoulder. "Jason, I'm okay now. Let me up."

He helped her sit. "So, what happened?" He spotted her glass on the table next to them and picked it up. "Here, I think you need more."

She took the glass and sipped. "I started pacing." She glanced up at him and then into her glass, and took a sip. "I saw the family tree and thought I'd find your name. Is your name really Proctor?"

"No!" he exploded. He hated the name, and everything attached to it.

A flash of fear crossed her face and she pushed herself

back into the couch.

She'd just fainted. He shouldn't be frightening her. In a quieter voice, he said, "My birth parents died when I was four. Kathleen and Reese adopted Jamie and me. They are my parents."

She gave him a quizzical look, but thankfully, let it pass and surprised him by taking his hand.

"I read more names." She squeezed his hand. "I…I found my grandmother's name."

"Marie Williams?"

She nodded as Kathleen gasped behind him.

He frowned. That's why he'd been uneasy when she mentioned that name. "It's not a rare name. It could be someone else." She couldn't have been drawn back to Rawlins like his mother. It was too scary to think that Rawlins was calling back its own.

"The birth date is hers. I can't believe my grandmother is from this town, too. I was staring at her name when everything blacked out. I don't know why I fainted."

Kathleen stepped closer and squeezed Jason's shoulder. "I believe you have some second cousins. I could introduce you to them."

Shauna smiled. "I have family again."

She looked pleased. She'd been so sad when she'd talked about her father. Even when Jason was away from his family, he knew they were there for him, but she had no one. And he had to dash her hopes. "Mom, not until Shauna's safe. We can't introduce her by her real name."

Shauna's shoulders slumped.

Footsteps galloped down the stairs. "Mom, is dinner ready yet?" They all turned at Abby's voice.

"Almost, Abby. Come on in." Abigail's hair was chin length was light brown. The last he'd seen her, it had been almost to her waist.

Jason stood up. "Hey, Abby." He opened his arms and a grin spread across her face as she launched herself into them.

"Mom didn't tell me you were coming. How long are you going to be here?" Her hold nearly choked him.

"For. Ev-er." He tickled her ribs and she squealed.

Abby released him and locked her eyes on Shauna.

"Abby, meet Jason's friend, Rachel," Kathleen said.

Shauna fluttered her fingers. "Hi, Abby."

"Hi, Rachel." She raised an eyebrow to Jason and mouthed, "Girlfriend?"

Jason lifted a shoulder. He'd let her draw her own conclusions.

***

So that's what it's like to have siblings. Shauna had always wanted a brother or sister, but after her mother left when she was seven, it had been only Dad and her. And Grandma. They'd had dinner with her every other Thursday until her death when Shauna was sixteen. They used to play board games and go for walks. Grandma was always interested in Shauna's hobbies, friends and school work. She missed their conversations. Maybe if her grandmother had told them about their family, Shauna would have known these cousins that Kathleen mentioned.

The front door opened and a blond haired man walked in with another man who was almost a replica, but younger. They had the same pale blue eyes, straight nose and broad shoulders.

"Dad, Tony. I want you to meet my friend, Rachel." Jason's words drew the others into the library.

Shauna's senses had returned to normal and stood. Jason frowned at her, and she shrugged. He probably thought she might faint again. He was overreacting. It wasn't as if he should be that concerned about her. They hadn't even known each other twenty-four hours.

With introductions completed, they gravitated to the dining room. Jason set the plates out as Kathleen and Abby each brought in two dishes. Shauna enjoyed watching them work together.

The roast looked as delicious as it smelled. The mashed potatoes were piled high, steam rose from a gravy boat and the carrots were coated in melted butter.

Jason hovered at the doorway. "Mom, do you need help with anything else?"

"This was the last. Let's sit down."

Jason kissed the top of his mom's head. "Thanks for making my favorite meal."

She patted his chest. "It's a celebration."

Shauna waited to see where everyone sat before choosing a seat. Jason surprised her when he took her hand and escorted her to the chair next to him. Touching him didn't seem so scary with his family all around.

The table seated twelve. She grew up with a table for four. The table and chairs looked sturdy, but very old. A matching buffet stood against one wall with a massive tiled fireplace across from it. A china cabinet full of antique dishes stood against the end wall. Trees with sparse leaves dominated the wall paper with a pale blue background. Even with all the furniture, there was plenty of empty space.

Shauna leaned toward Jason and whispered, "This is a huge room."

He chuckled. "You should see the formal dining room."

Her eyes widened. "This isn't the only dining room?"

He smiled. "Nope. And then there's the large eat-in kitchen. I think the servants used to eat there."

"And where do they eat now? The formal dining room?" she asked, playfully.

He laughed. "Now there's only the housekeeper who comes in twice a week."

Abby bumped his hand with a bowl on his other side. He took it, put potatoes on his plate and passed it to Shauna.

Abby leaned forward to peek around Jason. "Rachel, how long are you going to be here?"

Shauna bit her lip and looked at Jason. "I'm not sure yet."

Abby frowned. "Are you on vacation? Don't you have to go back to work?"

"I quit before I came here."

Abby bumped Jason's arm with her shoulder. "He convinced you to stay, didn't he?"

She didn't know how to answer. She was supposed to pretend she was his girlfriend. If she really was, she'd say yes, but she didn't want to lie to Abby and then leave.

Jason came to her rescue. "Give it a rest, squirt. We're still working things out."

"Hey, I'm not a squirt anymore."

Jason patted her head. "You're younger and shorter than me, so you're still a squirt."

She glared at him.

"Rachel?"

Shauna smiled at Kathleen. "Yes?"

"What would you like to do while you're here?"

How could she answer that? Kathleen knew she was here to hide out. It wasn't a vacation. "I don't know."

"What do you like to do?"

She shrugged. "I used to enjoy going on hikes with my dad and playing board games with my grandmother. And baking. I…" She shook her head. Not going there. The only one she'd baked for in the last year had been Nick.

As the end of the meal neared, nerves set in. Now what would happen? She didn't know if she would fit into the family routine. She couldn't guess if they did more family stuff or disperse to pursue their own interests. She could always go to her room to read, except she didn't want the room she was given.

Tony picked up his dishes and headed toward the door, then turned back. "Jason, you want to play *Halo*?"

Jason looked at Shauna.

"It's okay. I brought a book." It sounded like his family hadn't seen him in a while. She didn't want to take him away from brother time and it wasn't as if she was his girlfriend. He was keeping her safe, nothing more. And for the first time in the week since the incident, she did feel safe. No one outside of the Rawlins family knew where she was. Jason hadn't even told Mark or Kristy where he kept Shauna hidden. This house and the family offered a calming balm she hadn't known she needed.

"Reese," Kathleen said, "why don't you play with the boys while Rachel and I get to know each other?"

Kathleen knew the real reason Shauna was there, so why did she want to get to know her? Kathleen and Reese stared at each other, and he frowned for a moment. He leaned forward and briefly kissed his wife's lips before standing. It was nice to see how much they still cared for each other.

Reese picked up his dishes. "Come on, guys. I'll join you in *Halo*. Be prepared to lose this time."

"No way, Dad," Tony scoffed and disappeared out the door.

After the women finished taking care of the rest of the dishes, Abby went up to her room.

"Come join me in the library, Rachel," Kathleen said.

Once they were comfortably seated in front of the fireplace, Kathleen started right in. "Your grandmother never told you about Rawlins?"

Shauna shook her head. "I asked her a couple of times where she grew up, but she just said, 'Oh, it's someplace you never heard of.' And then she changed the subject." Shauna twisted her hands in her lap. "What's so bad about Rawlins that she left and wouldn't talk about it?"

"Nothing's wrong with it now, but back then…"

Kathleen bit her lip and stared at Shauna, as if gauging how well Shauna would take what she had to say. "Since you have ancestors from here, I think I should tell you about Rawlins. Like you, I wasn't born here and knew nothing about it. My parents left right after they got married. I came after I got a letter from my Uncle Gerald's lawyer telling me that I'd inherited his estate. I hadn't known I had an uncle. I think, when the time is right, Rawlins calls its family home."

Cold flowed down Shauna's spine and she shivered. Kathleen made it sound like the town, outside of the people, was alive.

Kathleen took a deep breath and a far away look came into her eyes. "My first night on the road to get here, I had a vivid dream about waking up in the room that is now Jamie's. I came into the hallway, stood at the top of the stairs and saw Reese walk in the front door. Then I woke up in my motel room. The next night, in the dream, I woke in the same room and rushed down the stairs. Reese came in and called me Kat. He touched my cheek and barely kissed me, then the dream ended. I thought I was really awake. It still feels like a real memory."

Kathleen watched Shauna too intently, and a smile spread across Kathleen's face. "The next morning, I had time to explore the town, and a shop called *The Magical Moment* intrigued me. I stepped through the door and froze when the man behind the counter looked up. Without my saying a word, he called me Kat. He was the man from my dreams. It turned out he'd dreamed of me also."

Shauna wasn't surprised her voice shook, since her insides quivered. "Did that moment from your dream ever happen?"

"A few weeks later, it did."

Shauna's hands trembled. Her dreams couldn't be the same.

Kathleen rubbed Shauna's arm. "Sh—Rachel, are you all right?"

She shook her head. "It's…um. I've had dreams about Jason for the past couple of weeks that seem very real. In Jamie's room." She lowered her head and covered her eyes with her hand. "And I only met him yesterday." She wished she hadn't let that slip. It was hard enough telling her best friend about the dreams. This was the guy's mother.

She took a quick peek at Kathleen and pressed her lips together.

Kathleen didn't seem repulsed by Shauna's statement. "It's okay. I'm not judging you for a dream you had no control over."

Shauna stared into the dark fireplace. She'd have control over it if it happened for real. Maybe Kathleen would judge then, but Jason was protecting her, nothing more. The chances of anything happening were slim.

"But you and Reese both had the same dream," Shauna said. "Jason didn't seem to know me when we met at the club. He didn't have the dream, so it won't happen." It was less reassuring than she'd expected, because the disappointment roiling in her chest at that moment told her she might have wanted it. A surprise, since she'd never wanted a man's touch.

"Ah, well..." Guilt washed over Kathleen's face.

"What is it?"

Kathleen hesitated. "Jason told me that he had a dream about you last night."

A fist twisted in her stomach. After hearing Kathleen's dream story, chances were her and Jason's dreams were the same. Her face flamed, imagining that he'd seen her naked, touched her, and did all those things she'd enjoyed in his dream. "So, this is going to happen?"

Kathleen shrugged. "I only have my experiences to compare it to. All I can say is that it is only going to happen if you want it to. In your dream, did you want it? Look forward to it?"

Shauna let her mind wander to her dream. Oh, yeah. She nodded. "I wanted it." Bad.

"So, right now, you don't want it to happen, so it won't."

Shauna took a deep breath and relaxed. It wasn't like Jason would force her and that's not how the dream went. It would only happen if she allowed it to. She smiled. "You're right." She took Kathleen's hand and squeezed it. "Thank you. I can't believe how simple that is. I just hope I don't have any more of those dreams." She'd been so overwhelmed with what they did in the dream, she hadn't thought about the fact that she was excited and wanted what was happening. She wasn't ready for that, and maybe never would be.

"Now that we've settled that, let me tell you about Rawlins. My ancestor, Joseph Rawlins, brought his family and other residents from Salem, Massachusetts out here after the witch hysteria died down, because his eight-year-old daughter, Hannah, had a dream that the two of them would be hanged as witches."

"Wow. That's a lot of trouble to go through because of a child's dream."

"Hannah had made accurate predictions before. She gave her father details that she couldn't have known about how they would die."

Like details about sex she'd never experienced. "Do you believe she could do that?" Hannah didn't die, so the dreams could be used to avoid that thing from happening.

"Yes. Twenty years ago, I had dreams that predicted deaths of young girls. I helped solve the murders so the deaths could end."

"You can do that? I always thought that was made up in books and movies." She rubbed her hands on her arms.

"You look cold. Do you want me to start a fire in the fireplace?"

"You don't need to go to any trouble for me."

"It's no trouble." Kathleen waved her hand at the heap of wood on the grate and cheery flames burst from the logs.

"Whoa!" When she first met Kathleen, she'd seemed so…normal. Shauna didn't expect her to be a magical, scary witch with paranormal powers. Shauna hoped Kathleen didn't use her powers to hurt people. It still didn't seem real and Shauna had seen the flames. Real logs burned, not a gas log turned on by remote control. She couldn't believe Jason had brought her to a place like this.

"You get used to it. I hope we can find out what other abilities you have, Rachel."

"Other?" This was not at all what she expected when she arrived. Jason's mother was petite, well-mannered and soft-spoken. Now she was telling Shauna about making predictions and showing off her fire-starting skills. She wouldn't have believed it if she hadn't seen it with her own eyes.

"Hannah taught me, but she already suspected what abilities I had, since they're usually inherited."

This was going too fast. It was as if she had decided to find out about her family, but it was thrown in her face. Then to find out she could have weird powers. Maybe her father and grandmother have powers and chose not to tell her about it. Maybe it was better to not have any abilities.

"How did Hannah teach you?"

"She came in my dreams."

Shauna's mouth dropped open. Dreams.

Kathleen squinshed her eyes. "I'm really going about this all wrong."

Shauna held up her hands. "Look, can you let me get used to this part first? Maybe tomorrow we'll talk more about it."

"Yes. I'm sorry, Rachel." Her eyes darted around. "It's a lot to take in. I understand your shock."

"I…I think I'll read for a while before I go to bed. Good night, Kathleen." Shauna fled the room. As she neared the stairwell, she remembered she didn't want to sleep in Jamie's room. The explanation from Kathleen about the dream eased her mind a bit, but she still didn't want to be in there. Following the sounds of the men playing their video game, she stopped in the doorway of the family room, watching them having fun together.

Jason saw her and paused his game play. "I'll be back in a few," he told Tony and his father. Jason joined Shauna at the doorway.

He leaned against the doorframe. "How is everything?"

"I'd like to go to bed, but I don't want to use Jamie's room. Is there somewhere else I can stay?"

"Sure. You can sleep in my room."

No way. She opened her mouth and closed it.

Jason sucked in a breath. "Sorry. I should have worded that differently. You can take my room and I'll take Jamie's."

Her face felt like a sunburn, and she wondered if he'd done that on purpose. She headed up the stairs. "You and your mother, too," she mumbled.

Jason put his hand on her arm and squinted. Great.

Now he was he angry with her. "What was that?"

"Your mom has overwhelmed me with family and Rawlins secrets. I had to get out of there to digest it all."

Jason paled and released her arm.

It wasn't the reaction she expected. If Kathleen had special powers maybe Jason did, too. Maybe he turned into a werewolf during a full moon and he probably thought Kathleen had told her his secret. Not that she believed in werewolves, but she'd never believed there were real witches in Salem who could start fires with a wave of a hand or that dreams were premonitions.

Concern for his pallor warred with her confusion. "Are you all right?"

He nodded. "Fine. Let's talk more tomorrow."

***

After watching Shauna race up the stairs, Jason marched into the library, and dropped down on the couch beside his mother.

"What did you tell Shauna? She looked upset."

"I kind of overwhelmed her with a little history."

His eyes drilled into her. "What specifically did you say?" He'd never used that tone with his mother before and tried to calm himself. He hoped she hadn't told Shauna his history.

"I told her how and why Rawlins was started and about Hannah."

"And?" That couldn't be all that had Shauna so nervous.

"I started a fire for her." She waved her hand, and he knew what she meant. "I told her how your father and I met in our dreams."

He leaned back against the couch and ran a hand through his hair. "And you told her I had the dream?"

She nodded.

"Mom." He tamped down his exasperation. "I told you what type of dream it was, and now you've got her worried about her virtue." He glared at her. "It can't happen. You know it can't." There wasn't anything that made him more afraid than the possibility of becoming evil.

"Jason—"

"No more, Mom. I'm exhausted. I'll talk to you in the morning."

He left the library and put his foot on the first step when he remembered he'd left his brother and father in the family room. He closed his eyes, too tired to continue playing.

He caught their attention at the family room door. "I'm going to bed. I only got four hours sleep last night, and I think I'm sleepwalking right now. Good night."

"Night, Jason," Tony called out.

"See you in the morning, Son," Reese chimed in.

He trudged upstairs and eyed his bedroom door on the way to Jaime's room. One golden eyed woman had spun his life out of control. He was hired to protect her and already he wanted to do more. Things he couldn't allow himself to do.

Chapter 4

"Shauna, dear."

"Mmm." Her brain was still half asleep.

"Hey, sweetie."

That voice was so familiar, but it couldn't be. Shauna forced her eyes open. She hadn't been asleep that long, and it was still dark out. A small, low-wattage light glowed on the dresser. It hadn't been on when she went to bed. She sat up and looked around. Someone sat on a rocking chair in the corner that she hadn't noticed earlier. Jason taking his duty of protecting her a little too far? Except the shape was too small to be Jason.

Shauna had no idea how someone had gotten into the room. She could scream, and Jason would be beside her in seconds. Leaning forward and blinking her eyes, she finally made out the features. Her heart pounded, and a matching beat pulsed in her head. She massaged her temples.

"Grandma?" It had to be a dream. Grandma had died seven years ago. It didn't feel like a dream, but was so real like those dreams with Jason before she met him. She shook her head. She loved her grandma, but she didn't want her coming back from the dead. "Are you a ghost?"

"No, dear. I'm a spirit in your dream. Ghosts visit while you're awake." Her toe pushed against the floor and the chair started to rock. Grandma had loved her Canadian Maple rocker.

A spirit just explained to her that ghosts were real. "This is too much." She flopped back on the bed. If someone had told her a place like Rawlins existed, she would have insisted they'd visited a movie set. Kathleen had told her about an ancestor visiting her. Maybe it was possible. Shauna peeked into the corner then propped herself up again. Still there. Grandma seemed solid enough, as if she were still alive. But even Grandma had said this was a dream.

"No one ever tells you in a dream that you're in a dream," Shauna said.

Grandma continued rocking and smiled.

It was too confusing. The room seemed the same as before, a bit dim, but everything normal. The only thing not right about it was her grandmother.

Shauna tipped her head. "How did you know I was here?"

"I sensed you when you realized I was from Rawlins. I tried to talk to you…" She looked away and pulled in her bottom lip.

"You did?"

Her grandmother nodded. "I'm sorry, dear. I surged in too quickly and made you faint."

"That's what happened?" Her thoughts had spun out of control before she blacked out.

Shauna drew her knees up under the blankets and wrapped her arms around them. It almost reminded her of times when she slept over at her grandmother's, watching a movie, eating popcorn and talking. "Grandma, why didn't you talk about living in Rawlins?"

"I never wanted you to come here. If I talked about Rawlins, you would have wanted to explore the town I grew up in."

"You're right. But why didn't you want me to come? How did I end up here anyway?"

"There's been an evil in Rawlins since the town's

founding. I could feel the press of evil building, pushing against my chest, so I left as soon as I finished high school. My parents couldn't sense it. They didn't understand. I didn't want my children to grow up with that."

"Evil? What kind of evil? Bad people?" Grandma said evil, with a capital 'E'. Shauna drew the blanket up around her shoulders.

"It's worse than bad people, dear. Some of them start out as decent people, who only want to strengthen their abilities, but once they've given in, evil controls them. To gain more power, they kill. Others are born evil. Those are the worst. Your powers have been awakened by coming here, so that puts you in danger. You need to leave."

"You knew I had abilities? What are they? Why didn't I know?"

"Most often, types of abilities are inherited."

"Did Dad have them?"

"I don't know if he did. Rawlins seems to be the trigger. I didn't sense powers in you when I was alive, but I do now. I think it's because you're here."

"But I had—" No way was she going to discuss those dreams with her grandmother. She didn't seem to know about them, and Shauna wasn't going to enlighten her.

"Had what?"

Shauna dipped her head. She'd never been able to successfully lie to the woman. "I had a dream about this house a couple of weeks ago. Now it seems like a premonition."

"That's a passive ability. The others, you must consciously use. I'll teach you to protect yourself and then you have to leave."

"Grandma, I can't leave. I'm hiding from my ex-fiancé. I'm in danger from him."

Her grandmother stared past Shauna's shoulder and

rubbed her chest. "I don't sense evil, but maybe it's because I'm not alive." She turned piercing eyes on Shauna. "That Proctor boy brought you here for a reason. It's his family that has embraced evil. They brought it with them from Salem. He plans to use you to bring it back."

"No, he wouldn't do that. He hates his natural father." At least, she thought so, since he didn't want to be a Proctor. If Jason's father was evil the way her grandmother said, no wonder Jason hated him. "It's only by chance that he was the one hired to protect me."

"Nothing is chance where this town is concerned. We'll start your lessons tonight with levitation."

"How is levitation protection?" The discussion was unbelievable, as if Grandma really thought Shauna could levitate. This was definitely a dream. Talking to her grandmother, abilities, evil people. Might as well play along.

"It depends on how it's used. Now, let's see. How about if you lift that brush on the dresser. Like this." The object rose about six inches into the air and hovered before gliding back to the dresser. "Now, you try it."

"Just like that? Sure. Rise up, brush." She waved her hand.

Her grandmother gave a familiar huff. "Put in some effort. Imagine the brush floating and where you want it to be. Now, really concentrate. You have to unlock the skill. Once you've got it, you barely use any effort."

Shauna sighed. "Fine." She raised her eyes above the brush and willed it to lift to the same height her grandmother had raised it. The brush stayed in place. She glared at it and willed it to do her bidding. One end lifted up and dropped down, but the brush didn't rise.

She clapped her hands and turned to her grandmother with a wide grin. "It moved. Did I do that?" She clapped her hands and turned to her grandmother with an ear to ear grin.

It wasn't much, but she'd never done anything like it before.

"Yes, dear. Try again." It was the long-suffering voice. Grandma knew how to push her. "Ask its permission to make it rise, then imagine your hand picking it up."

Nodding, Shauna formed a need in her head and asked to brush her hair as she imagined reaching for the brush. It rose, flipped over and came toward her. She gasped and lost her concentration. The brush dropped on the end of the bed.

"Very good. Now make it go back to where it started."

Shauna nodded and pictured her hand returning it to the dresser. It remained in its resting place. She frowned at her grandmother. "Why did it work before and not now?"

"You haven't fully unlocked the skill yet. You didn't try as hard."

She bit her lip and squinted at the brush, adding energy to the image of lifting it. It rose and returned to the dresser.

"I can't believe I did it. But I can only do this because it's a dream. You can do anything in a dream." She could probably fly if she wanted to.

Grandma smiled. "Now try something heavier." Her grandmother looked around the room. "Pick up your suitcase."

"I could hardly lift it with my hands, how can I do it with her mind? Isn't it too heavy?"

"If you can pick it up yourself, you can easily levitate it. With more practice, you can even levitate things that are too heavy to pick up."

"So, I could levitate a—horse?"

The older woman raised an eyebrow. "Yes, but I don't know why you'd want to. Try the suitcase."

Shauna smiled as she focused on lifting it. The case tipped up onto its wheels, but refused to leave the floor. Maybe she couldn't lift something that heavy. Her abilities might not be as strong as her grandmother's. She glanced at her grandmother, who nodded at the case.

Determination kicked in as Shauna stared at the luggage and the case rose from the floor and dropped to its side on the bed. She gave her grandmother a triumphant look.

"Hey, I wonder if I can unzip it." She moved her imaginary fingers to the zipper pull and worked it around three sides of the case and flipped the top open. "It really worked!"

A money clip on the dresser caught her attention. She raised it, spun it around and lowered it back down. The lamp beside her was bigger. She lifted it as far as the cord would allow and lowered it, misjudging the cord dragging beneath. The lamp started to tip, and one side touched the table. With more concentration, she brought it safely down.

"Okay, maybe I better not levitate breakable things for a while." She scanned the room for her next object.

"Shauna."

She'd almost forgotten her grandmother was there. "Sorry."

"You need to be able to protect yourself with this."

Shauna bit her lip. This wasn't just for fun or to make things easy. Her grandmother thought she needed this. "So, how do I protect myself?"

"You could pick up someone who's going to attack you and drop him. You could throw something at him."

"It doesn't have to move slow?"

The older woman pointed to a shelf. "There's a baseball up there. Throw it to me."

Shauna lifted the autographed ball off its stand. It hovered. She frowned. Maybe if she imagined it hurling at Grandma. It spun and her eyes followed it across the room. If Grandma didn't catch it, the ball would hit her in the chest and Shauna would feel awful if a spirit felt pain. She didn't have to worry. Her grandmother's hand flew up and there was the telltale slap of leather hitting a palm. It worked!

"You did great, Shauna. I'm going to let you sleep now. I want you to practice this, so that you can do it with barely a thought."

The light on the dresser winked out, and Shauna felt as if she'd been awake for hours.

***

Shauna stretched in the morning light and scanned the room. Unbelievably well rested after the weird dream she'd had, her body felt energized. She sat up, and dropped her feet to the floor. Her foot hit a soft lump, and she froze. Her clothes were scattered over the floor with the suitcase upside down on top of the pile. So it wasn't an ordinary dream. She'd knocked the suitcase off the bed while she'd slept. Shauna whipped her head around to look at the chair in the corner. A baseball sat in the middle of the seat.

Her hands covered her mouth. "Oh. My. Gosh."

The door flew open and she gasped. Jason's gaze darted into every corner before settling on her and her pile of clothes on the floor. "Are you all right?"

"Ah, yes. You heard me?"

He continued to study the room, the clothes, then Shauna. His gaze fixed on her breasts. The thin tank top didn't hide her reaction, as her nipples tightened. Her cheeks warmed. No, no. He didn't need to see how she responded to just a look. She crossed her arms over her chest.

He glanced at the floor by her feet and then at her face. "I was passing the door and heard a noise. Why'd you dump your clothes on the floor?"

She could make up something about forgetting to take her suitcase off the bed, but Jason was one of the few people who would believe the truth.

"I had a dream with my grandma."

He raised an eyebrow, crossed his arms and leaned against the door frame.

"And this morning I thought it was only a dream, and I didn't move my bag back off the bed." She felt silly with her arms still across her chest after he copied her, so she pulled her legs up and wrapped her arms around them.

A smile ticked one side of his mouth. "What's the bag got to do with your dream?"

She wanted to show off her new ability, if it was real. If it didn't work, he'd never know what she was trying to do. At this stage, concentration seemed to be key. Her invisible hand wrapped around the handle of the suitcase and lifted it up and back onto the bed. She smiled at him and his stunned expression.

He took several steps into the room. "You learned that while you slept?"

His hair was wet from his shower. She would love to levitate him to the bed so she could run her hand through it. She blinked. Her mind didn't need to go there. "Is that so surprising in this house?"

"Well, not in this house. But you seemed so normal when I met you two days ago."

"So, I'm not normal?" She set her fists on her hips and tipped up her nose. "Are you repulsed by my new ability?" Maybe he preferred a woman without magical skills.

His mouth dropped open and he rubbed his cheek. "Um, half of this town isn't normal. I guess it's normal for here."

He got out of that one.

"You seem to have recovered from yesterday's talk with my mother."

"Yeah, practicing with Grandma helped."

"It must have been—interesting seeing her again."

Her heart warmed. "It was nice. It wasn't like I was

talking to a ghost. It was really her. Just weird that we talked about spirits and special powers."

Jason chuckled. "I grew up with all this, but I can imagine how you must feel."

"Have you talked to an ancestor like your mother and I have?"

His smile was gone, replaced with a scowl. "No! And I don't want to."

Shauna's hand flew to his arm. "Sorry, Jason. I didn't mean to be so thoughtless." No one would want to talk to one of them. "I'm sorry. I forgot that…how you felt…sorry." There was no good way to finish. He'd said he hated his father, but, even worse, her grandmother had told her that the man was evil.

Taking a deep breath, he let it out slowly. "It's okay. I'm sorry I snapped at you."

He stepped back. "It's Sunday morning. Mom always makes a wonderful breakfast, so come down when you're ready." He walked out, shutting the door behind him.

She stared at the closed door. Grandma thought he could be evil. Maybe Shauna shouldn't trust him. All of his biological family must have been evil. Maybe they learned to be evil or maybe they inherited it. Part of Jason could be evil, even though he grew up with different parents. Shauna drew in a deep breath. More than she'd ever expected had happened since she'd run from Nick.

Chapter 5

Since she had this new levitation ability, Shauna decided she'd practice it by putting her clothes in the dresser. Her guess was she'd be there at least a week. Checking space, she rearranged some of the clothing so she could use two drawers. Momentarily, guilt kicked in for taking Jason's room, but she pushed it aside. She wouldn't sleep in the room that her dreams occurred in.

Her eyes widened on the bed. This was where Jason slept, his warm, maybe naked body, tangled in the same sheets she'd slept in the night before. And again tonight. She raised her hands to her warming cheeks, never having thought she could blush when she was alone.

She concentrated on lifting each piece of clothing, folding it mid-air and settling it into the drawer. No bending or walking made it go so much faster. When that drawer was full, she pushed it closed with her mind, and opened the second drawer, continuing her practice. Once the floor was clear, she emptied her smaller bag. She squinted at the closet doorknob. It turned and the door opened. She stared at her two bags and mentally ushered them into the closet, sealing them inside. She was going to enjoy using this new super power. That was until her forehead started to ache. She rubbed her temples. Maybe she'd done too much.

Following voices to the kitchen, she stopped in the doorway, unsure of her reception, but more so wanting to enjoy watching how the close family interacted. She wasn't sure how long Jason had been away from his family, but they welcomed him back as if he'd been there all along.

Shauna's mother had left when she was seven, so for most of her life, it had been only her father and her. Except for his last two years, they'd been close, but nothing like Jason's family. They laughed over something Tony said. She could only guess at what it would have been like to grow up surrounded by love and laughter like that.

She hovered in the doorway until Reese spotted her. "Rachel, come on in."

"I feel like I'm intruding on your family time." Jason pulled out the chair beside him. She couldn't very well take another chair, and accidentally brushed his arm as she sat, leaving a tingle in her shoulder.

Jason dropped two pancakes on her plate from a stack in the middle of the table. Abby pushed a plate of sausage links toward her, then Shauna accepted a bowl of mixed fruit.

"Orange juice or coffee?" Kathleen asked from where she stood at the counter.

"Coffee, please. Black. Thank you. This looks delicious." She cut a sausage link and popped a savory piece into her mouth as Jason set the maple syrup pitcher next to her plate.

Breakfast was very much like dinner. Conversation swirled around, and Shauna was happy to be pulled in and included.

All conversation stopped when Jason proudly said, "Rachel mastered an ability already."

Shauna's face grew warm as everybody stared at her. "Jason!"

"It's all right, Rachel. Everybody here has abilities. Mom, her grandmother came to her like Hannah did with you."

"Rachel, that's wonderful," Kathleen said. "I wasn't sure of the best way for you to find out about your abilities."

"Um, Grandma said that we'd start with the ones she has…had. She said that you usually inherit them."

"So, what can you do?" Abby asked with excitement.

"Watch!" She lifted the platter of pancakes from the end of the table and set them in front of Jason. "Grandma called it levitation."

Abby squealed and clapped her hands. "Wow! It took me forever to learn my abilities."

Shauna grinned. "Abby, what can you do?"

"I can start fires and read the history of objects. I'm not as good as Mom, but better than Dad." She turned to her father and gave him a big smile.

"What do you mean by reading a history?" Shauna asked.

"I'll show you. Just a second." Abby raced out of the room and returned with a book. She set it on the table. "This was in the library when Mom inherited the house."

Shauna flipped open the cover. It was an original *Alice's Adventures in Wonderland* printed in 1865.

Abby closed the book and picked it up. "I think I was about ten when I first read this. I loved it, but the best part was watching its history. A little girl got this book as a birthday present from her aunt. She read it over and over. When she grew up and had a little girl, she read it to her and eventually gave it to her daughter to read on her own."

Shauna frowned. "How do you know this?"

"When I hold the book and concentrate on it, I can see it like it's happening in front of me." She looked at her mother. "Mom can even hear them talking."

"Whoa. That's impressive. You would be a really successful antique dealer. Nobody could fool you."

Abby smiled. "Maybe that's what I should do." She put the book beside her plate and resumed her seat.

"I wonder if I can do something like that," Shauna

mused.

Abby clasped her hands. “After breakfast, I can show you how.”

“All right. Let’s give it a try.”

“And after that, I’ll show you around town,” Jason said.

Her stomach fluttered. It shouldn’t do that. Jason was protecting her, nothing more. A dream didn’t mean anything.

***

Shauna leaned back in the seat as Jason drove to Rawlins town center. “I had no success with reading the history of objects. Nothing at all. I know I should be happy that I have at least one ability. I mean, levitation seems more useful, yet I’m so disappointed that I can’t read objects.”

“That’s all right,” Jason said. “It’s pretty amazing that you can levitate objects. I wonder if you can levitate yourself.”

“Whoa! That would be fun. I’ll have to give it a try. What can you do?”

His deep blue eyes drew her in, and her stomach did crazy things. She’d never felt so many butterflies tickle her stomach before. It wasn’t the nerves of doing something scary. It was an excited nervousness that caused her to imagine Jason kissing her and running his hands over her body. He returned his attention to the road, and she closed her eyes, took a deep breath, and tried to calm the flutter that had her heart racing.

She didn’t know why, but she’d always been too nervous around guys in high school, and turned down everyone who asked her out. In college, she’d thought she’d gotten over it when she had no problem talking to men in class, and casually around campus. But the moment they showed a greater interest, a deep, cold fear invaded her.

Nick had been…something else. She'd only seen him a few times before her father died. He'd been friendly, and she could talk to him, probably because he hadn't shown a greater interest. After her father died, he swooped in and handled so many things, and held her as she cried. She only just realized that she'd never kissed Nick. He'd kissed her cheek, her hand or the back of her neck, but rarely on the lips. And she'd never returned those kisses. Maybe he'd sensed her fear of intimacy, and was giving her time to get used to him. She should never have accepted his proposal.

Dreams of Jason snuck past all her defenses, and made her crave a touch she'd never imagined. It was harder to push those thoughts away, and return to the conversation.

She nudged his arm. "Hey, you haven't answered my question. Are you afraid to tell me what your special powers are?"

He glanced at her then stared out the windshield. "I can see in the dark."

She laughed. "I can, too. Sort of. How is that an ability?"

He turned onto a side street, made a u-turn and parked the SUV in front of a store called *Mystical Moment*. A woman with short, blonde hair came around the side of the building.

Jason opened his door. "Perfect timing."

Shauna grabbed his arm, stopping him from getting out. She shook her head. "Uh-uh. I need more."

He sighed, ran a hand through his hair, stared straight ahead. "You know those goggles the military use at night to see on missions?"

"Mm-hm."

"I can do that. Without the goggles."

"You have infrared vision? That is so cool." She never would have expected that to be an ability.

He shrugged. "It's been helpful."

"Have you used it on missions?"

"Yeah, but I can't say more." This time, she let him exit the SUV, and he came around and helped her out.

"Hi, Jason," the blonde said. "I haven't seen you in a while."

"Hi, Anna. I'd like you to meet my friend, Rachel."

Shauna held out her hand. "Hi, Anna. Nice meeting you." She immediately liked the woman with the short, perky nose and green eyes that crinkled when she smiled.

Anna's eyebrows rose. "Must be serious. You haven't brought a woman home before."

She had it so wrong. That was the impression they were letting people take, so she had to let it slide.

Anna jangled her keys. "I'm not officially open for fifteen more minutes, but come on in."

Shauna figured they'd have to stand outside for a while. "Thanks. That's so nice."

Jason grinned. "Perks of my dad owning the shop." He took Shauna's hand, tugged her toward the building, and they stepped in.

Anna closed the door behind them. "So, Jason, what brings you back here?"

"Actually, I'm moving back. I'm setting up my business here."

Her eyebrows drew down. "And what business is that?"

Maybe Anna assumed Jason would join Reese in his business.

"Security."

"Isn't Rawlins too small for that kind of business?"

"Yes, but I'm going to set up in Amherst and live in Rawlins."

"Oh, good. And, Rachel, are you moving to Rawlins, too?" Fortunately, Anna dropped her keys into her purse and stuffed it under the counter, and didn't see the surprise on Shauna's face.

"Uhm."

Jason jumped in. "She hasn't decided yet."

It was a good thing he thought faster than she did, or else Anna might have made assumptions about the arrangement. It would have sounded strange if he asked her to live with him and she hadn't made up her mind. Jason and Shauna should have worked out all the details of their cover story.

Anna came back around the counter. "I was disappointed that you couldn't come to my wedding."

"Oh, yeah. Congratulations." He took her hand and kissed her cheek. "I was out of the country when I found out. How is Alan? Still doing construction?"

"Yes. His brother joined him and they've got two other guys working for them."

"Hey, that's great."

"Now I've got to get stuff done before I open the store. Feel free to browse." She slipped through a door behind the counter.

Shauna surveyed the store. Shelves of small bottles and jars lined the left wall and the back wall on both sides of the counter. Two tables held baskets of various items. On the right, a wicker loveseat, chair and table made a cozy corner.

"My parents officially met here," Jason said behind her.

Shauna frowned. "Officially?"

"They'd already met in their dreams," he reminded her. "Dad knew they'd meet, but Mom hadn't realized her dream was a premonition. She almost fainted when she saw him."

Shauna knew how that felt, times ten. Her face grew warm as images from the dreams with Jason invaded her. She turned, but not before seeing one corner of his mouth tip up. She picked up a bottle, pretending to study the label. He was probably thinking of their dreams, too. Her face flamed hotter and her breathing became shallow and fast. Closing her eyes, she took a deep breath.

A hand grasped her shoulder, and she jumped.

"Sorry. I didn't mean to startle you. Are you okay?"

He was so close she could feel the heat from his body at her back. She nodded and stepped away from him. His hand slid off her shoulder. She found Jason extremely attractive and kind, but didn't know of she'd have these intense feelings about him without the dreams. She wished the first time they'd met had been at the club, not jumping ahead to such…intimate moments. The thought had her nerves tied in knots. But maybe without the dreams she would have had the same chilled fear she felt when other men showed an interest in her.

Taking another step forward to put more distance between them, she feigned interest in the bottles on a shelf and read labels. "Mugwort, Nettle, Poison Hemlock. What is all this?"

Jason stepped along side her. "They're ingredients for potions."

"Seriously? Like magic potions?"

"Of course."

She waved her hand at the shelves. "They sell enough of this stuff to stay in business?"

"Yes. Well, that and the natural skin care and cleaning products, not to mention candles for creating the ambiance for the potions or a romantic dinner." He lowered his voice. "I'll have to show you Mom's potion book at home."

She held her breath. Just the sound of his voice made her want his arms wrapped around her and his lips on her…anywhere.

"Are you ready to discover more?" Jason asked.

She blinked, back in the present. He couldn't be talking

about what she was thinking. "Sure. Show me what else this town has to offer."

Jason took her hand and pulled her to the door. She looked back as the woman returned from the stock room. "Bye, Anna. It was nice meeting you."

Jason never looked back. "Yeah. Bye, Anna."

"Bye, guys."

He didn't release her hand until she'd gotten back into his SUV. Sometimes he seemed to like her and others, he pushed her away. She wished she knew what was going on in his head.

On Main Street, Jason pointed to a somewhat modern looking brick building. "There's town hall. That's the Historical Society, which used to be town hall. It has the original of the Rawlins' Family Tree that Mom gave them. Some of the founders' journals are in there. That's Dad's real estate company. He owns a lot of rentals here and in the surrounding towns." He pointed to a building with a sign reading *Ballard Real Estate and Rentals*.

"Your dad owns two businesses?"

"He also owns a restaurant in Amherst. I'll take you there some time."

"He keeps busy."

"Yeah, but Mom helps him."

Jason parked on the side of the street and shut off the car. "So, that pretty much covers Rawlins." Across from each other were *The Black Kettle Restaurant* and *Cozy Corner Diner*. "How about lunch at one of our two restaurants?"

"Okay. Which do you suggest?"

He smiled. "They both have good food, but not as good as Dad's place."

"Loyal, are you?"

He gave her a lopsided smile. "Of course. How about

the *Cozy Corner*?"

"I don't know anything about either one, so that's fine with me."

They entered a diner with a long counter and stools running along it. Booths with high backs lined two walls. The seats were covered in dark green vinyl. Jason led her to the fourth booth and pulled out two menus from behind the condiment rack, handing one to her. She ignored the subtle glances from other customers. A waitress hustled up and set glasses of ice water in front of them.

"Jason! It's been years since I've seen you. What are you doing back?" She put her hand on his shoulder. Shauna had known Jason for less than three full days, yet it bothered her to see this woman touching him. The blonde had her hair pulled back into a tight pony tail, the end a large ball of fluff. She stood so close to Jason, that if he leaned, his cheek would brush the woman's overly large, and probably fake, breasts. Her lips were strawberry red, and her blue eyes were framed with false eyelashes.

Jason grimaced at Shauna before turning his face up to the waitress. "Hi, Vanessa. I've moved back to town."

She leaned in closer and lowered her voice. "Maybe we can get together for old times sake."

It bothered Shauna even more that the other woman totally ignored her.

"I'm going to be pretty busy." He nodded toward Shauna. "This is my friend, Rachel. Vanessa and I went to high school together."

"Yeah, we dated for a while." She gave Jason's shoulder a possessive squeeze.

He leaned back in the booth and shrugged his shoulder. Shauna thought he'd tried to dislodge the woman's hand, but it didn't work.

Jason cleared his throat. "We're ready to order. I'll have

the baked stuffed chicken."

"I'll have the same." Maybe that would get Vanessa out of there.

Vanessa wrote down their order and squeezed his shoulder again. "It's good seeing you, Jason."

Shauna audibly let out a breath when Vanessa walked away with an exaggerated hip swing. "So, how long did you date? She seemed awfully possessive."

"Only about three months in junior year. I don't know what that was about." He leaned forward, lowering his voice. "And we never had sex."

She willed away a blush, but was pleased Jason hadn't been intimate with that woman. And wonder why he'd told her. "You must have broken up with her." Shauna surprised herself, stating the fact instead of asking. She must have really been jealous.

His mouth gaped open. "How did you know?"

"I don't think she's gotten over the breakup." She knew she'd have a hard time recovering from a breakup with Jason, and she wasn't even with him, but high school seemed an excessively long time for Vanessa to be hanging on.

"So, what do you think of our little town?"

She scanned the customers nearest her and leaned forward. "Do most of these people have special abilities?"

"At least half can do something. Maybe only the occasional premonition dream. I can't sense who has abilities, although there are some who can."

"This is so weird."

Jason put his hand over hers. "You'll get used to it."

"I probably won't be here long enough to get used to it."

Maybe she wanted it to be longer. Just the touch of Jason's hand on hers sent warmth up her arm and straight to her heart. Already, she didn't want to leave Jason. Thinking about it made her heart ache. The quick and amazing connection to him still puzzled her. Shauna didn't know if she felt something genuine for him or if these feelings were forced on her.

It also bothered her to think about leaving the town where her grandmother grew up. Her family had been in Rawlins for generations. Maybe it was time to return to her roots.

Except her grandmother didn't want her here.

Chapter 6

Jason wrapped his fingers around hers. "What do you have to go back to?"

Shauna raised her eyebrows then looked down at their joined hands. She was already thinking along those lines, surprised that Jason would ask. "I only have Kristy."

He rubbed his thumb across the top of her hand. "Give it time. This place may grow on you."

She pulled her hand away as Vanessa carried two plates toward them. If looks could kill, Shauna would have dropped to the floor. She'd never made an enemy so quickly. Never actually had an enemy before. Maybe it was a new ability.

The chicken was moist and tender and the stuffing perfectly seasoned. She didn't care for the canned green beans, but the potatoes and gravy were delicious. The rest of the meal was spent learning more about each other and their families. When Vanessa brought the check, she slipped a piece of paper into Jason's pocket. "Give me a call." She sauntered away.

It was bad enough the way Vanessa was all over Jason before, but now she slipped him her number in front of Shauna. She couldn't believe anyone would be that brazen. Her palm itched to slap the woman. She didn't want to be anywhere near that tramp again. "I don't think I'm going to be eating here any time soon. That woman hates me."

"I'm sure it's not as bad as that."

"If she could shoot daggers out of her eyes, I'd be dead.

Come to think of it, anything's possible in Rawlins. What ability can Vanessa use against me?" So much for cat fights over a guy in Rawlins.

Jason chuckled. "Daggers? I wouldn't think so." He reached into his pocket, pulled out the paper Vanessa had stuffed into it, crumpled it and dropped it on the table. Next, he took out his wallet and left money beside the check.

"Ready to go?"

Shauna was thrilled that Jason didn't accept Vanessa's number, but she didn't want him to know how she felt. He might not feel the same way. She glanced at the ball of paper and back to Jason. "Do you really want to leave that? It's like throwing her offer back in her face."

"I don't want anything to do with her, and I don't want her to think there could be anything." He stood and escorted Shauna out of the diner.

"Let's go back to the house," Jason said. "You haven't had the grand tour yet."

***

After parking in front of the house, Jason led Shauna inside and turned to the first room on the left. "This is the formal living room."

Shauna stepped into the room and looked across the foyer to the room opposite. "It's twice the size of the family room." Deep chairs sat in clusters of three and four, and a thickly cushioned couch shared a cluster with two chairs. All were covered in a velvety dark purple fabric. Small walnut tables stood beside or between most of the furniture.

"It's the party room, although we haven't had very many." Leading her to the next room on the left he waved his hand to present it. "And this is the formal dining room."

It was as large as the living room with a table that could

seat at least twenty.

"It's beautiful, but I like the dining room we ate in last night better."

"Me, too. Now, let's go to the library."

"I've been there already."

He gave her a mischievous grin. "Ah, but you haven't seen everything it has to offer." In the library, he walked to the right, back corner. "Now, you have to keep this a secret." His face became serious and she wondered why the change. "I want you to know about the secret room in case you have to hide out. After all, we did bring you here for your protection."

With all their exploring in Rawlins, she'd almost forgotten why she was there. She smiled, realizing how safe and secure she felt. "A secret room? I guess that's not so surprising in an old house."

"At least not this house." Jason ran his fingers under the left edge of a painting. He stopped and with a soft click, a panel popped open an inch. He pushed the door closed. "Now, you do it."

Shauna stepped up to the painting, her arm brushing his chest. He stepped back as if he didn't want her to touch him. She glanced at him but couldn't read his expression. She reached along the edge, found the button and pushed it.

The door popped open, and Jason pointed. "Now put your fingers in the slot on the edge of the door and pull it open."

She did, and stared into a dark room, until he flipped on the lights. Shauna followed him into a cozy room with thick blue carpet on the floor, probably to deaden any sound. A table and two chairs sat in front of a bookcase. In a corner sat two overstuffed chairs with a floor lamp between them. Other than the lack of a bathroom, it was a perfect hideout.

After pulling the door closed, Jason said, "When the

door's closed, it interlocks with the frame all the way around, so no light will show, even if the library lights are off and the lights in here are on. You'll be safe in here."

"Has this room ever been used?"

"As far as I know, not as a hideout. Uncle Gerald hid journals and books in here."

"Why hide books?" She walked over to the bookcase and pulled one out. "Hannah Rawlins' journal? Is this the Hannah Rawlins that your Mom mentioned?"

"One and the same. She wrote about her abilities and killing the evil people back in her time. So, they're not exactly journals for public consumption."

"She actually—killed people?" She shivered. Maybe she'd done it in self-defense.

"She killed murderers. They were getting stronger from their ritual killings. She did what had to be done."

Shauna slipped the journal back into the bookcase. She wasn't ready to read it yet, if ever.

"Did you say your Uncle Gerald had a journal in here, too?"

"Yes. I've read Hannah's, but I never could get myself to read Gerald's."

"Why not?" The look of revulsion on his face scared her. "Never mind. Forget I even asked."

Jason ran his hand through his hair. "It's all right. Uncle Gerald wrote about his investigation of the last serial murders in Rawlins. It turned out that my biological father was the one who committed them. I couldn't bring myself to read it."

She squeezed his arm. "I'm sorry. That must have been really hard for you."

"I don't remember him or my biological mother. I was only four when they died. I don't want to remember them."

Without a thought, she wrapped her arms around his

waist, froze for a second when her arm grazed his gun, and put her head on his shoulder. A part of her needed to comfort him, and another part was telling her she was crazy.

He stood still and stiff for a couple of seconds before he wrapped his arms around her, too.

After a few more seconds, it didn't feel like she was offering comfort to him, but herself. She wanted to unbutton his shirt, open it up and drop a kiss on his bare chest. He wanted something similar, if what she felt against her stomach was what she thought. Reluctantly, she stepped back and looked up at him. The sexy face from her dreams. Already, cold invaded without his arms around her. Before she could stop herself, she stood on her toes, and brushed a kiss on his cheek. His eyes widened.

She didn't know why she'd done that. She turned to leave before he could see her blush, but found she was trapped by the locked door. Tugging and pushing the handle didn't release the door. Maybe she could levitate the latch, except she couldn't see what she was doing. "Um, Jason, how do we open the door?"

She still faced the door and didn't know he'd come up behind her until his chest brushed her back as he leaned around her to push a button beside the door. He moved away before she could react, but she'd already done more than she should have.

***

"Here's the release." He could have stepped beside her to push the button, but he had an overwhelming need to touch her again. He already missed her warmth wrapped around him. That simple, chaste kiss on his cheek made him feel more, want more, than any kiss he'd ever been given. This was dangerous. He didn't want to want her. He didn't know what could happen if he made love to her—whether he'd take power from her or cause her physical harm. And there was the chance that making love to this virgin could turn him evil. He wouldn't take the chance. But her arms around him…He was worse than screwed.

Shauna swung the door open, and Abby jumped. She'd been working on homework at the desk. "Oh, you scared me!" She put a hand over heart, then scrunch up her face. "What were you two doing in the secret room?"

More than they should have been. Only then did Jason remember that he should have shown Shauna where to peek out, to make sure the room was empty. "I was giving Rachel a tour of the house."

"But we don't show that room to anybody."

He shrugged. "Rachel's special."

Abby squinted, but didn't say anything. For once, his little sister kept her mouth shut.

He took Shauna's hand and pulled her out of the library. He led her up the stairs and paused beside the second door on the right. "This is Abby's room. It used to be mine. It's the only one, besides the master bedroom, to have its own bathroom."

"How did you rate? And why does Abby have it now?"

He tapped his chest. "Being the oldest, I got the best. Then when I went away to college, I thought it was a waste that no one would use that bathroom, so I traded rooms with Abby. You wouldn't believe how upset Tony and Jamie were." He chuckled as he remembered the arguments. "But it was my room, so my decision."

"How did you choose Abby?"

"She's the youngest, so she'd use it the longest."

"And she's your favorite."

He glanced down the hall and leaned toward her. "I can't say that."

Jason led her up the second flight. They stopped at the top landing.

Shauna stepped beside him. "I didn't know there was a real third floor."

"We don't use it much. It used to be servants' quarters. Now if one of the girls has friends over, they come up here to party in peace. Or occasionally, Mom takes in a family for a few weeks who've lost their home."

"That's sweet of her." Shauna walked down the hallway, peeking into the open doorways. Each identical room had a window, bed, dresser, and a bar to hang clothes on.

She stopped at a small windowless bathroom. "All these rooms and only one bathroom to share."

She opened the last door, a storage area. He hadn't been up there in a few years. He guessed it looked a lot like any attic of an old house.

"Have you explored in here? It looks like so much fun." She didn't enter the semi dark room and after a few seconds, she sighed.

"What's wrong, Shauna?" Jason said from behind her.

"I miss my dad."

He pointed into the room. "And this made you think of him?"

She chuckled. "In a long, convoluted way."

He leaned against the door frame, crossed his arms, and smiled. "Tell me about it."

"You asked for it. I was thinking that the house I grew up in didn't have an attic like this and not even an overstuffed basement. There's a ping pong table and a pool table there. My Dad and I played a lot until the last few years. I miss him."

"I'm sorry."

"He was all I had, but it's getting easier. Mom left when

I was seven, so he was mother, father and friend to me."

Jason ran a knuckle down her cheek. He had so much love in his life. His family would be there for each other no matter what. It must have been devastating to suddenly have no one.

"That's why you needed Nick's help when you lost your dad," Jason said.

She nodded, tears shimmering in her eyes. "I fell apart. I don't know what would have happened without Nick."

He wished he could have been the one to help her through her loss. He wrapped his arms around her. It was his turn to offer comfort. He wanted it to be more than comfort. His heart beat so strong that he thought she'd hear it if she pressed her head to his chest. Emotionally, holding her was right, but his head said to get far away from her.

He pulled away. "Let me show you the basement."

***

They walked down to the kitchen in silence. As Jason slid back the lock on the basement door, she wondered why someone would put such a substantial lock *inside* the house. It was almost like they wanted to keep someone imprisoned down there. Jason flipped on the light and they descended the stairs. The room was huge, and light didn't reach into the corners. Three walls were fieldstone, the other was plaster with two closed, six-panel wood doors with crackled gray paint. A fairly new heating system stood next to the open wooden stairs.

Jason pointed to one door. "That's the spell room. It has as many kinds of potions and herbs as *Mystical Moment*, and all the equipment you need to create spells." He pointed to the other door. "That has more storage."

Shauna turned the doorknob on the first door, but it was

locked. "No one's allowed to make spells?"

He shrugged. "I've only been in there with Mom. I've never had an interest in creating spells."

She didn't want to make spells either. She didn't know what could be done with spells, but couldn't imagine herself working a spell for anything.

The second door opened easily. She flipped the light switch and dim light revealed shelves of dusty objects. She walked along the shelves, afraid to touch anything. "There's some really old stuff here."

"Mom had the historical society come a long time ago and take away whatever they thought had value. So, if you visit the society's exhibits, you'll see some of their display items say *Donated by Kathleen Ballard.*"

"That was nice of her."

"Yeah, she thought they were going to waste in this damp, old basement."

Shauna continued along the shelves. She picked up an occasional object. "I'm surprised they didn't take more." At the end of the shelves, she stopped and stared at a newer patch of cement on the wall, about the size of a door.

"I wonder where this used to lead."

"I don't know. As far as I know, it's always looked like that."

Shauna shivered and backed away, but her eyes stayed glued to the gray patch, bordered by stones. A door slowly shimmered and solidified in front of her. It was made of old wood planks with a rusted doorknob, but she had to be imagining it. If not, there had to be a reason the door had been removed. It might reappear when something wanted a person to go through it. No. It couldn't really be there. She didn't want to, but she found herself reaching for the door. She needed to touch it to know if it was a wood door or a cement wall. She took one step, two steps and another. She closed her eyes as her fingers touched damp wood.

Ice curled up her arm. That wasn't possible. She tried to pull her hand away, but it wouldn't move. Frigid fingers crept over her elbow and higher. Fear sliced through her, and she wondered what would happen if it reached her heart. It was already pounding so hard, she'd probably have a heart attack before it got that far. She opened her eyes and felt the cool, rough cement. An indescribable shiver passed through her. What was that? She let out a breath and wrapped her arms around herself.

She needed to leave, but she couldn't take her eyes off the wall. "Jason, I need to get out of here." Her voice sounded kind of squeaky.

She sensed him staring at her. He wrapped an arm around her shoulders and tugged her toward him. Relief filled her as she finally broke free of whatever had held her. She fled across the floor, up the stairs and up the next set of stairs, hearing Jason call out to her as she shut the door to Jason's room. She leaned against the door, and drew in a long breath.

Shauna had no idea what had happened. What she did know was that she would never go into that room again. It was pure evil, and the worst thing she'd ever felt. It was worse than the anguish she'd felt when her father died or the fear when she'd run from Nick. She hadn't even known one could feel evil, but she knew that's what it was when it reached out to her.

There was a knock on the door, then Jason's voice. "Shauna, are you in there? Are you all right?"

She couldn't answer. The doorknob rattled and the door pushed against her back. She took a breath and let Jason into the room. His concern reached her like a comforting hug. Shauna dove forward and wrapped her arms around his waist and pressed her head into his chest. She hadn't realized she was shivering until his heat seeped into her. His cheek rested on her head.

After a few minutes, he asked, "Shauna, what happened?"

She gazed up at his worried face. It was too soon to let him go. "There used to be a door there. I saw it. I…I don't know what happened. I needed to touch it. Then I felt so much evil. I didn't know you could feel evil." She tightened her hold on him and snuggled her head back into his chest. "At that moment, I was more scared than I'd ever been of Nick."

His arms tightened around her. "I won't let anything happen to you." He held her a few more minutes, then pulled her arms away. "Why don't you bundle into the blankets and rest for a bit?"

He closed the door as he left. Cold invaded again, but this time it was because Jason turned his back on her. Again.

***

Shauna hadn't bundled in blankets, but rocked in the rocking chair. Pretty strange kind of chair for a guy to have in his room. Maybe Jason's mom had put it in there. She felt closer to her grandmother in this chair, not only because that's where she'd sat in the dream, but as a young girl, Shauna used to climb into her grandmother's lap and they'd rock. That's what she needed after that strange encounter in the basement. She tipped her head back and closed her eyes, her feet pushing rhythmically against the floor. She almost felt Grandma's fingers soothing her forehead.

After a short while, Shauna pulled in a deep breath and stood, stretching her arms over her head. She'd find a book in the library and read for a while. She'd get a lot of that in while she was in Rawlins.

She nearly reached the library door as Abby's frustrated shriek rang out and a pencil sailed past, almost clipping Shauna's shoulder. Shauna retrieved the pencil and waved it as she stepped into the room. "I come in peace."

Abby's hands flew to her mouth. "Oh-my-god. Did I hit you?"

Shauna chuckled and dropped the pencil on the desk. "No, but it was close."

Abby picked up the pencil and tapped it on the paper in front of her. "I'm so sorry. This stupid math assignment is driving me crazy. Dad usually helps me with it after dinner, but it didn't work out Friday night, and Saturday was a bust, and now it's Sunday and everybody's gone. I want to go to my friend's house for dinner and I can't go until my homework is done."

Shauna held back a laugh, not wanting to irritate Abby. Shauna scooted around the desk and studied the papers. "Ah. I see what you're doing wrong."

Abby's eyes widened. "You do?" She swatted her paper. "This is beyond Mom, and Tony sometimes helps, but he's always busy."

"I'm an accountant. I've probably cracked more math books than you ever want to see."

Abby giggled. "I'm not going to be an accountant." She pointed at the table on the other side of the room. "Can we sit over there while you help me?"

"Sure." Shauna waited for Abby to gather her homework and followed her to the table, taking the seat beside her. Shauna picked up a pink eraser and started rubbing out some of the numbers. "Let's go back to where you're good."

A half-hour later, Abby tucked her papers into a notebook and grinned. "Thanks, Rachel. I can't believe how easy you made it seem."

Shauna shrugged. "I used to tutor some girls in high school and college. Sometimes you just have to explain a procedure a little differently than they've heard before."

Abby grabbed her books and stood. "Well, it worked for me. Thanks, again. Now, I can go to Caroline's house."

Shauna sauntered to a bookshelf full of paperbacks and selected a sci-fi novel. She hadn't tried out the window seat yet and thought the light would be nice this time of day.

Jason's voice caused her to jump and spin around. "Thanks for helping Abby. You sure know your stuff."

She scanned the room. "Where are you?"

A hand fluttered over the couch in front of the fireplace. She took hesitant steps and stopped next to the end table. To reach her, he'd have to go around the chair beside her or scramble over the table. Or maybe she'd stopped there so she wouldn't go after him. He lay stretched on the couch, his hands behind his head. Every sexy inch spoke to her of dreams she wanted to become reality.

His eyes darkened and that sexy expression appeared. Maybe he was reacting to the way she practically drooled over his body. She spun around and made a beeline for the window seat.

Chapter 7

Shauna took her time walking down the stairs, listening. Her fingers skimmed the banister, afraid her fuzzy brain would cause her to stumble. The house hadn't been this silent before, as if it was empty. Well, it was Monday, well past eight-thirty, so everybody was probably at work or school. Except, Jason should be here. He couldn't still be sleeping and he wouldn't leave without telling her. As she was about to enter the kitchen, a man cleared his throat in the library and she changed direction. Jason was reading a paperback on the couch.

Just inside the doorway, she stopped. "Here you are. I was beginning to think everyone had left."

He gave her a crooked smile. The one in her dreams that he gave her just before…Not going there. He probably saw her blush.

"Good morning, sleepyhead."

Sleeping late always made Shauna groggy. She rubbed a hand over her eyes. "Sorry. I don't usually sleep so late."

Looking at the mantel clock, he asked, "Can you be ready to go in forty minutes?"

"Sure. Where are we going?" He must have remembered how fast she'd gotten ready at the motel.

"I have an appointment with Dad at eleven to look at houses."

"So, you're not going to live here?" She hadn't really thought about it, but it took her by surprise. She had still lived with her dad.

He laughed. "I love my family, but no."

"Okay, I can be ready." She ate a quick breakfast, prepared for the day and was back in the library a short time later.

Jason looked up. "You're done already? It's only been thirty minutes." His eyes traveled from her head to her toes and back to her face. "Are you really a woman?"

She sent him a frown and flipped her hair. "My hair's still wet, but I'm ready."

"My sisters take at least an hour and a half to get ready in the morning. You're amazing."

"You must be easily amazed. It's not a big deal," Shauna said, glad he appreciated her effort.

Jason set his book down and sauntered toward her. No, he was just walking to the front door. She kept thinking—hoping—there was more between them.

A spot was open in front of *Ballard Real Estate and Rentals* when Jason pulled up to the curb a short time later. He opened the door for Shauna and as she stepped out of the car, she felt a sudden chill. She rubbed her arms, spotting Vanessa across the street. The woman glared before continuing her walk to the *Cozy Corner*.

Jason stopped beside Shauna. He glanced in the direction she stared as Vanessa entered the diner. "What's the matter?"

She shook herself, hoping it would make the chill leave. "That felt so weird."

"What did?"

"Vanessa stared daggers at me, and I had such a prickly chill. It was almost like she pelted me with sleet. She hates me."

"You two didn't even talk for a minute. How could she hate you?"

Sometimes men were so dense. "Because I was with

you at the diner, and now I'm with you again. Vanessa seems like the kind of woman to cause trouble."

"I haven't even seen her in six or seven years and haven't dated her since high school. She has no right to feel that way."

"She may not have the right, but that doesn't mean it isn't so."

Jason shook his head and sighed. "Come on."

***

Jason held the door for Shauna and they entered Reese's office. He waved them over.

"Hi, Dad."

"Hi, you two. Have a seat. I've come up with a few houses."

Shauna fidgeted beside him. He knew she wasn't comfortable doing this with him, but if she wasn't nearby, he'd be worried. Reese turned on the monitor and Jason leaned forward as pictures of the first house displayed.

When a house interested him, Jason asked her what she thought of it. She had some good comments and was more willing to give her own opinions after that, without being asked.

After seeing many average sized houses flash by, a mansion came on the screen. It could have been a castle with its granite block walls and slate roof. Black shutters graced the windows and the double front doors. He tensed. No. He didn't want to get near that house. Just the thought of it scared him. He'd probably have nightmares if he tried to sleep in it, and then the nightmares would try to take him over.

"Whoa," Shauna exclaimed. "That's beautiful…and huge."

"Dad, why is this on the list?" His hands gripped the armrests so tightly, his fingers hurt. It took everything he had not to scream.

Shauna's mouth dropped open. He couldn't tell if she was surprised at his reaction or if he was scaring her. He took slow breaths, and got himself under control.

"It was on the market, and I wanted to make sure you didn't want to buy the old family home back. Besides, it's right next door to us." His father knew its history, and shouldn't have considered it.

"I wouldn't mind living next door, but I can feel the evil coming off that house. There's no way I'd want to venture into it, let alone live in it again."

"You lived in that house?"

He glanced at Shauna. "Delete it from the list, Dad." He glared, trying again to tamp down the anger.

Reese tapped his finger on the mouse, and the picture disappeared. "It's gone. I'm sorry, son." His mouth was a straight line.

The tension eased as they continued through the list then went back to the ones that Jason was interested in. With Shauna's help, he chose five houses.

"I'll set up appointments for tomorrow for you to see them," Reese said as they stood to leave.

"Dad, can you join us for lunch?"

"No, thanks. I'm picking your mom up from *Mystical Moment*. She made a picnic lunch for us."

"All right. Enjoy." Jason gave Shauna a sideways look as they headed out the door. "So, I guess we're going to *The Black Kettle*." No sense causing her distress when it didn't matter to him which place they ate.

She placed her hands on her hips. "Yes, since it's the only restaurant in town I'm willing to set foot in. We could go back to the house and find something there for lunch."

"No, we'll eat at *The Black Kettle.* Let's walk."

***

Once seated at a table for two in the busy restaurant, Shauna didn't know where to look first. The restaurant was more than just a cutesy name in a town with witches, it was decorated with everything she could imagine when thinking of stories of witches. A small cauldron sat beside the cash register with a sign stating *Tips*. Pictures of witches from movies graced the walls, as well as magic wands. Old books stood on small shelves scattered about the walls. Shauna wasn't close enough to read the titles, but assumed they were spell books and witch stories. Some of the shelves also held jars and bottles, and she wondered if they contained ingredients for potions. A couple of old brooms stood in one corner. She shivered when she saw manacles dangling in another corner.

She leaned toward Jason, inches from his ear. "I can't believe how blatant they are with all this."

He chuckled. "It's sort of an open secret. No one talks about it, but they know others have abilities."

Fortunately for Shauna, Jason didn't know their waitress. She relaxed and enjoyed her roast beef sandwich and potato salad. Halfway through the meal, she noticed that some of the older customers were looking at her and then looked away when she caught them.

She leaned toward Jason. "Some people are staring at me. Don't they get many strangers here?"

He glanced around. "They get enough, but you're here with me, so they're probably wondering who my beautiful friend is."

Her heart pounded. "I just thought of something. Some of these people are my grandmother's age. They probably knew her. It would be wonderful to someday talk to them about her."

His eyebrows lowered. "Let's hope she didn't look much like you at your age."

His breath on her cheek was almost a caress and had her gazing into his eyes, eyes that held the same expression before he kissed her in her dreams. Her lungs must have become paralyzed, and she couldn't look away from him.

Jason sucked in a breath, and pushed back in his chair. "Maybe we should leave."

Before she had a chance to respond, she was hustled out and into the car, trying to figure out what she'd done this time to set him off.

***

Back at the house, Shauna decided to read in her room for the rest of the day, not wanting to be in Jason's way with the strange mood he was in. And she knew precisely what she wanted to read, only she had to talk to Jason about it. "Would anyone mind if I read Hannah's journals? I could catch up on Rawlins' history." It was still so eerie that she'd ended up in the town her grandmother had grown up in. Had Rawlins somehow drawn her to itself, like Kathleen said?

"Since you're part of Rawlins, I don't think Mom would mind."

"So, I can—go into the secret room and get one?"

"Sure."

They stood in the doorway of the library. Shauna glanced at the corner, where the hidden door was, and back to Jason. "It feels like I'm breaking in." She kept looking over her shoulder as she walked toward the hidden door. She had Jason's permission to enter, but it still felt wrong.

Jason laughed. "You could go to the Historical Society

to find out about Rawlins if you want. But you'll find out more about its early history from Hannah's journals. The things that nobody is supposed to know."

"Nobody, except Rawlins and Ballards?"

"Exactly."

She turned back when she reached the blank wall. "Can I take the journals out and read them in the library? I don't have to read them in there, do I?"

"You can take them up to my—uh, your room, if you want."

"Thanks." She opened the door, turned on the light, then stepped to the bookcase. There was an unnatural silence in the room that she hadn't noticed when she was inside the room with Jason. Calming waves washed over her, as if some kind of spell reduced fear if someone had to hide. Maybe the intent was to deter an invader.

She gave herself a shake and pulled out the first of Hannah's many journals, set it on the table and returned to the shelves. She hadn't taken time before to check out the other titles. There were books about paranormal abilities, spell books and historical books of events spawned by beliefs in magic. She couldn't resist pulling out a few and scanning the pages. She slid Gerald's journal partially off the shelf and checked behind her. She thought Jason wouldn't want her to look at it, and she really didn't want to find out what he'd written about Jason's father. She pushed it back in, not feeling ready for it. Picking up Hannah's first journal, she left the room and closed the door.

Jason was seated on the couch reading a Dean Koontz novel. His mood seemed improved, so she settled onto the opposite end and opened up the journal. The thick pages were yellowed. What did they make paper from back then? She barely detected a dry, dusty smell.

"I can't believe I'm holding a book that was written in

1697."

Jason smiled at her. "Yeah, it is pretty amazing. Hannah was quite the woman. No one back then knew how impressive she was."

Shauna was surprised at the pride Jason seemed to have for his mother's ancestor, especially since he wasn't a blood relation and it was probably one of his ancestors that Hannah killed. It made her want to read the journals even more.

She ran her fingers over the cover. "It doesn't feel safe to touch."

"It has protective spells on it, otherwise it would have fallen apart ages ago."

She gently turned the page. It was difficult to read at first, the writing faded and nothing like the printed words she was used to. Although written in English, the language was different from how it was spelled and spoken today. She became engrossed in the story of how Hannah's family and others fled Salem after the witch trials ended. Some of their own had been killed, and her father was afraid that Hannah's growing ability would cause the hysteria to return, centered on her.

Occasionally, a sound from Jason would distract her. Shifting in his seat, putting an ankle across his knee or leaning forward with his elbows on his thighs. Each move caused her to follow the play of muscles, remembering a dream where her hands roamed freely over his back, his thighs, his—she forced herself back into Hannah's story.

A closing of the front door startled her, and she looked up. Outside, light was fading. She hadn't notice the hours fly by. Voices in the hall and the smell of food forced her to leave the story. She hurried to the secret room, and set the journal on the table. She and Jason followed the sound and found Abby putting two boxes of pizza on the buffet in the dining room.

Kathleen saw them. "Jason, Rachel, can you get plates, glasses and drinks?"

"Sure, Mom."

In the kitchen, Jason pulled plates out, but Shauna stopped him. "Wait. Let me levitate them into the dining room."

"Ah, no thanks. You know how old this china is? Mom would have a fit if she saw you using your brand new ability to move them. Why don't you do it with the silverware?"

"Spoilsport. All right." She picked up glasses and levitated silverware, one after the other in front of her, following them to the dining room.

The four of them had been seated only minutes with plates of pizza when Reese and Tony arrived home and joined them.

"Pizza! Yes!" Tony said.

Jason laughed. "What every teenager wants for every meal."

"Of course," Tony said as he loaded a plate with a few slices.

Halfway through the noisy meal, Reese said, "Jason, I've scheduled three houses to visit tomorrow starting at ten. The other two are on Wednesday at two."

"That sounds great, Dad. Thanks."

Shauna spoke to Jason. "It feels weird for me to tag along with you everywhere. I could stay here while you look at the houses." She didn't want to see the house that he ended up buying and imagine him in it after she left.

"No, you're coming." He leaned into her. "I can't protect you if you're here, and I could use a woman's perspective. I never bought a house before."

"All right, but I haven't bought one before, either. I don't want to be in the way." She was probably safer in the house than wandering around town for everyone to see. Did he really think her best protection was with him?

After Shauna placed her dishes in the dishwasher, Kathleen touched her arm. "Rachel, could we talk?"

"Sure, Kathleen." She followed her into the formal living room, hoping it wouldn't be as disconcerting as the last time the two had a private talk.

"I'm coming, too," Jason said.

Maybe he was he afraid his mom would reveal something else that would frighten her.

Jason closed the pocket doors behind them.

Kathleen sat on the couch and waved to the chair. "Have a seat."

Shauna sat in a deep chair while Jason joined his mother on the couch.

"Shauna, I had a dream last night where I gave you my necklace." She reached behind her neck, unhooked it and held it out to Shauna.

"Mom. You've never taken that off. I thought it was fused closed." Jason's eyes widened.

"It was, but after my dream, I had no trouble opening the clasp."

Shauna didn't understand the talk of a fused clasp and had no idea why Kathleen would want to give a near stranger a valuable necklace. "Kathleen, I can't accept it."

"Shauna, you have to. Uncle Gerald left this to me because he placed a protection spell on it. I was never able to remove it. This morning I unhooked it for the first time in nearly twenty years. You're meant to have it now. I don't know why, but you need it."

"But maybe you still need protection." Two weeks ago, it would have sounded strange to talk about an object giving protection, but she'd seen enough to know it was likely true.

"I still have the ring." Kathleen held up her hand and wiggled her fingers. "I did a spell this morning to increase the power of both since I'm separating them." She leaned forward, holding the necklace closer to Shauna.

Shauna hesitated as the necklace swung from its silver chain. Finally, she reached out and took it. The dark blue stone seemed to swirl with life and still felt warm from being against Kathleen's skin. It was surrounded by small diamonds and intricate silver filigree. She looked at Jason. He shrugged and looked unsure. Shauna wasn't sure what to think of putting on a necklace she might never remove. Kathleen seemed so sure she needed it. With the danger she was in because of Nick, every bit of protection would be valuable.

"All right. Thank you." Shauna held the ends of the clasp in her hands and connected it behind her neck. A sudden warmth heated her fingers. "Oh. The clasp got hot."

"I should have warned you that would happen when it fused."

"What?" Shauna reached to the clasp, but it wouldn't open. It was done. She had only partially believed that the same thing would happen with the clasp as happened with Kathleen. It was almost like she had something alive around her neck. Would it eventually sense that she didn't need it anymore and she could pass it back to Kathleen or someone else? "So, what will it protect me from?"

"Magic. Not something you would have had to worry about before you came here. I haven't sensed evil in Rawlins for years, and I haven't had any dreams about trouble. All I know is that you need that necklace, so it's yours.

"Thank you for caring about me." Her hand went to the warm stone.

Kathleen stood and put her hand over Shauna's. "I do care. You're always welcome here." She studied Shauna for a few seconds, glanced at her son, then left the room. She seemed to convey a message Shauna didn't get.

Shauna turned to Jason. "This is such a strange place. I'm not used to believing in magic."

"I grew up here, so it doesn't seem strange to me. But coming back after being gone for three years sure makes me see it differently."

That was the scary part, wondering what the necklace would protect her from. Maybe there was something, other than Nick, that she required protection from, something in Rawlins that she would never have otherwise encountered.

Chapter 8

House hunting had been a fruitless endeavor with the promise of more appointments the next day.

"How about a walk in the state forest?" Jason asked.

Fresh air in the woods sounded heavenly. Ages ago, she used to go with her father. Nick had no interest in nature, and neither did Kristy. She loved looking for wildlife and the occasional wildflowers. "That would be wonderful. Would you mind if we went back home to change first?" The weather had turned out warmer than she expected, and she didn't want to sweat in front of Jason. She also needed her hiking shoes.

At the house, Shauna raced up the stairs and into her room. She tugged off her clothes and pulled on shorts, t-shirt and socks, then put her hair in a pony tail and raced halfway down the stairs before noticing Jason watching her from the bottom. She nearly stumbled and came to a stop to catch herself. He'd changed into cargo pants and a t-shirt, looking more casual than she'd seen him before, and maybe more sexy. His eyes glinted with that light that told her he liked what he saw. She finished the rest of the stairs more slowly.

The side pocket on his right leg bulged. That must be where he hid his gun. Something always reminded her she wasn't there on vacation.

A half-hour scenic drive north on winding roads brought them to the state forest. Four cars were already parked in the dirt lot, and Jason pulled in at the end.

"It's been ages since I've done this," Shauna said as

they got out.

Jason chose a trail, and they walked side by side on a wide path.

She glanced at him and back down the trail. "My Dad and I used to hike once or twice a month. That's one of the things I miss the most about him. But we hadn't gone for the last couple years before he died. He seemed...different. On our hikes, we used to talk about everything, his work, my work…" Her love life, which was nonexistent, but she wasn't going to share that with Jason. "I tried to get him to date again, but he said nobody could replace my mother. She left us. What was so great about her?" She sighed.

Jason surprised her when he took her hand and squeezed it. "I didn't mean to make you sad."

"No, I'm not really. It brings back some good memories, too. Thank you." Now was not the time to be lost in memories, not when just a touch from Jason sent warm tingles up her arm and through her body.

The edges of the trail were grassy, like they'd been mowed. Oaks and maples dominated with an evergreen here and there to give off a piney scent. A tunnel of overhead branches with the sun peeking through in spots curved over the slightly sloping trail.

"Tell me about this trail," Shauna said.

"It leads to Manning Lake. There's a two mile path that goes all the way around it. Once at the lake, we can take the path or turn around and head back."

"Let's decide when we get there."

His voice had gone husky. "You look like you'd have no trouble doing the whole trek."

With a quick glance, she caught the reason for that voice. It was that sexy dream face. Her face grew warm, so she hurried down the trail.

As they approached the lake, the view opened up.

Shauna stopped and gazed. "It's beautiful." Trees surrounded the long, narrow lake, and boulders bordered the shore in many places. A field of water lilies floated on the smooth surface of the lake with their white or purple blossoms. She stepped closer to the water and sat on a large, flat, sun-warmed rock. Jason sat beside her, not close enough to touch.

"I don't think I'm ready to walk all the way around the lake. Maybe next time." She leaned back on her hands and lifted her face to the sun. She took a deep breath and was overwhelmed with Jason's scent. A hint of clean sweat, maybe how he'd smell if they made love. She cut off the thought.

She opened her eyes to find Jason staring at her. Her heart skipped a beat and sped up. A few times, she'd caught Nick looking at her like that, and it had made her uncomfortable, but with Jason, she wanted to touch him, feel his lips. Unable to stop herself, she touched his face, cupped his cheek then slid her hand to his neck. She leaned toward him and he met her halfway. Their lips touched. He nibbled her lips as he pulled her body close to his and kissed her harder. She'd never been kissed like this. Nick's kisses had always been overly appropriate as if he was afraid he'd scare her. Which he would have.

Jason's tongue tickled her lip and she opened to him, moaning when his tongue met hers. His breaths came faster than hers. One of her hands slid up into his silky hair and the other wrapped around his back. She wanted more and pressed closer to him. Visions of his naked body flashed into her mind and she moaned. She wanted to touch it for real, feel his warmth.

His kisses were more intense than the dreams, and her body so desperately wanted more.

***

He couldn't get enough of her. He slipped his hand under her shirt and smoothed it up her back. It slid over her ribs and slipped under her bra, nudging it up. Jason cupped her full breast, and ran his thumb over her taut nipple. She moaned and he kissed her more deeply. He wanted to lay her on the rock, and leaned forward, his arm brushing his gun. He froze, realizing what he was doing. It took every ounce of control to release her, and draw away from her responsive body. He propped his arms on his legs and rubbed a hand on his face as he slowed his breathing.

He wanted her, but he couldn't do this. He thought she'd be safe from him out here, where anyone could happen by. It was that dream. He knew how much pleasure they could give each other. Maybe the Rawlins' evil had given them both the dream so that he could fulfill some kind of legacy. If they made love, he might draw power from her and be changed.

It scared him to think he could harm her or become like his biological father. The people that he thought of as his real parents deserved better than to have him do something that could hurt them. He didn't want to be the one responsible for bringing evil back to Rawlins. He didn't want to be that evil person. He couldn't take a chance.

"I'm sorry. We need to leave." He stood, staring out over the water. Shauna's breathing matched his. Deep breaths brought more control. Despite his attraction to her, she was bad news. He shouldn't have allowed himself to be tempted.

"Did I do something wrong?"

Her quiet voice was barely audible, but the hurt came through. He hadn't meant to hurt her. She must think he was the worst kind of scum. She'd so willingly returned his kisses, and he'd cut her off before they'd gone too far. Before any kisses would have been a better stopping place. Some protector he was. He'd gotten so lost in her kisses that anything could have happened before he had a chance to react.

Although he kept his eyes on the lake, he waited until gravel crunch under her feet, before he spoke. "No. It's me. I'm sorry." If he saw her face right now, he'd want to fold her into his arms to reassure her. They'd both be lost. He stood up and started down the path, pausing until her footsteps came up behind him.

He hated doing this to her. She was the first woman to never leave his thoughts and she was the one he couldn't have.

***

Walking behind Jason, Shauna couldn't figure out what she'd done wrong. It wasn't her, or so he said, but he was kissing and holding her like he really cared and then suddenly he wasn't. Maybe he couldn't stand the way she kissed. His eyes wouldn't meet hers. She was starting to care for him, but he kept twisting her emotions, pulling her in only to reject her. Women changed their minds less than he did. It would be a whole lot easier on her if he decided to either keep his distance or get closer to her. Doing one and then the other threw her in turmoil.

This was new territory for her. She'd never before felt this need to kiss and touch a man like she had with Jason. The dreams were intense and felt like memories. Now she knew what he could make her feel with kisses and she wanted to experience all of it for real. That didn't look like it was going to happen. Or maybe it would, and he'd reject her again. That would be worse. She wished the dreams would fade.

Nobody before Jason had penetrated the shell surrounding her. She'd shied away from dating, let alone having boyfriends, so she had no experience on how to deal with guys' attitudes. Any guy's interest in her had repulsed her. She'd decided that sex wasn't for her, until the dreams about Jason. Knowing how Jason could make her respond, he was the one she craved to have sex with. And he'd just rejected her. It felt like he'd torn a piece out of her heart.

She was tempted to levitate a stick into his path to trip him, but that was too mean, and she couldn't use her new ability that way.

The uphill return trip was more difficult than walking to the water. Jason ignored her, walking so fast she couldn't keep up. He disappeared around a bend and she ran. Her thighs burned and she couldn't catch her breath. She stopped, bracing her hands on her knees, willing her breathing to slow. Now she wished she'd pushed him into the lake.

Maybe she'd taken a wrong path. This seemed so much farther than their walk in.

Once her breathing returned to near normal, she started walking again. Jason came around a turn in the path. "I'm sorry, I lost track—"

"You already said that." She stalked past him. It felt like they'd had a silent argument. Maybe he angry because she kissed him first. Except, he met her halfway. He was the one who pulled her closer. He was the one to push his tongue into her mouth. He was the one to practically drop her and turn away. He was too frustrating.

Jason followed her back to the car. He beeped the locks, and she snatched the door open and slammed it closed before he could help her. She kept her face turned to her window on the drive home. He didn't need to see her humiliation. A quick kiss and done would have been fine. A friendly little kiss she could have understood, but he'd taken over the kiss, made her want so much more from him. And then he'd left her to trail behind him.

It was a silent, uncomfortable ride back to the house. Shauna exited the car as soon as it stopped and scurried into the house. She reached her bedroom and closed the door, leaning her head against it, and let silent tears run down her cheeks. not even knowing why she was crying.

Now she knew what Jason's kisses could do to her. They were so much more than she'd experienced in the dreams, but now she craved to finish what they'd started, knowing the rest would be more intense than anything she'd ever imagined.

Shauna couldn't face Jason over dinner. The best thing to do was take a nap, and they'd let her sleep through it. She lay down on top of the comforter and went through some relaxation exercises. It worked better at night when she was actually tired. It took starting over a couple of times as thoughts of Jason intruded. Finally, sleep claimed her.

Chapter 9

Shauna waited on the bed in Jamie's room for Jason to return from the shower. Her hands shook and she clenched them into fists. She wasn't sure how he would react when he found her there. Footsteps came down the hall and stopped outside the door. Her heartbeat kicked up. It was Jason. The doorknob turned and she bit her lip, tugging the blanket higher to make sure she was totally covered. She didn't want him to know she was naked until she knew he had the same longing for her.

He stepped in and his eyes widened. Without saying a word, he closed the door, his eyes on her. He seemed indecisive. Maybe he'd tell her to leave. It could easily go either way.

He seemed to accept her silent offer, and gave her that sexy, one-sided smile. With his first step, every muscle in her body tightened. Now that it was going to happen, she wasn't sure she was ready. She labored to draw air into her lungs as each slow step brought him nearer. She tried to smile, but ended up catching her lip between her teeth. He dropped the robe off his shoulders. She wanted him as much as he clearly wanted her. Shauna imagined her hand running down that muscled chest. He slid in beside her and pulled her close to him, warm body to warm body. Oh, yeah, he wanted her. His lips touched hers gently before he growled and deepened the kiss. She ran a hand through his damp hair...

***

A long time later, yet still dark out, Shauna stretched, feeling like she should purr. Her body felt good, tingly. She'd had that dream again. It wasn't exactly like before. This time she'd started out naked in the bed. His eyes had glowed when he'd seen her. He'd made love to her slowly, and she'd treasure every second. After waking, her desires frustrated her. She wanted the real thing. She wanted his hands on her. She wanted him inside her.

She hadn't had the dream since she met Jason. Why now? Maybe it was because of what happened at the lake. Because they'd kissed and Jason had pulled away from her. It was confusing that she couldn't be mad at him anymore because of the dream. Like fake make-up sex.

She tunneled her fingers through her hair dark hair, and picked up Hannah's journal from the nightstand. Hopefully it would take her mind off Jason.

***

Jason sat at the library desk with his open laptop. He checked his email and sent a quick message to Mark, letting him know Shauna was safe. She hadn't come down by the time he finished, so he went upstairs, knocked on her door, but she didn't respond. He assumed she didn't want to see him after the way he'd treated her.

Dinner was tense for Jason. He told everyone that Rachel was tired and went to bed early. He felt eyes on him during the whole meal, like they all knew there was more to it. He could tell them it was his fault, but he couldn't fix it. It wouldn't help. He tried talking about the houses his dad had taken him and Shauna to see that day. It wasn't the same as the day before when she joined in.

"Jason, I set up appointments for those two houses," Reese said. "Come to my office about two. Allen should call tomorrow with appointments for offices on Monday."

"Thanks, Dad. We'll be there." He might have to drag Shauna out. Everything would have been fine if he hadn't given in and kissed her.

Finally, dinner was over and the dining room and dishes cleaned up. He stood in the kitchen with his parents, feeling like an awkward teenager again.

"Dad, can we go for a walk?"

Reese glanced at Kathleen and back to Jason. "Sure, son." He kissed his wife's cheek and they headed out the front door.

"Does this have something to do with Rachel?" Reese asked as soon as they hit the sidewalk.

"Yes, but it's complicated. Let's go sit on the park bench."

They crossed the street to the park and strolled another hundred yards to the bench.

After they were seated, Jason stared ahead of him. It wasn't quite as bad as when he was a teenager, but bad enough.

"Remember when I told you about my ability to detect virgins?"

"I remember you were pretty upset," his dad said.

"I promised myself that I would never have sex with a virgin. I even broke up with my girlfriend to make sure of it. I've been careful since then. Except Rachel…is a virgin and I shouldn't want her. We went for a hike this afternoon and when we sat down for a rest, I kissed her. I almost lost control." The near panic in his voice reminded him of discovering that ability when he was fifteen.

"Jason, you're nothing like Nathan. I think you have to start out with an evil heart for that to take hold of you. I heard stories about the horrible things Nathan did, even back in middle school. You've never been like that."

Jason glanced quickly at his father and away. He'd seen the concern in his father's eyes.

"Just the fact that you're so worried about it shows that you're better than him," Reese said.

It sort of made sense, but it was a risk he was afraid to take. "Thanks, Dad, but I don't know if I can trust that. Maybe it would only take that one virgin to make me someone else. Still, I was hired to protect Rachel, so I can't send her away. I'm afraid for her and of myself if I let anything…intimate happen between us."

"What about getting someone else to protect her?"

Jason shook his head. "Mark could probably find someone else to protect Rachel, but it pains me to even think about never seeing her again. I'd worry that whoever was protecting her wasn't doing a good enough job."

"Your mom told me that both of you had premonition dreams of each other."

Jason nodded. "But mine didn't happen until after we met. Maybe it was just my imagination because I'd met her."

"But they both happened in Jamie's room. Your imagination wouldn't have put you in there."

Jason almost smiled. "Mom told you that? If it was only my imagination, it would have been only sex and no scenery." His face heated and he glanced at his dad. "Sorry, I shouldn't have said that out loud." He ran a hand through his hair.

Reese gave a chuckle. "I never expected to be talking to my adult son about sex this way. I'm not pushing you to have sex. I just think that if you two are meant to be together, then you don't have to worry about being taken over by evil. Making love with the woman you love isn't the same as having sex for your own benefit. Nathan didn't care about those girls in high school. He only wanted power." He put his hand on his son's arm and waited until Jason looked at him. "It's what's in your heart that matters."

The discussion with his dad about this particular ability had been difficult the first time. Before it had been about avoiding sex. Now it was about having sex with the woman who might be the right one. "You've given me a lot to think about."

"You could explain the situation to Rachel."

Jason gave his father a horrified look. "Dad, I've never talked about this to anyone, but you."

"If you're thinking of pursuing a relationship with her, she needs to know the risk, however slight it is. And if you decide not to chance it, it's only fair to explain that it really isn't her."

Jason rubbed his forehead. "Yeah. Okay. She'd at least understand why I've been Jekyll and Hyde." Maybe there was hope for the two of them.

***

"Shauna, dear, we need to talk."

"Mmm." Shauna opened her eyes. The light on the dresser was on. Looking around the room, she found her grandmother sitting in the same chair as before and sat up. "Grandma, you're back."

"I came to teach you another ability and to discuss that boy again. Oh, and did you practice levitation?"

Shauna squirmed. Only her grandmother could make her do that. "Yes. I did it that morning to put my clothes into drawers. And then occasionally to see that I could still do it."

"Shauna, you must practice so this comes as easily as lifting a finger."

"I am. I'll do it more. Now what do you want to teach me this time?" She bounced a little on the bed.

"I want to see if you can create bubbles."

"Bubbles? Like soap bubbles and a wand?"

"Shauna, what use would that have? These are protective bubbles."

"Like Kevlar against bullets?" Shauna smiled. Maybe she could get Grandma to smile.

"Yes, dear. That's one use."

"Really? I was kidding. This bubble could keep out bullets?"

"Yes, and if you were in a fire, it would keep the smoke out and most of the heat. It would protect you from wind and cold."

"Would it work if I was attacked?"

"Yes, dear, as long as your attacker wasn't already touching you. Then he'd be in the bubble with you. So, do be careful."

"Grandma, have you ever had to use your bubble?"

"Only for inconsequential things, like being caught in a rainstorm or a windy day. You do have to be careful where you use it. People can't see the bubble, but they can see the effects of it. If you were in the rain and used the bubble, people would see that you weren't getting wet and maybe how the water detoured around you."

"But it doesn't matter in Rawlins, right?"

"People don't flaunt their abilities, dear. Once, everybody in Rawlins knew that others had abilities. Now, there are people living here that know nothing about Rawlins' origins.

"All right, I'll be careful. How do I begin?"

"First start by forming a bubble. You can pretend you're blowing soap bubbles."

Shauna pictured herself dipping a wand into a bottle of bubbles and slowly blowing on the soapy film. It popped before it got large enough. She tried again and again without success.

Frustrated, she said, "This isn't working Grandma. Is there any other way?"

"Another way is to build your bubble. Picture the top of it forming and work your way down the sides and enclose the bottom."

Shauna imagined a film of soapy liquid hovering in front of her. It dripped evenly down the sides and curved inward, connecting at the bottom. A one-foot sphere floated in front of her. It looked like a regular soap bubble with a bit of a golden glow from the light.

"I did it!"

"Now reinforce it, dear."

Shauna frowned at her grandmother.

"Recoat the whole surface a number of times."

Shauna did as directed.

"Now touch it."

Shauna poked a finger at it. The side gave a little and started to move away.

"Grab it and hold it."

Shauna gently clasped the bubble in her hands. "It's squishy like a balloon."

"Now let it rest on your hand and pop it."

Shauna stared at the bubble. She imagined a pin pricking it and the bubble burst. "Well, that's not going to protect me very well."

"We have to work at getting it bigger and stronger. Stand up, Dear."

Shauna crawled out of bed and curled her toes on the cold floor.

"Picture the top of a bubble over your head and let it flow down the sides, closing it beneath your feet."

Shauna's bubble slowly increased in size. When it reached the floor, she lifted each foot and let the bubble totally envelope her. She pushed on it with her palm. "Wow.

This is so weird."

"Now make it stronger. Right now, it would only keep out rain."

Shauna poured down more coatings on her bubble. "How do I know how strong it is?"

"It's like looking through glass. You know when you're looking through thicker glass. Maybe tomorrow you can encapsulate something in the yard and shoot arrows at it."

"Why didn't I think to pack arrows in my suitcase? Maybe I'll find rocks." Shauna had hoped to get a chuckle from her grandmother.

"You've done well, Shauna. Now I want to talk about that Proctor boy again."

Shauna sighed. "Grandma, his name is Jason Ballard. He's no longer a Proctor."

"He still has Proctor blood. The evil of his father is waiting for release."

Shauna leaned forward and raised her voice. "No. He's not like that. He's good. He's caring. Nothing is going to change him."

"You already love him, don't you? He's put a spell on you."

Frustration warred with a small niggling of doubt. "I don't know if I love him. Maybe. Nobody put a spell on me." Shauna remembered her necklace and lifted it. "Shouldn't this protect me from a spell? Kathleen gave it to me for protection."

Her grandma stood in front of Shauna and touched the necklace. "Well, I'll be. It does have a protection spell on it. I think I like Kathleen." She straightened and stared at her granddaughter. "So, he can't put a spell on you, but there are many other ways to harm you. Be careful around him." She touched Shauna's shoulder, startling her. "It's time for me to leave. I'll let you sleep. Remember, I love you."

Shauna wrapped her hand around her grandmother's surprisingly warm hand. "I love you, too, Gram."

Bubbles. She didn't need a bubble to protect her from Jason, except maybe a small one to protect her heart.

Chapter 10

Shauna grabbed her clothes, holding them to her pajama clad chest, and headed down the hall to the bathroom. The door opened just as she got to it, and she froze. Jason clutched a towel at his waist. Shauna lowered her gaze to his chest, where the damp hairs held her attention. It was the first time she'd seen his chest outside of her dreams. She wanted to touch him to see if he felt the same, to see if he responded the same. She skimmed down to his tight abs, and the towel barely covering him and wished she had the courage to pull it off. Fresh from the shower, he smelled of soap and shampoo, but soon his own special scent would reassert itself. She knew how to hasten it. He always smelled delicious in her dreams.

She dragged her view to over his shoulder, into the steamy bathroom. Other mornings, when she'd seen him on his way to or from the bathroom, he'd worn a robe. And the only time she came face-to-chest with him, and he wore only a towel.

It was too late to turn around and go back to her room. She wanted to look at that chest again, but if she did, she'd have to touch it, feel how warm it was. And he'd push her away. She rather pretend he hadn't rejected her yesterday, and not risk getting rejected again.

"Morning, Rachel." It was a slap in the face that he'd used the fake name when nobody was around. Maybe it was another way to distance himself from her.

"Hi, Jason." She sounded like a hurt wimp instead of the

courageous woman she wanted to be.

She stepped aside to let him pass, dropped her head, and closed her eyes. He didn't move past. Maybe he'd go away if she ignored him. He'd probably try to humiliate her again. A finger touched under her chin, startling her into opening her eyes, as he tipped her head up.

"We need to talk."

She shook her head. "There's nothing to talk about."

"There's plenty to talk about. Let's go to the park after breakfast." Slowly, he leaned toward her, kissed her forehead, then continued to his sister's room.

Shauna watched him disappear behind the door as she covered her open mouth. Something was different. He kissed her. After what happened the day before, she didn't think he'd get near her again. His rejection still twisted her heart. Her dreams were probably causing these feelings, this wanting, but that didn't explain his actions.

A new thought struck her. Maybe they were dreams sent to compel her to have sex with Jason. Could that be all it was? A false urge. That could ruin her. Because, under it all, she knew she was falling for him.

Weeks ago, she wouldn't have believed she could be compelled to do something. She also wouldn't have believed a necklace would protect her from it. She touched her necklace. It eased this particular concern.

Shauna rushed through her shower and breakfast, soon stepping out the front door with Jason. It startled her when he took her hand. His heat traveling up her arm and settled in her fluttery stomach. She was too confused to think of anything to say. The day before, he couldn't stand to kiss her and today he kissed her forehead and held her hand.

They crossed the street and angled toward a park bench. Jason sat and pulled Shauna down beside him. She sat sideways, so she could face him. Her knee pressed against his thigh.

His lips thinned and his left foot tapped. "When I was sixteen, I gained a new ability."

She leaned closer. This was important, and he wasn't comfortable telling her about it. She touched his thigh and his eyes dropped to her hand as if she just scorched him. She started to pull it away, but his hand clamped down on hers. He glanced at her eyes and then stared down at their hands.

"I knew which girls were…virgins." His face turned red.

If that was so, he knew that she was a virgin, too. Now her face grew warm. "Um, how could you tell?" Maybe that's why he stopped kissing her the day before. He didn't want to take advantage of a woman with no experience. But she hadn't been protesting.

"They sort of have this glow around their head—"

She giggled. "You mean, like an angel's halo?"

He didn't smile at her remark, and his hand tightened on hers. He was serious. "No, it's around the whole head."

"What kind of ability is that? I thought abilities were supposed to help you."

His voice turned gruff. "Well, if you're evil scum like Nathan Proctor, it would help."

"But you're not. What did he do?" Maybe she didn't want to know, but it seemed Jason needed to tell her.

"He compelled virgins to have sex with him. It increased his power. He probably wiped out the entire virgin population when he was in high school."

She couldn't imagine how hard it was for Jason to learn his father was that revolting.

"I'm sorry, Jason. I'm not sure I know what's worse—that your birth father was evil, or what it felt like for you to learn what he was like, or that…you have the same ability.

His shoulders lifted and dropped. "So, I vowed to never

have sex with a virgin. I was too worried that I'd get an increase of power, and that I'd like it, and wouldn't be able to resist taking more. I even broke up with my girlfriend after I got the ability. I couldn't take a chance."

Jason released her hand and touched her cheek. "You're the first virgin I haven't been able to walk away from. I was drawn to you from the moment I saw you at the club." He dropped his hand to the bench and looked away. "But I can't touch you. I'm too afraid of what will happen."

All these mixed messages because she'd never had sex? "Gee, I thought it was the virgin who should be afraid or at least nervous. Hey, I don't even feel like a virgin anymore after—those dreams." Maybe he didn't know she'd had them, and she'd just unwittingly blurted out her secret. She blushed. She couldn't believe they were talking about this. If his were the same, he'd know what her body looked like, how she responded to his touch. "Um, did you know about…the dreams?"

"Yeah." He glanced at her and away. "I suspected when you turned the radio off in the car when the song about dreams came on. After a couple of other things, I was sure you'd had the same dream as me."

"So, maybe it doesn't matter after the dreams."

"You're still physically a virgin. I still see you that way."

"Oh. So the only way you'd touch me, is if I go find some random guy to have sex with and then come back to you?"

His head snapped around. In a loud, angry voice, he said, "What? No!"

Nervous laughter bubbled up at his reaction. She'd wanted her first time to be special, but if it was the only way Jason would touch her, could she do it with someone else? A shudder passed through her. No. "I couldn't do that, but it does leave us with a problem."

Jason pressed his lips together and remained silent.

It dawned on her that she'd never had an interest in having sex with Nick. It actually scared her a little. With Jason, she thought about it all the time. She wasn't sure if the desire came from her dreams or the growing feelings she had for him.

"So, we're at an impasse." She couldn't believe they were talking about having sex, or not. Mostly not.

He lifted her hand to his lips and teased it with kisses. "For now."

For now? Maybe it wasn't hopeless. Shauna set both feet on the ground, and scooted closer to Jason. He put his arm around her, and pulled her closer. She tipped her head onto his shoulder, more comfortable with Jason than any man before. Despite his words, she didn't believe he would turn evil. Shauna trusted him. And she wanted to find out if what she'd experienced in her dreams was real. She had no idea when or if they'd have sex, but at least she understood him better.

After a long, comfortable silence, Jason said, "I've got some emails to respond to and other things to set up before seeing houses this afternoon, so we should head back." He took her hand and pulled her up as he stood. They held hands until they reached the house.

She stopped beside Kathleen's car as he headed to his. "I have to get my laptop." He opened the rear door and leaned in, and as quickly closed the door without his computer in hand. He took his keys from his pocket and opened the front door.

She'd seen the laptop on the seat. "Jason, are you leaving?"

"I have to go." His voice sounded as if he spoke to himself. He didn't look at her.

He hadn't said anything before about having to go somewhere. She settled a hand on his arm. "Jason, did you remember something you were supposed to do?"

His eyes darted around, and he clenched his jaw. "I have to get my laptop." He opened the back door and paused, then closed it.

"I have to leave." His voice was flat again. He reached for the driver's door.

Shauna stepped in front of him, thoroughly confused. She set a hand on each of his arms.

"Jason! Stop now. What are you doing? That's twice you said you had to leave."

His eyes scrunched. "I'm not leaving. Why would I say that?"

Something wasn't right. She held his arms more firmly. "You're the one who said it. Why would you?"

He stared at her hands on his arms. "Shauna, remove your hands, and see what happens. If I start to leave again, touch me and make sure I get into the house."

This was one of those weird things that could only happen in Rawlins. With only a touch, she was preventing someone from making Jason leave. She lifted her hands from him and watched his eyes. They were beautiful. She'd never seen eyes as dark blue as his, like warm pools she could swim in. Then his eyes glazed like he was deep in thought.

"I have to leave."

"Jason, come into the house." She grabbed his arm and pulled. He resisted for a second before he followed her. As soon as they were through the door, she called out, "Kathleen, we need you!"

The woman rushed down the stairs, and didn't have time to ask a question. "Kathleen, if I'm not touching Jason, he says he has to leave. I stopped him, but he doesn't remember that he was leaving."

Kathleen stepped closer. "Ah. This is one of the reasons I was led to give you my necklace."

Shauna reached up to the object. "It's your necklace that's keeping Jason here?"

"I think the necklace protected Jason from a spell. Now that he's in the house, he's okay because the house has protection. Someone seems to be compelling him to come to them." Kathleen's brows drew down as she looked from one to the other. "Any ideas who and why?"

Shauna and Jason glanced at each other and shook their heads.

Kathleen bit her lip. "Well, for now, let's protect you against it. Jason, get one of those medallions that you used to wear. We'll put a protection spell on it."

He hurried up the stairs while Kathleen took Shauna into the library. She hesitated then said, "Maybe I should have you wait out there."

"Are you going into the secret room?"

Kathleen lifted her eyebrows. "You know about it?"

Shauna nodded. "Jason showed me in case I have to hide from Nick."

"All right, then." Kathleen stared at her for a second. "Jason's the one who showed you and…" Kathleen walked into the corner and opened the door to the secret room, disappearing inside.

And what? Shauna wanted her to finish.

A moment later, Kathleen returned with a book.

"This is my spell book." She skimmed the pages and found the one she wanted, then set the book on the desk.

Jason stopped in front of them. "How's this, Mom?" He handed her a silver moon and star pendant on a silver chain.

"That'll do. Now, I'm going to hold this and the three of us are going to recite this spell." She pointed to it. "Read it through a few times. Get it in your head so that when we read it together, you mean every word."

Shauna nodded. She picked up the book and held it for all to see. The spell was shorter than she expected, and she read through it several times.

Jason stepped back. "I can't read this spell. My ancestors are evil. There's no way I'm calling them."

Kathleen touched his cheek. "You're my son. My ancestors are your ancestors."

He shook his head and took another step back. "His blood still runs through my veins."

Shauna's heart broke for him. He had a wonderful family who loved him as their own, but it always came back to his biological father.

Kathleen's shoulders dropped. "All right. Rachel and I will read it. You can hold the book."

"And I don't want to wear it forever, so don't seal it."

Kathleen glared at him. "Jason—"

"Mom—"

"All right. All right. We won't read the last line."

Shauna handed the book to Jason and read through the first part of the spell twice more. "I'm ready."

Kathleen cupped the necklace in her hand. "Rachel, put your hand over mine. Start…now."

"We call forth the force of our ancestors to put your protective power into this object we hold. May it shield the wearer from the influences of black magic."

Shauna made sure she meant every word. As the last words left her mouth the necklace warmed for a few seconds. "I think it worked."

Kathleen nodded and handed the pendant to her son. "Here. Put it on."

He slipped the chain over his head and strode out the front door.

The two women followed him. They stood on the wide porch for several minutes.

"I think I'll go get my laptop now." He sauntered down the steps with Shauna not far behind. Pulling the computer from the back seat, he turned and almost bumped into her. "Sorry, I didn't realize you were so close."

"I wanted to make sure you'd be all right." She smiled. "I guess it worked. I wonder who you've made angry because you didn't come to them."

Jason tipped his head and touched the medallion. "Maybe I should take this off and you and Mom can hop in the car and see where I go. Then you can put the medallion back on when we get there."

Kathleen stepped beside them. "That's not a good idea. The longer you're under their control, the harder it will be to break it. And we don't know what situation we'd be walking into. Maybe we wouldn't be able to get the medallion back on you."

Shauna grabbed his arm. "I agree with your mom. It's too dangerous."

Jason pursed his lips and gave a curt nod. "No doubt they'll step up their game."

She shivered. They didn't need this happening on top of her concern about Nick. He put his arm around her, and they sauntered back into the house.

***

After lunch, they joined Reese to look at more houses. He pulled into the driveway of a house with a For Sale sign. The house sat back farther from the street than its neighbors, with several trees shading the front yard. The uniformly green grass smelled freshly mowed. Flower beds encircled the tree trunks closest to the house. Rectangular gray stone covered the two-story house. Shauna didn't have time to count the many windows. An open, attached two-car garage sat on the right of the house.

Shauna squeezed Jason's hand. "It's beautiful."

"We go in this way," Reese said, leading them into the garage and to the connecting door to the house. He knocked and the door was opened by a barefoot man with shoulder length, blond hair.

"Hi, you must be the realtor. I'm Guy Fiore." He held out his hand.

Reese shook it and handed Guy his card. "I'm Reese Ballard and this is my client, Jason and his friend, Rachel." He waved behind him. They entered the house.

"I'm in heaven," Shauna said as she slowly spun in the kitchen. She loved all the natural oak cabinets and the black granite counters. A center island with a black cook top on one end provided seating with tall chairs on the other. A cinnamon scented candle burned in the center of a large dining table with eight chairs, in front of patio doors that looked out over a large backyard.

Guy smiled. "I'll let you get to it. If you have any questions, you'll find me in my office trying to beat a deadline." He walked out of the kitchen.

"This is the best kitchen yet," Shauna whispered.

Jason laughed. "You already gave it away with the heaven comment. You might as well speak up now."

"Oh, sorry. The perfection stole my common sense."

Reese led them through the dining room with French doors overlooking the manicured backyard bordered by woods. The main feature in the living room was a large red brick fireplace with a gas log. They peeked into the office where Guy worked. One wall was all shelves with cabinets on the bottom. Behind the next door they found a half bath. The last room on the first floor was a family room, with pocket doors pushed open. A squishy rust colored carpet covered the floor and a big screen television hung on the wall over a stone fireplace.

"Let's go upstairs now," Reese said.

Each of the four bedrooms had two windows and a walk in closet. A full bath on each side of the hall separated the bedrooms.

The master bedroom, at the end of the hall had four windows, two in front and two on the side wall. Between the side windows, sat a black tile fireplace with a tiled mantel. The huge walk-in closet and bath were at the back of the house.

Shauna stepped into the bathroom. "Oh, I love this." She could imagine Jason leaning back in the Jacuzzi tub and climbing in with him. She fanned herself and turned away, and the thought of watching Jason showering behind the clear glass shower doors didn't help. She caught her reflection in the mirror. Yeah, Jason would easily guess what she was thinking about. She ran her hand across the smooth gray granite counter with his and hers sinks.

She glanced at Jason, who was grinning at her. "What? You haven't made any comments yet."

He touched her cheek. "I'm enjoying seeing your comments on your face."

This turn-around in him confused her. She may have known what his problem was, but that didn't mean he was ready to move ahead.

They finished the tour of the house and stepped out onto the back deck. Tall privacy fences bordered the sides.

"I think I see a path leading from the yard," Shauna said, standing on tip-toe to get a better look. "We, uh—you could go for hikes right out your back door."

"That would be great," Jason said. "I think I'm ready to see the next house, Dad."

"Let me thank Guy."

He went into the house while Jason and Shauna rounded the garage and got into the car.

The second house was nowhere near as nice as the first, but Jason seemed to be reserving judgment.

Reese leaned back in the chair at his desk in the office. "So, what do you think?"

"I'd like to make an offer on the first house we saw today."

Shauna tried hard not to show her happiness. Of all the houses they'd seen, it was the only one she had fallen in love with. Jason liked it, too. She had to remind herself it wasn't hers.

"Excellent choice. That's the one I liked, too," Reese said and pulled a contract out of his desk. He started filling in blanks. "I think the house is fairly priced, but I'm sure you could get it for less. What would you like to offer?"

"Three-hundred-twenty-five-thousand."

Reese filled in the blank. "Anything you want to request?"

Jason turned to Shauna. "Is there anything I should ask for?"

She was surprised he asked her. He treated her like a girlfriend since their talk, yet they hadn't resolved anything about the virgin situation. "You could ask him to leave the chairs at the kitchen island. They match the cabinets perfectly and might be hard to replace."

"All right. Put that in, Dad, and tell him it's cash and he can move ASAP."

Shauna gasped. "You're paying cash?" She put her hands up. "Sorry, it's none of my business. That's more than I need to know." But she was curious. How did a twenty-five-year-old man have enough cash to pay for a house?

"That's okay, Rachel. It's from my inheritance."

She hoped it wasn't from the evil dad. If that was the case, she was surprised that he'd take the money. He didn't want anything else to do with the man. Again, something she didn't need to know.

"Sign here, Jason, and I'll send it over to Guy's realtor right now." He smiled. "Your mom's going to love that you'll live only two blocks from our house."

"Wow. I can't believe you found such a perfect home," Shauna said with a smile.

"I don't have it yet. Maybe he'll get a better offer."

Reese stood. "I'll fax these off."

Jason smiled at Shauna and touched her leg. "About my inheritance."

"No, it's okay. You don't have to tell me anything."

"I want to." He let out his breath. "When I was eighteen and Jamie sixteen, we were told about it, and had to decide if we'd accept it. We ended up with a little over three-quarters of a million each and this is the first time I've touched it."

"I can't imagine trying to make that kind of decision in your teens."

"My first reaction was to reject it. Jamie and I talked about it for weeks. Our first decision was that we'd be united in whatever we decided. We talked and Jamie wrote down all the pros and cons. One of the pros was that if we didn't accept it, an evil branch of the family would get the money. In the end, we decided that the money wasn't going to turn us evil, and we'd talk to each other before spending it.

"So, you're still okay with it?"

"Yeah. I called Jamie before I came back home to tell her I'd be using it to buy a house and we rehashed our decision."

He stood. "Let's get out of here."

Jason's hand was at her back as they walked out of the office. Shauna shivered and scanned the street for the cause.

Vanessa leaned against the side of the cafe, glaring at her. Why did Vanessa have to be taking a break now? "That woman so hates me."

"Vanessa? This again?"

"You must have missed the look she gave me."

"She smiled at me."

"Of course, she did. Hey, do you think that maybe she's the one who tried to compel you to go to her this morning?" If Vanessa could get Jason to come to her, there could be all kinds of things she could get him to do. Like force him to have sex with her. Maybe fall in love with her. Maybe love potions were real.

The woman crossed the street. "Oh, no. She's walking this way." Shauna tugged on his hand. "Jason, let's get to the car."

Vanessa reached them before Shauna had a chance to convince Jason to take off. The woman ran a finger down Jason's arm and he flinched away. "Hi, Jason." She glared at Shauna. "You won't be able to keep him because you don't belong here. He's supposed to be with a woman who has powers, and that would be me."

Vanessa spun and marched back to the café, and glanced back once over her shoulder, blasting steel arrows of pure evil—directly at Shauna.

Chapter 11

Shauna rested her head against the headrest and closed her eyes to block the bright sunshine The low vibration of the car relaxed her. They were off to see the realtor who worked in Reese's commercial office.

It had been a nice weekend. Spending time with Jason's family had been wonderful. The way they interacted with each other was fun to watch. Even though Jason had rarely been home the last few years, to his family, it was like he'd never left.

There'd been only one awkward moment.

Abby leaned toward her. "So, when and where did you and Jason meet?"

Jason's parents knew the truth, but she should have expected to be asked this by one of the siblings. Stick as close to the truth as possible. "We met at a dance club—"

Jason reached over and gave her hand a squeeze. "Months ago. I saw her across the dance floor and couldn't take my eyes off her." His stare was so intense, she could hardly breathe.

Had he really seen her like that?

Jason's family made her feel like she belonged. His sister and brother didn't know that she was in their house so Jason could protect her. They wanted to get to know Jason's girlfriend. He'd never brought a girlfriend home before, so they thought it was serious. She didn't want them to be disappointed when she had to leave.

She had to admit her feelings— she was the one who

would be really disappointed. Even more than the family, she was falling for Jason. After all this was over, her life without him would be empty and lonely. Even more so than before, because now she knew what she would be missing.

Jason touched her hand, and his eyes flashed with concern. "Are you all right?"

Maybe she'd made a sound. He could probably read her face.

"I'm fine." She hoped her smile looked real.

He parked in the lot beside the Amherst realty office. At the door, Jason pulled it open and Shauna went in first.

The gray haired man stopped typing, his brown eyes peering over his glasses at them. "You must be Jason." He stood, rounded his desk and held out his hand. "Allen Peters."

Jason took his hand. "Thanks for your help, Allen. This is my friend Rachel."

After they were seated, Allen went through the available offices for rent. Jason chose four to look at and they headed out.

After a three hour search, they'd found Jason's new office. One was too small, one was too dark, another had a weird layout, but then there was the almost perfect office. Its wide windows overlooked the street and let in lots of light. A large, open office area filled the front, and the back held three offices, each with a window looking out onto an alley. Not a great view, but there was light.

They returned to the Allen's office and sat around his desk. He rifled through file folders in a drawer and pulled out a lease agreement. "You actually chose one of your father's units."

"Why didn't you tell me before?"

Allen shook his head. "He wanted you to choose what would work for you. He didn't want to influence your decision because he owned some of the offices. He *is* going to give you a break on rent, though."

"He doesn't have to do that."

Allen held up a hand. "You'll have to take it up with him. I'm just doing what he asked me to."

"All right. We'll go with his price, but can you put in the contract that we'll renegotiate the rent after six months?"

"Of course. Good luck with that, though."

A short time later, Allen handed Jason the keys, and he held Shauna's hand as they left the office. The bright sun blinded her for a few seconds.

"Now you'll need to go shopping for office furniture. Do you think you should paint the walls? Do you need to buy computers, printers and a copier? What about a sign or paint it on that big window? Oh, and you should put up vertical blinds. Do you have a name for your company?"

He shook his head. "I think you're more excited about this than I am."

"Aren't you excited?" She wanted to kiss his lips, but she pecked his cheek instead.

He wrapped his arms around her, leaned against his car, and kissed her. It was exactly what she wanted, but she pulled back, knowing she needed more than what he could give. His hand grabbed a fistful of her hair, and he deepened the kiss. Warm tendrils raced to her core, her heart pounded, and her lungs starved for air.

He kept sending her mixed signals. He'd kiss her until she didn't know where she was, and other times, he pushed her away. She never knew what to expect. She knew now why he didn't want to make love with her, but it was driving her crazy. Each time he kissed her like this, she hoped he'd lose control and take it further, but his steely resolve always won out.

He pulled back and rested his chin on top of her head.

"That may have been a mistake."

She stiffened and tried to push away from him. He was doing it again. She shouldn't give in next time.

"Uh-uh." He kissed her forehead. "Not that kind of mistake. It reminded me of a dream."

Her cheeks heated, and she wondered what he meant, if the kiss wasn't a mistake.

He took her hand. "Let's head back to the house."

***

He shouldn't have pulled her into his arms and kissed her. Her taste still filled him and he had the need to taste even more of her. He still had no solution to his problem. He glanced at Shauna, glad she wasn't looking at him as he worked to recover from that kiss.

They'd only driven about fifteen minutes when Jason's phone rang. "What's up, Dad?"

"Did you find a suitable office?"

"Yes. It's one of yours. Thanks for the discount." It wasn't a surprise his father would help him.

"I didn't think you'd take it for free. The main reason I called is to let you know that Guy Fiore sent a counter offer on the house."

"Okay. Accept it." He smiled, knowing it would bother his dad, who loved to negotiate. The only one Dad wouldn't negotiate with was his mom, almost always letting her win.

"But I didn't even tell you what it is. That's not negotiation." Reese didn't hide his irritation.

"Do you think it's reasonable?"

"You could probably get it down a few thousand more."

"Then it's not worth it. Accept it." He didn't need to risk losing the house quibbling over nothing. Soon enough, he could have Shauna all to himself in his own house. His gut twisted with need and fear.

Reese huffed. “Fine. Guy says he can close and be moved in two weeks.”

“That’s great. Thanks, Dad.” He ended the call.

Shauna squeezed his arm. “You got the house?”

He grinned at her. “Yes. Let’s celebrate.”

She clasped her hands, and her eyes glowed. “Your house and office on the same day. That’s wonderful.”

“Let’s go to Dad’s restaurant. It’s not far. You’ll love it.”

Within five minutes they pulled into the parking lot of *The Village Restaurant.*

Her eyes traveled over the building. “It looks really old.”

Jason tried to see it with her eyes. His dad had always owned it, so he’d never paid attention to the structure. Five-year-old kids didn’t notice how a place looked, only being interested in the food. It looked like a well-maintained building that had been on this corner for a hundred-and-fifty years. The cream-colored siding had been freshly painted, as well as the green shutters on each side of the leaded windows. Every tile of the slate roof was perfectly aligned.

“It’s not,” Jason said. “That’s the look Dad was going for.”

“Well, he succeeded.”

“Almost all my dad’s properties have something interesting or unique about them. I hope I have as much concern for my clients as Dad does for his renters.”

“You will. Your concern proves it.”

He smiled and held the restaurant door for Shauna. They stepped up to a podium.

The hostess looked up, her dark brown hair swung back from her face, and her eyes widened. “Jason! I didn’t know you were in town.” She stepped out and gave him a quick hug, the top of her head barely reaching his shoulder.

"Hi, Amy. I've been back a couple of weeks."

"How long are you staying?" She led them to a table.

"I'm moving back. Rachel and I are celebrating my purchase of a house and renting of office space."

He caught the curious appraisal Amy gave Shauna. Occasional girlfriends had come in when he worked at the restaurant, but he'd never brought in a woman for a date. Amy stopped beside a table, waited for them to be seated and gave them menus.

Amy touched his shoulder. "I'm sure your mom is ecstatic that you've moved back."

He smiled at Amy. "I believe she is."

A quiet chime indicated the front door opening, and Amy hurried away.

Shauna stared after the hostess. "It looks like you two know each other well."

He grinned at her, sensing her worry about competition. It excited him that she could be jealous. "I worked here for a few years during high school and on breaks from college. Amy did, too. She was a hostess and waitress then. I bussed and then waited. She's the manager now." He leaned toward her and took her resistant hand. "And she's happily married with a two-year-old."

The tension left her. Yeah, she was his if he could figure out how to have her without being invaded by evil. He was falling for her, hard and fast. He should find someone else to protect her so he could try to forget. But he knew he'd continue having the dreams. There was no forgetting Shauna.

When she'd said that she could have a one-night stand to solve his problem, the words twisted his gut. He didn't want her in another man's bed, even if it meant she could safely be in his after that. If there was a way for them to be together that didn't involve Shauna giving herself to another man, he would find it. He would be the one to introduce her to the delights of love, and it would be better than the dreams.

He gave her a smile and drew circles on her hand with his thumb. Watching her breathing change, he lifted her hand to his lips and kissed it. She gasped. He grinned and picked up his menu. Without looking at it, he said, "I recommend the roasted chicken."

He was playing with fire, and hoped he didn't get burned.

***

Shauna took a quick glance around. No one seemed to have noticed. What was he doing to her? After turning her inside out, he casually gave her a meal recommendation. Her brains were scrambled and he'd only kissed her hand. But that look in his eyes told her he wanted to do so much more. She wanted his lips on other places and blushed when the dream almost assaulted her with the feel of his hands and lips running over her body. She raised the menu to hide her face as she concentrated on pushing the dream out of her mind and worked at slowing her breathing. Had anyone ever had this kind of problem before? Finally, she looked up at him.

"You did that to make me think about…" the dream. She couldn't finish it out loud.

He smiled again. "Maybe."

Ever since telling her about his problem, and she confessed to having dreams about him, he touched her and kissed her more. He seemed to be less afraid of what could happen, or he had a whole lot more self-control than she did. He kept her on edge.

She leaned forward and whispered, "Are you purposely trying to drive me crazy?"

He grinned. "Maybe. It's driving me crazy, too, but I can't help myself."

The waitress arrived to take their order. Shauna hadn't checked out the menu, so took Jason's recommendation on the chicken and didn't regret it.

After they were almost done eating, Jason asked, "So, will you help me shop for furniture?"

"Me? Not your mom?"

"I'll probably get her opinion, but you'd be more fun to shop with."

He gave her a smile that she couldn't refuse. She liked this fun Jason. She just hoped he didn't back away again.

"I'd like that. Do you already have some furniture?"

"I've got some furniture in storage from my apartment. Mom saved some pieces from my other parents' house that she thought Jamie or I would want, after thoroughly sanitizing them, of course."

She wrinkled her forehead. "Sanitize? Why?"

He leaned close to her and lowered his voice. "She made sure they didn't have any kind of spells on them." He straightened up. "Two pieces came from Salem with the first settlers."

She was awed. "You've got furniture that's over three hundred years old, and it's not in a museum? I don't even know my family history before my grandmother."

Jason frowned. "I wish I didn't know my family history." He smiled. "But we can remedy your ignorance."

"Thanks. I think." She hoped her ancestors weren't evil people like Jason's.

Chapter 12

After Jason pulled into a parking space at the furniture store, he tugged his gun out from behind his back and locked it into the glove compartment. Sometimes Shauna forgot he had it.

"Why are you leaving it here?"

"It's kind of hard to test chairs and beds for comfort with a lump in my back."

"Oh." Beds? She hadn't thought about testing beds.

The first area they entered was living room furniture. Shauna scanned chairs, couches and tables as far as she could see. Since she lived in her father's house, she'd never had to buy furniture, and hadn't a clue how to start. Jason lay on a couch with his eyes closed. Maybe he was trying to find out how an afternoon nap at home would feel.

A tall, blond man strode up to her. His broad shoulders looked like he moved the furniture around for exercise. "I'm Brad." He held a card out to her, glancing down at her left hand when she accepted it. He took a half step closer, and his voice became husky. "Can I show you some pieces? What are you looking for?" His gazes darted down to her chest and back to her face.

She jumped when Jason wrapped an arm around her. "She's with me and we'll let you know when we've made our selections." His voice was the gruffest she'd ever heard it.

The man held his hands up. "No problem. I'll check on you later." He left them.

Jason's arm tightened around her. "No, you can't have sex with him. He won't solve our problem."

"What! Jason, I already said I wouldn't do it."

"I saw how he looked at you."

"Yeah, but you didn't see me respond." She giggled. "Are you jealous?"

"No. Maybe. Let's look at furniture."

Shauna's heart beat double-time. He'd staked his claim, and she found it sexy. Not sure what to do about it, she took his advice and headed to a cushy recliner. After sitting, she tipped it back, kicked the footrest out and closed her eyes. She could fall asleep in this, just the right amount of cushioning and smooth fabric. "Jason, you have to try this recliner." She startled when his lips touched hers. One quick kiss and she wish for more.

His faced hovered and he smiled. "I couldn't resist." He pointed to a loveseat. "I think that's better. Both seats recline." He turned back to her. "We can lie back together. Who knows what could happen after that?" A blush rose up her neck, and he kissed her again.

Who knows? Like nothing anytime soon. She understood his reasons for holding back, but the kind of kisses he gave her made her want a whole lot more—sooner rather than later.

He talked as if they were going to be together, as if they were a couple looking for furniture for their house, not his house. She'd be leaving once the threat from Nick passed. But she had nothing to go back to. The house she grew up in wasn't a home anymore without her father. No job, because her fiancé-boss was probably a killer. Her best friend lived two hours away, so they didn't see each other as much as they used to.

She flipped a lever on the side of the chair and the footrest collapsed. Jason led her to the loveseat he'd pointed out and sat, drawing her down to sit beside him.

"See, you can have your own seat, all the way over there, or you can snuggle closer." He patted the cushion beside him.

She shook her head and tipped the seat back. "It's comfortable, but not as cozy as the other one."

"Oh, this one can be cozy."

She flipped the footrest down and jumped up, nervous about what he'd meant.

Jason came up beside her and took her hand, pulling her through the dining room furniture. A couple sat at a table, conversing, as the woman pointed to other tables.

"I've got dining stuff covered." He continued on to the bedroom furniture. "This is where I want to look."

She glanced around, then at him, felt the heat rising to her face and turned away. He needed a mattress for his own bed, but she didn't know how many guest beds he wanted

Shauna roamed slowly through the department, studying each display in the huge showroom as Jason trailed behind her. She retraced her steps to a cherry set. "I love this carved headboard." She ran her fingers along the swirls and leaves. "And the top drawers are carved, too." The set included the king size bed, two nightstands, a double dresser with a mirror and a chest of drawers. "You need a big set for your huge master bedroom. You could get an overstuffed chair and an end table, too."

"I like it. What about the guest rooms?"

She went back to an oak set. The headboard was simple with three inset panels. The other pieces were plain and sturdy. "This would be nice with the nightstands and one dresser."

"That'll be good. Now for the best part. Let's choose mattresses." He took her hand and led her deeper into the store, toward a wide variety of mattresses and box springs.

She dragged her feet, and he tugged her arm. "Are you afraid to get horizontal with me in a public place?"

Her heart kicked up a notch. His hot and cold drove her crazy. Focus on public. "Jason, you're having way too much fun with this." She tried to turn it less personal, but it hadn't been anything but personal the whole time they were in the store. Maybe he'd finally accepted that he'd be all right with her, and was ready to move ahead, and this was a way to show her. "So, what kind of mattress do you like? Soft? Firm?"

"Probably in the middle. What about you?" He ran a finger from her ear to her chin.

She had to swallow before answering. "Probably in the middle, too." She stepped back from him and started pushing on mattresses, pillow tops, memory foam. When she got to the fifth one, she said, "Try this one."

"I will if you will."

"But it's for you." And she didn't want to lie next to him in a bed in public. It would probably give her dream images overload.

"I want your opinion."

"All right." She sat on the bed. He went to the opposite side, laid down and pulled her down beside him.

"Jason!" she shrieked, and slapped her hand over her mouth. She glanced around. No curious observers. Maybe it happened all the time.

There was a sparkle in his eye. "You can't check it out by only sitting on it. Put your head on the pillow."

She stuffed a pillow under her head, but didn't relax. His hand on her waist was doing crazy things to her breathing. She'd never been in bed with a man before. Technically, it was *on* a bed with possible customers around the corner. She scooted closer to the edge of the mattress. She would be better off seeing what his next move was rather than be surprised by it again.

She patted the bed. “This one feels nice.”

Jason’s eyes sparkled with humor. “It does, but it felt better when you were closer to me.”

She put her hand over her eyes. Maybe she didn’t want to see. This was an all new Jason. She liked him, but the sudden change was almost too much. Maybe this was his normal when he wasn’t worried about evil taking over.

Jason chuckled. “Is that like a kid who thinks if she can’t see me then I can’t see her?”

She left her hand over her eyes. “No, it’s more like, if I can’t see you I won’t want to…” He is driving her nuts.

“Want to what?” He lowered his voice. It was the sexy one. He knew exactly what she was going to say.

She uncovered her eyes, pushed herself up to a half sitting position and glared at him.

His chuckle was cut off when his phone rang. He frowned at the number and put his phone to his ear. “Jason Ballard.”

His frown deepened. “Kristy. You aren’t supposed to have this number. What phone are you calling from?”

Kristy’s voice was too muffled to understand the words.

“All right. That should be fine, but Mark shouldn’t have given you my number and you can’t call again.” He listened, looked at Shauna and gave her a devious smile. “Yeah, she’s right beside me on the bed.”

Shauna choked as he handed her the phone with a chuckle. “Jason!”

She sat on the side of the bed, her back to him.

“Hi, Kristy.”

“You’re in bed with him?”

“Not really.” She glared at him over her shoulder. “Jason is buying a house, and we’re looking at furniture. You happened to catch us trying out a mattress—in a store.”

"Well, that's too bad."

"Kristy!"

"Anyway, I called to tell you Nick dropped by my apartment to find out where you were. I told him you went to visit a friend, but I didn't know who or where. He didn't believe me." Only then did Shauna recognize the terror in her friend's voice. "He grabbed my throat and told me I had twenty-four hours to figure out where you were."

Shauna reached for her own throat as it constricted. "When was that?"

"Yesterday after work."

"And you didn't run? Kristy, you have to get out of there. Now. Before he comes back." Shauna had no idea if he would hurt Kristy, but the man was capable of ordering a murder. He might try to use Kristy to make Shauna come back.

Jason touched her back and held out his hand. "Let me talk to her." He took the phone. "Kristy, did you say Nick asked you about Shauna?" His jaw tensed. "Tell your dad. He'll get you out of there. Have him contact Mark when your plans are made." His lips thinned as he popped the battery out and pocketed his phone. "How did that woman talk Mark into giving her my number? Now I'll have to deactivate this phone and use my backup. And let Mark know I've done it."

Shauna would have laughed, except now Kristy was in danger because of her. "You don't know Kristy. When she wants something, she gets it. When we were kids, I don't know how many times I got into trouble for letting her talk me into doing something." She sighed. "We should probably leave." It was amazing what one phone call could do.

He ran a finger along her jaw. "We still have shopping to do. It's not like your ex is waiting for us in the parking lot."

Nick could kidnap Kristy before she had a chance to hide, and it would be Shauna's fault for running away from him. He'd met Kristy a few times, so he knew Shauna would go to her best friend when she ran. She had to believe Mr. Collins would keep his daughter safe.

Nick had gotten one step closer to finding Shauna. With Jason around, she'd been able to push her ex out of her mind, forget how afraid she'd been. It all came screaming back when Kristy was threatened, reminding her of her fear. Jason, and all his hang-ups about evil had been a distraction.

She took a deep breath, trying to bring back the carefree feeling she'd had before the call. She stood and stared at the rest of the mattresses. Fun and games were over now that Nick invaded her thoughts. She had needed the reminder that she wasn't Jason's girlfriend, but a client he was responsible for protecting. She shook her head. "I can't do it."

He stood, came around to her side of the bed, and wrapped an arm around her waist. His playfulness was gone. "Let's go find that sales person."

***

Shauna stepped out of the car in front of the Ballard home as Jason exited the other side. A teen boy zigzagged his bicycle from the street to the sidewalk and to the street again. Jason pushed the door closed and walked toward the front of the car as the boy rode his bike directly at Jason.

"Jason, look out!"

The teen picked up speed, and by the time Jason looked up, he was unsuccessful in sidestepping the bike. The impact flung Jason's arms wide and whooshed air from his lungs with a grunt. He tumbled onto his back as the young man flew over his handlebars and expertly rolled back onto his feet.

The boy ran back to Jason and squatted beside him, his back to Shauna. "Sorry, man. You all right?" After a few seconds, he hopped back on his bike and sped away.

Shauna ran to Jason's side. "Are you okay?" His eyes remained closed. The door to the house flew open and Reese hurried outside.

"Reese, Jason got hit by a bike!" She glanced down at Jason, and frowned at her.

Reese knelt beside his son, his brow wrinkled. "Jason, does anything hurt?"

"The back of my head is probably going to have a goose egg." He pushed himself to a sitting position with a little help from Reese and touched the spot. "Yeah, it's there already. And I'm sure I'll have a huge bruise from landing on my gun." He pulled it out with from his waistband and winced.

Reese frowned. "What happened?"

Shauna stared down the now empty street. "A teenage boy on a bike plowed Jason down. It looked like he did it on purpose."

Jason rubbed his forehead. "He wouldn't have done it on purpose. He could have been hurt, too."

"You didn't see him until the last second. He looked at you and he ran you down."

Reese glanced at each of them. "Did either of you recognize him?"

They shook their heads. Shauna scanned the street. "Maybe it was it a distraction." Nick could be here already and had hoped to snatch her while Jason was down, only Reese came out and stopped a potential abduction. "Maybe he picked your pocket."

Reese took Jason's arm. "Rachel, let's help him up."

She grabbed the other arm. "Let's get you inside and put ice on that lump."

They helped Jason to his feet. He swayed a couple of seconds, then shook them off. "I'm fine." He checked his pockets. "Everything's there." He walked on his own into the house and headed for the library.

Shauna brought him ice, wrapped in a towel and handed it to him.

He took it and held it to the back of his head. "Thanks, Rachel." He sat back and closed his eyes.

She felt like she'd been dismissed but didn't want to leave him alone. "If you need anything…"

He waved her off. Maybe she should have taken him to the doctor.

"I'm going to sit here with you and read Hannah's journal." She retrieved the book from the secret room and sat on the opposite end of the couch, hurt by his switch to impersonal after the progress she thought they'd made in the store.

***

Shauna sat at the kitchen table, a plate with two pieces of peanut butter toast in front of her. The family had left for the day and Jason was still upstairs. He usually got up before now, but the bump on his head must have affected him. She'd check on him if he wasn't up by the time her toast was gone.

He'd behaved strangely at dinner the night before. Where normally, he was playful with his brother and sister, he was more serious. He didn't speak to Shauna unless she directly asked him something. Normally, he made sure she was drawn into the conversation. At least his family was more comfortable with her and filled in. Maybe the headache was worse than he let on. It wouldn't be surprising.

He'd mentioned nothing about the house and office or furniture shopping. It had been a wonderful day, yet he acted as if it never happened. She was excited and wanted to talk about the house, but it was Jason's house, and it was his place to tell his family. Even Reese kept glancing at him with a quizzical look and frowned at his wife. Who wouldn't talk about a house he'd just put under contract?

Footsteps galloping down the stairs alerted her that Jason was coming.

He stopped in the doorway. "Oh, hi…Rachel."

"Morning, Jason." Whenever they were alone in the house, he always called her Shauna. It was almost as if he didn't remember her, and had struggled to remember the name he'd used.

He looked like he hadn't slept well.

"How's your head?"

He ran his hand down the back of it. "It's a little sore to the touch, but the headache is just at an annoying level now."

So, he had had a headache last night. "Do you think you should go to the doctor?"

His jaw clenched. "I've had worse."

He rounded the table and pulled a cup out the cupboard. Selecting a k-cup, he popped it into the coffee machine and within seconds the scent of coffee filled the room. He rummaged in the cupboards and sat in the chair farthest from her with a bowl of cereal and his cup.

With forced cheer, she asked, "So, what's the plan for today?"

He lifted an eyebrow. "I'm going to work on my webpage."

He seemed surprised she'd asked.

"Oh. I guess I'll read more of Hannah's journal."

"Mom's letting you read Hannah's journals?"

This didn't make sense. He couldn't have forgotten. "Jason, I've been reading them for days. You're the one who showed them to me."

"Um. Okay."

"Maybe you should go to the doctor."

"No. I have a lot on my mind. I'll be fine." That sounded final.

After clearing her dishes, she went to the library and retrieved Hannah's second journal.

Twenty minutes later, Jason entered the library, his laptop under his arm. He sat at the desk and opened the computer. And ignored her.

He treated her as a stranger and was practically rude to her. She stared at two pens beside him and rolled them off the desk. He frowned and picked them up. She thought he'd realize that she was the reason they fell, but he didn't look her way. She huffed and flopped back in her seat.

A couple hours later, Jason closed his laptop and walked out the front door. She thought he was heading for the stairs, but he left the house before she could react. He didn't say he was leaving. Every time when he went somewhere, he took her with him. For the first time ever, she was alone in the Ballard house. He was supposed to protect her, and now she felt he was the one who needed protecting.

Reading wasn't holding her interest because her mind kept wandering to Jason. She wanted to know where was he, how long he'd be gone, and if he was in trouble.

She put the book back in the secret room then paced the library. Five miles must have passed under her feet before a car pulled into the drive and the engine turned off.

As he came through the front door, she met him in the hall.

He spotted her and lifted a bag. "I thought you might like dessert."

Her hand covered her stomach. With all the worrying, she hadn't thought about lunch. *Cozy Corner Diner* was scrawled across the bag. Her stomach twisted into knots. With the way he'd treated her so far that day, she was surprised he offered her dessert.

"Did you happen to see Vanessa when you were there?" She couldn't help the jealousy that flared up.

"Yeah, she was working." He lifted the bag again. "Come on. I'll dish this out."

She shook her head. "I can't." She pushed her hand harder into her stomach, hoping that would stop it from twisting. "Maybe you should throw it away."

She raced up the stairs, into the bathroom and leaned against the door. Her breath came in gasps and gradually slowed, taking the worst of the panic with it. Now the worst was her pounding head.

If Vanessa knew Jason was buying that dessert for her, she'd probably put some kind of spell on it. She cracked open the door. The hallway was empty. Her open bedroom door beckoned. She paused beside the bedroom then retraced her steps to the kitchen. She should face him. He was trying to be nice, but impersonal. She could handle it.

Jason tossed a plastic container into the trashcan and looked up at her. He pointed at two plates with chocolate cake on them. "Dessert?"

She shook her head and pushed her hand into her stomach. "No thanks. I'm going into the library while you enjoy it."

He shrugged. "Suit yourself."

She'd been settled on the couch in the library for twenty minutes when he sat on the other end. She glanced up from the journal. Jason stared at her, then leafed through the pages in the book in his hands.

It was as if he was trying to figure her out, but she

thought he'd done that already. Despite the fun in the furniture store, he'd done a complete about face. They were more distant than the day they'd met. Something wasn't right with Jason.

Chapter 13

The bathroom door closed behind Jason and Shauna slipped into his room. Everyone else had gone for the day. Glancing around, she realized that despite her not sleeping in this room, she would still make love here for the first time. It was her decision, and that made it feel less preordained.

She grabbed the bottom of her tank top and took a deep breath before pulling it over her head. At the pajama waistband, her fingers froze. She was ready for this. With determination, she pushed the pants over her hips and let them drop to the floor, then slipped under the covers that smelled of Jason. She'd never been naked in a bed before and the cold sheets were a shock. She scooted until she found the spot that was still warm from Jason's body. It felt right with his scent surrounding her.

The room was the same as the many dreams she'd seen it in—the antique bed, dresser and chair, the pale pink walls, the ceramic ballerina on the dresser. Would Jason be the same as in her dream?

After being so playful at the furniture store, Jason had become distant. Now he treated her like a stranger. The hot and cold had to stop. In fact, the last three days had only been lukewarm and cold. She knew he was worried about what would happen to him when they made love, but he didn't have evil in him. It was time to force his hand or whatever. This time, she wouldn't let him back away. He wouldn't refuse if she was already in his bed. She was giving her consent by tucking her naked body under his blankets.

Fear quickened her breaths. Maybe she was making a mistake. Jason may have changed his mind about her. Maybe he didn't want to be tempted by the virgin anymore. Didn't want to take a chance with her.

Before her nerves overtook her, the door opened and he stood in the opening in his navy terry robe. His eyebrows rose, but that was soon replaced with the sexy smile that always caused butterflies as he closed the door. His eyes seemed different, but it was probably the darker room.

"This is a pleasant surprise." He walked to the bed.

She bit her lip, her nerves getting the best of her. She'd expected him to ease her mind or ask if she was sure. His eyes deepened in color. He breathed faster, untied his robe and dropped it to the floor. After a quick look at his muscled chest and the glint of his pendant, she carefully kept her eyes on his face as he opened the drawer beside the bed and took out a small crinkly package. He slipped in beside her and gave her a kiss as he ran a hand down her side.

He held the condom out to her. "I didn't expect a guest of my parents to jump into my bed, but I can't turn down an offer like this."

She stared at the small package but had no idea what to do with it. Of course, it was a condom, but she didn't know what it looked like inside the wrapper. Didn't know how to use it. He knew this was her first time and shouldn't expect her to figure this out. Was he making fun of her inexperience? She shook her head and bit her lip. And then it hit her. The condom had so distracted her, the words had only just sunk in. He'd said she was a guest of his parents.

She studied his eyes. Jason didn't remember her. Maybe it was because he'd hit his head. Or it could be some kind of spell. Right now, he'd have sex with any attractive woman in his bed. She couldn't be that nameless woman. She'd waited too long for the right person, the right time.

She shook. "I've changed my mind. I need to leave." She pushed his shoulder.

"You've got to be kidding." He chuckled. "It's too late to change your mind."

Tears blurred her vision. She couldn't believe she'd ended up in this position. "No, Jason. We can't do it like this. Please." She'd never been afraid of him before, but now terror filled her.

He pushed her down and held her in place as she struggled. He captured her hands and pulled them over her head as his knee trapped her legs. She'd been nervous and excited when she'd come in, but now only panic filled her. Her breath rasped like she'd run for miles. She tugged her arms, but they barely moved. He wasn't the man she loved anymore. His cold eyes belonged to a rapist. He didn't care if he hurt her, it was all about his pleasure. She was just his to use and discard.

He leaned over her, his mouth inches from hers. She didn't want his kisses like this. She twisted her head from side to side. "No, no, no." Each word louder than the one before.

He froze. For several seconds, he stared at her then frowned, as if trying to figure something out. He grabbed the sides of his head, screaming, and rolled onto his back.

Once freed, Shauna pushed up, scrambled off the bed, and threw on Jason's robe. She snatched her clothes from the floor and ran to the door. Then she glanced over her shoulder. His body was relaxed, as if asleep. After that scream of pain, he couldn't possibly be asleep. Maybe he'd passed out.

She couldn't believe that she was worried about him after what he'd almost done. She remained rooted to the floor, waiting for his next move. If he came after her, she'd have time to race down the hall to the bathroom and lock herself in.

A few minutes later, Jason opened his eyes and groaned, rubbing his temples. He sat and spotted her. "Shauna, what are you doing here?" He frowned. "What's wrong? Is someone here?" He swung his legs over the edge of the bed but remained seated. "You might want to close your eyes while I—you're wearing my robe. I'll put pants on, and then you can tell me what's going on."

It sounded like the real Jason, and he'd called her Shauna for the first time in days. Relief washed through her, and with the release of fear, tears slid down her cheeks. She closed her eyes and rested her head on the door. Clothes rustled and a zipper rasped. A hand touched her cheek, and she jumped.

"Tears? Shauna, what's wrong?" He took her hand and led her to the bed, sat and pulled, but she resisted. The horror was still too fresh.

He frowned. "It's all right. You know I'd never hurt you."

She warily lowered herself to the bed beside him, tense and ready to run. This sounded like the real Jason.

She released her pent-up fear and sobbed. Jason's arms went around her, and he rubbed her back, murmured to her, kissed the top of her head. When she'd calmed, he used the edge of the sheet to wipe her face.

"Can you tell me what's wrong?" His eyes filled with worry.

She squeezed his arm. "I came in here when you went to shower."

"Shower?" His hand went to his still damp hair. "I don't remember showering. You were at the door when I woke."

She shook her head. "No. I was in your bed when you came back from the shower."

He rubbed his forehead. "Why can't I remember that? After leaving the furniture store yesterday, I had trouble keeping both hands on the wheel on the way home. You'd think I'd remember seeing you in my bed."

"Yesterday? That was three days ago!"

His eyes widened then closed for several seconds. He opened them and squinted at her as if trying to read her mind.

"Have I been passed out for three days?"

She shook her head.

"Tell me what's happened."

"You've been kind of strange since that kid ran you down with his bike. Even your family has been worried."

He crinkled his eyes. "I remember being knocked down. Got the wind knocked out of me, and my head exploded." He massaged his temples. "That's it. That's the last thing I remember until a minute ago."

"Your dad was coming out, so he helped me get you into the house. We put ice on the lump. And you acted as if I was here visiting your parents. You called me Rachel, like you thought that really was my name."

"You came in here this morning when I was acting that way?"

She shrugged and closed her eyes. "I-I thought you were just trying to distance yourself from me. I wanted to show you how…that I wanted to…that I…."

He pulled her close. "I'm so sorry I've been sending you mixed signals. I can't imagine how hard it's been for you."

***

Jason ran his hand through his drying hair again. What happened to him that he couldn't remember the last three days? And during that time, he couldn't remember Shauna.

"Tell me about this morning."

She stiffened and didn't meet his eyes. "I waited until I heard you go in the shower and I came in here."

"And what did I do when I came back?"

"You smiled at me. You seemed pretty happy to find me here."

"Well, what guy wouldn't be?" Too late to take it back, Jason realized it was a cold thing to say after making Shauna cry. How badly had he hurt her? Fear weighed heavily in his chest, afraid of what he'd done.

He closed his eyes. There was a small piece of cold, black evil inside him. It hadn't been there before. He worked at walling it up. The feeling was mostly gone, but he knew it was there. He was afraid that it would break out again.

She blushed. "I was too nervous to peek when you dropped your robe and climbed in beside me and then you tried to, um…"

"What did I do?" Jason listened intently as Shauna described his deplorable behavior. More tears followed.

Jason hugged her in a tight embrace, surprised she let him. "Shauna, I'm so sorry. Did I–he–hurt you?" What Shauna described was so foreign to him that he couldn't think of it being him.

"No. You screamed, grabbed your head and then I think you lost consciousness for a few minutes."

"Thank God." He shuddered at what could have happened. If he'd raped her, there would have not only been the trauma for Shauna, but he was sure it would have released evil in him. And he would have lost her. A pain stabbed his heart. Fortunately, he hadn't touched her, but he could have done irreparable damage. Maybe she'd be too afraid to let him touch her again. He didn't want to see fear in her eyes when she looked at him.

She frowned. "Why?"

"I think that's what pulled me out of whatever it was. You changed your mind and I—he was going to force you. Deep inside, I couldn't do that." He kissed her forehead. "I'm so sorry I put you through that." He'd overcome the evil he still felt lurking, and stopped before hurting her.

He held her chin between his thumb and forefinger and looked into her still wary eyes. "That wasn't the real me. Even before I met you, I wouldn't have forced a woman to have sex. That other me didn't know or didn't care that you're a virgin. That me wouldn't have taken the time you needed to be comfortable. That me was only interested in himself." He hugged her. "That me doesn't love you the way I do."

The corners of her lips curled up. "You love me?"

He rubbed his thumb across her lips. "More than anything. I was attracted to you from the first moment I saw you, despite the fact you're a virgin. And the more time I spend with you I fall deeper in love." He grinned. "Probably every woman I know would have thrown fits over the way I've pulled you in and pushed you away, but you've taken it well. Your patience with Abby and her homework has been terrific. Your sexy innocence drives me to distraction."

Shauna tipped her head back and raised her eyebrows. "Isn't that an oxymoron? And what happens when I'm not innocent anymore?"

Jason kissed her nose. "You'll still be sexy. And probably will still drive me crazy."

Her eyes widened. "I hope that's a good thing." She burrowed her head into his neck. "I love you, too, even though you drive me crazy. You make me feel safe, but maybe that's the bodyguard part of you."

Shauna professing her love was the most beautiful thing he'd ever heard. "None of the other times I've been a bodyguard compare to this with you. Of course, I did my job, but it hurts if I imagine something happening to you."

He ran a hand down her spine. He'd been so intent on their conversation, he hadn't thought about her wearing only his robe, with an easily loosened tie. Now, he thought how easy it would be to uncover her, and pushed the thought away. She needed time and reassurance. And he needed to figure out what had happened.

"All right, then. One more thing and I'm kicking you out." He kissed her again and watched for her reaction to his next words.

"I realized that because I love you, my main concern is for you and not what I'm getting out of having sex. I think I'll be okay because I'm not like Nathan Proctor." He gave her a small smile. "I am going to make love to you, but not today."

Shauna put her hand over his lips. "Don't mention him." She slid her hand down his neck to his chest and frowned. "This isn't your medallion."

"What?" His moon and stars pendant was replaced with one stamped with a Celtic knot. He'd always had it tucked under his shirt, so no one would have noticed the change. He yanked on it, but it didn't break. Taking the chain in both hands, he pulled until it snapped, and dropped it on the nightstand. "When did I start acting strange?"

"Right after that kid on a bike knocked you down."

"His must have done it so he could replace my medallion with this."

Shauna rubbed the place on his chest where the medallion had been. "He did come back to you as you lay on the ground. He apologized, but I'll bet that's when he switched it."

"It has to be the same person who's trying to compel me to come to them."

"I still think Vanessa's the villain. That didn't work, so she made you forget me."

He still didn't see a reason why Vanessa would go to this trouble for him. They'd barely spoken to each other after the short time they'd dated. "She's delusional if she thought she had a chance with me by wiping my memory of you. And then there's Nick, but it's pretty unlikely he'd create a spell of any kind."

"I doubt he knows anything about magic." Shauna glanced at the medallion. "We'll have to put protection on another medallion for you."

"We can do it after dinner and have Mom sanitize this phony one before we throw it away. Now, you should escape before I do something I shouldn't." He wished he could take the words back since he didn't want to remind Shauna he'd almost done something horrible.

When she reached the door, he stopped her. "Shauna, I know this was a disaster, but it'll be wonderful when the time is right for us. I promise it will be better than your dreams." His eyes lingered on her lips and it took a monumental effort not to go to her.

After the door closed, he fell back on the bed, let out a long breath and closed his eyes. He'd come so close to destroying Shauna and everything they could have together. He'd never felt evil inside himself before. He'd felt it for a couple of seconds after he opened his eyes and stared at her. His love for her drove it into that small space, but it left completely when he removed the medallion. He never wanted to feel that again.

Chapter 14

In the library, Jason sat at the desk and opened his laptop. He had a view all the way to the front door with the stained-glass peacocks. The morning light transferred the picture to vestibule floor. He'd gotten grounded for a week once when he was caught bouncing a basketball against that door.

With his memory of Shauna restored, he still had three lost days and no amount of questions or concentration brought them back. In a way, he was relieved. He didn't want to remember how he'd attacked Shauna or how he felt as he did it. He tamped down the building anger at the faceless person who'd done this to him.

His report to Mark was late. It was surprising the cavalry hadn't arrived. He would have sent the troops if he was lead in a protection detail. He clicked on the oldest message in his email account from Mark, sent while Jason wasn't himself. Its date was the day after his report was due.

Hey buddy,

This is the first time you're late with your report. Is everything okay there? How's Shauna? If I don't hear from you, you know I'm heading up there.

Mark

Jason found his own message, with the same date, in his sent folder.

Hi Mark,

Everything's great. I found an office. I've been working on my website, planning my ad.

Who's Shauna and why do I need to send you reports?

Jason

Jason could imagine how poorly that question went over even before clicking on Mark's next message.

What do you mean, WHO'S SHAUNA?!! Now is not the time for jokes. If you don't give me a real report within twenty-four hours, I'm hauling up there and dealing with YOU.

Mark

Jason fell back in the chair. If Mark didn't hear from him today, he'd be charging in.

How was he supposed to fix this? He couldn't tell Mark that a witch had put a spell on him to make him forget Shauna. Well, maybe he could. Mark knew about Jason's special night vision. He might be able to take the leap and believe that someone could cast a spell that gave a person amnesia. Jason needed to send Mark something to explain the lapse.

Hi Mark,

Sorry about that last message. I got a knock on the head and don't remember the last three days, but everything's fine now. Nothing to worry about. Shauna was safe with my family the entire time. She's good, perfect even.

I won't take pay for protecting her any longer. I care for her and keeping her safe is more important than anything. Please let Jack Collins know that he doesn't have to cover this anymore. I know how much he cares about her, so I'll still send you reports.

Also, a few days ago, Kristy called. Why did you give her my number? The info about Nick contacting Kristy should have come through you. I'm afraid that this may have caused a breach. I pulled the battery on my phone and am using the backup.

Jason

When he wasn't himself, he'd put the battery back into his phone. This morning, he'd removed it again. Mark probably knew where they were. He would have tracked both Jason's phone numbers, but worse, for three days Nick could have tracked him.

He'd barely started going through the rest of his email messages when his computer signaled a new message. It was Mark.

Glad everything's good there. You'll have to tell me the whole story sometime.

I knew with the way you drooled over Shauna at the club, that you'd get her in your bed. Refusing pay for her makes this sound serious.

Sorry about Kristy getting your number. She kept asking me for a way to contact Shauna, but I stayed strong, which wasn't easy. Then I woke to find her checking the contacts on my cell. She must have watched me access my phone's security. She'd already found your number by the time I wrestled it from her. Since she's the one who talked her father into hiring us, I think she's just worried about Shauna.

From that, you can probably tell, I'm seeing her. She's the first woman I've taken on a date to the shooting range. Man, that woman can shoot. AND she talked me into spending the first week of her "vacation" with her.

I have one of the guys monitoring Nick. Except for when he harassed Kristy, he's been sticking to his normal routine.

Mark

Jason chuckled. Shauna was right about Kristy being able to get what she wanted. And it sounded like Mark was enjoying almost every minute of it. He hoped, for Mark's sake, Kristy wasn't doing it just to stay close to Shauna.

***

Shauna woke and stretched, her first thought of Jason. She felt his love in every glance and touch, even though he hadn't said the words again. It was like a dam had broken and he allowed himself to have feelings for her. The last few days, he'd been extra careful with her. He'd only kissed her on the cheek or forehead and an occasional, too short kiss on her lips. She guessed he felt guilty over what had happened and treated her as if she might panic if he showed too much passion. If the need to protect her hadn't overcome the spell, it could have permanently turned Jason evil and maybe rape wouldn't have been the worst thing he did to her. A shiver passed through her at the thought. What she needed was a new memory to replace the bad one.

The house was quiet, all family members gone except Jason. Shauna gathered her clothes and stepped into the hall. The bathroom door was closed. She'd thought Jason was finished and downstairs. Before she could turn back to her room, the bathroom door opened.

Jason paused for a second, then smiled and hustled down the hall, stopping in front of her. “Good morning.” He planted a quick kiss on her lips. They hadn’t met like this since the beginning. At least this time he wore his robe, although it gapped nearly to his waist.

She dragged her gaze up, past the real medallion, to his eyes. The twinkle told her that he knew what she’d been inspecting.

He grinned. “Like what you see?”

She tucked her bottom lip between her teeth and nodded.

He took a step back and his gaze traveled down her camisole and sleep shorts, then back to her face. “I do, too.” He ran a finger along the neckline of her top, making her shiver. On the second pass, his finger slipped a bit under the camisole.

Her breaths turned into short, shallow bursts. She didn’t know how he could affect her so quickly. His eyes glowed with warmth, not the cold lust from before. This Jason knew and cared for her. He lifted a shaky hand and buried it in her hair, pulling her into a kiss. Nervousness melted away, and she threw her arms around his neck, deepening the kiss. Her whole body responded to his against hers, aching in places only her dreams told her about.

Jason pulled back and gazed into her eyes. “Does this mean what I think it means?”

She nodded. His question made her even more sure. “I’m ready. I trust you.”

“Your room or mine?”

Her eyebrows shot up. “We can choose? I thought…” Her gaze focused on the door of Jamie’s room.

“It’s a premonition. A possibility.” He tipped his head toward Jamie’s room. “It doesn’t have to happen in there. It doesn't even have to happen at all."

She buried her face in his neck. "Oh, yes, it does."

He chuckled, backed her up into his old room, and closed the door. She could understand him not wanting to make love in his sister's room.

He tipped her chin up and she lifted her gaze to his. "I love you. That's why I feel mostly safe making love to you. I'm going to do everything in my power to make this good for you."

Shauna kissed his chin, which was all she could reach without going up on her toes. "I love you, too. That's the reason I want to do this with you." She grinned. "And to find out if it's anything like my dreams."

He nibbled her lips and steered her toward the bed. "Oh, this will be better than your dreams. I guarantee it."

The bed covers were still rumpled and he pushed them back further, then slowly slid her tank top off. Goosebumps sensitized her to his every touch. He feathered kisses along her neck, making her breath catch at his tenderness. His lips blazed a trail between her breasts and to her stomach. This felt so much more intense than any dream, and it was only starting. She might not survive if it was better than the dreams. His kisses followed the slide of her shorts. She dropped her hands to his shoulders, not sure if her legs would hold her. He gently pushed her back against the bed and moved her to the middle, his every action careful, as if she were a scared rabbit.

His robe dropped off his shoulders, revealing his muscled chest. She darted her gaze to his face where a hint of a smile joined the fire in his eyes. The bedside drawer opened and closed. Plastic crinkled, and hit the nightstand top. The drawer had been empty when she'd taken over the room, but he must have stocked it recently. He slid into bed and kissed her, their only contact their lips and his hand on her cheek.

Love swelled in her heart because of the care he took with her. In her dreams, they were…more active. She needed to let him know she was ready. She scooted closer to him. Maybe she wasn't quite as ready as she thought, but this was her Jason. She kissed his neck and snuggled into him. "I want this, but I'm still a little nervous. In the dreams, I was more sure of myself."

"The dreams probably weren't preceded by the evil me."

She shivered and tightened her hold on him. "I hadn't thought of that."

"I'm a little nervous, too. I'm almost sure evil won't enter me, but there's this little bit of doubt."

"Well, I know you won't let it in." She kissed him, pushing her uneasiness away with his. Sliding closer to him, she let the enchantment take over. They lay on their sides, and she stared into his clear eyes before he swooped in for a kiss. Her fear was gone, and all she wanted was to feel his heat, feel the intensity rise. Jason's hand skimmed over her shoulders and down her arms, every touch sending an electric longing to her core. She ran a hand down his back and was lost when his hand brushed over her breast.

***

It was amazing that this woman could love him with the whipsaw emotions he'd put her through. She knew the evil in his ancestry, but still believed that wasn't him. He'd worried that she wouldn't be able to get past what he'd almost done to her. Her trust meant everything to him, and he wouldn't destroy it.

He kissed her—everywhere. For the first time, he allowed himself to take it slow with a woman, to allow the excitement to build. Shauna shivered when he kissed behind her ear. He kissed her fingers, sucking one into his mouth. Her breathing accelerated and his mouth covered the tip of her breast. She moaned as his tongue teased her nipple. His composure almost shattered at her reaction—her arching back, her tight grip on his arm—and he sucked in a breath to rein in his desire. His lips slipped along her ribs and she giggled, scooting away. He followed her and moved lower toward her intoxicating scent, a blend of her arousal with the delicate fragrance jasmine.

His lips hovered over her core. "Shauna, are you sure?" He needed to know her gift was still freely given. Once he tasted her, he knew it would be too hard to stop.

She gave a quick nod, but he waited, poised above her. Her lips moved and formed the word yes. No sound came out, but permission had been granted. He kissed her, a caress on the most intimate part of her body. Shauna raked her fingers through his hair and lifted her hips to him. He slipped in a finger, and she gasped, her eyes flying open. Jason, pleased at her intense, surprised pleasure, held her gaze as he curled his finger and increased the speed of his tongue. Her eyes glazed before she closed them and tipped her head back, her breath racing. A wail of satisfaction tore from her and she tensed, before shuddering in an explosive release.

Jason sheathed himself, glad to have brought Shauna to fulfillment and ready to bring her to a higher ecstasy. He kissed his way up her body, claiming her lips as he massaged her breasts. She ran her hands up his back, and Jason eased himself into her, her tight walls squeezing his erection. He groaned and pushed further, pausing to gauge her response before driving in a little farther. Shauna drew a quick breath, pushing back against the mattress.

"Sorry, honey." Jason kissed her, and her fingers wove

through his hair. He caressed her breast, and she moaned in his mouth. His other hand slid over her hip to the sweet curve of her bottom before returning his fingers to her center. Shauna's breath hitched, and she arched against him. He nibbled down her neck to her shoulder, and she threw her head back, her mouth open in silent euphoria. She scraped fingernails down his back, and he thrust deeper into her warm body.

With the little control he had left, he slid deeper and pulled back again and again. Shauna met each slow thrust with a lift of her pelvis and her ragged breaths drove him until they moved in a rhythm only they could hear, their hearts in sync. He brought her to soaring pleasure, his name on her lips, and he followed her with a low roar. He dropped beside her, pulling her close, needing her in his arms. He'd never experienced anything like the overwhelming exultation, anything else paling to what surged through him now.

He gave her a quick kiss. "I love you." It was all he could manage with his racing heart and out of control breathing.

She pressed her full lips against his neck. "I love you, too. And you're not evil."

His arm tightened around her. He'd felt something extra, a surge of energy entering his body when he took Shauna. Maybe his abilities had increased.

"Did you feel something else? Something different? Some kind of power surge?" She giggled. "It was all different to me. I didn't expect it to be so…so powerful, even with the dreams."

Jason let out a long breath. They'd done it. Nothing bad had happened. He didn't feel the evil in his heart that he'd felt when he'd worn that other medallion. He pulled her closer and gave her a slow, lingering kiss, feeling lighter than any other time since he met Shauna. Maybe since he'd turned fifteen.

A small concern nagged him about the energy surge. He'd have to test out his abilities.

Chapter 15

At dinner with Jason's family, Shauna worried that one look at her, and they'd know that she and Jason had made love. Thankfully, the family seemed the same as usual.

Jason's leg bounced and he pushed his food around his plate more than ate any. He smiled at Shauna, but spoke to his sister. "So Abby, do you have a boyfriend?"

She shook her head and frowned at him. "I told you already that I broke up with Jeremy."

"No new guy?"

"No. With the creep he turned out to be, I don't want another guy. Why are you asking?"

He shrugged. "Just curious."

Shauna studied him, and one corner of his mouth tipped up. She remembered the discussion about Abby's old boyfriend. Had Jason forgotten? Maybe he was having some lasting effects from the spell he'd been under. Or maybe their lovemaking had affected him after all, but slower than expected.

Reese lowered his eyebrows as he gazed at is son, then turned to Kathleen. They stared at each other for several seconds, as if silently conversing.

Kathleen turned. "Jason, has your headache come back?"

He shook his head. "No. I'm fine, Mom."

Shauna hadn't thought of that.

"Hey, Tony, how's basketball going?" Jason asked.

She almost laughed at the obvious way Jason took

attention away from himself.

Up to that point, Tony hadn't seemed to be paying attention to dinner conversation. "It's all right. I'm not team captain, like in high school. Too much competition. I'm thinking about dropping it next year."

The rest of dinner was spent talking about sports and Shauna lost interest.

They stood after dinner, picking up dishes to take to the kitchen. Jason set his last dish in the dishwasher and straightened. "I need to take a walk in the park."

"Not without me." Shauna took hold of his hand.

He laughed. "Can't be separated from me?" He brought their entwined hands up to his mouth and kissed hers. She shivered in anticipation of more kisses. Would they have to wait until the house was empty to make love again? He so easily affected her.

Shauna tugged Jason through the front door. He stopped and pulled her into his arms. He kissed her neck then ran his tongue from there to her ear and nipped her earlobe. He whispered, "It's hard not to touch you now that I'm not afraid to."

He released her, but she still held on. She had to will strength back into her week knees. Stepping back, she took his hand again. He pulled her along.

She pointed behind them. "The park's in that direction."

"We're going to a different park. I want to see more people."

"Want to see how good your willpower is?" It seemed pointless to go to a different park when a perfectly good one was up the block from the house.

"I'll explain later."

This was not a leisurely stroll. There was purpose in Jason's steps. Maybe his goal really was to see people.

They got within sight of the park and Jason slowed his

steps. Shauna had a chance to catch her breath.

He frowned. "Sorry." He squeezed her hand and wiggled his eyebrows. "There are better reasons to make you breathe like that."

This was so unlike the Jason she was used to.

A cheer drew her attention to a soccer game surrounded by a crowd. Both sides of the field was filled with people, sitting on the grass, on blankets, in chairs and others standing behind them.

They circled the field. Jason didn't seem to watch the game, but the spectators. Maybe he was looking for someone. He led her to a park bench, pulled her onto his lap and kissed her cheek.

"Thank you." He leaned back, pulling her with him.

She frowned at him. "For what?"

"For being you." He touched her face. "It turns out there was a side effect of making love with a virgin, or at least with you."

She gasped. She was almost afraid to ask. The only difference seemed to be that he allowed himself to touch and kiss her more. She studied his eyes. She didn't sense that he'd gone evil. She really didn't want to know if it was bad, but she whispered, "What happened?"

"The virgin detector is gone." He hugged her. "Maybe whatever or whoever gives us these abilities realized I wasn't going to use it as it was intended and finally took it away. I don't know. I'm just glad it's gone."

"Jason, that's wonderful. I know how much it bothered you." She kissed him then pulled back. "That's why you asked Abby about her boyfriend."

"Yeah. I wasn't surprised when it had disappeared around you."

She dropped her eyes and blushed.

"But Abby didn't have one, either. I really thought

she'd—Anyway, I had to see more people to find out."

"I understand. Can we walk slower back to the house?"

He kissed her cheek. "As slow as you want." Somehow he made that sound like he wasn't talking about walking.

She took his hand and stood. He followed her up. They'd only gone a few steps when Vanessa approached from the soccer crowd. She wore a baseball cap with her blonde ponytail pulled through the back and overdone makeup, short shorts and a tight, faded *Charmed* t-shirt.

"Hey, Jason. It's good to see you."

They stopped and Shauna squeezed his hand.

"Hi, Vanessa."

Shauna would have ignored her and kept walking, but Jason was more polite.

"My little cousin's playing. Got to give family support." She rolled her eyes. "I haven't seen you since you came into *The Cozy Corner* a few days ago. I thought we were getting together." She ran a finger down the arm that wasn't holding Shauna's hand. He twisted slightly away from her.

Jason must have promised Vanessa something when he couldn't remember Shauna. Fortunately, it looked like his memory came back before he'd done anything he might regret.

"That's not going to happen, Vanessa. You remember Rachel?" He lifted their linked hands.

The daggers were back. Shauna could almost feel them as Vanessa flicked a glance at her and their joined hands.

Vanessa lifted her hands, palm up. "All right. The offer's still open if you change your mind." She turned and walked back to the game, giving a glance over her shoulder before melting into the crowd.

Shauna shook. "Ugh. That's nothing like the pleasant shivers that you cause." She covered her eyes with her free hand. "Never mind. I didn't say that."

He laughed. "I can't unhear it." He gave her that sexy smile that caused flip flops in her stomach. "I think we can arrange some of those shivers." He nodded. "Yeah, that'll work."

Shauna scanned the crowd. "Later, not here."

Jason started walking. "I'm going to hold you to that."

***

After a nice evening with the family, Shauna had gone upstairs to brush her teeth. When she stepped into the hallway, Jason stepped out of Jamie's room with his duffle bag in his hand. Was he leaving? Were they leaving?

"Um, what are you doing?"

"I'm moving into my room with you."

She hyperventilated. Was she ready for that? They'd only had sex once. She loved him and he loved her, but that seemed like a big step.

"Maybe I should have talked to you about it first." He set the bag down and walked up to her. She jumped when he touched her. He pushed open the door to his room. "Okay, let's talk."

He guided her to the foot of the bed and they sat together. This couldn't be the usual next step after having made love once.

"Tell me what's going through your head."

"We can't be in the same room in your parents' house." She twisted her hands together and he covered them with one of his.

"Because of the premonition dreams, my parents knew we'd end up together."

"But—They did? How come I didn't know that?" She only thought she'd had the dreams because it would be her first time having sex. It didn't mean that they would stay together.

He gave her a quick kiss, making her forget her next words.

"I'm twenty-five. I've never brought a woman home before. I know this started as only my protecting you, but in different circumstances, I still would have brought you home."

"Do they know we already had sex?"

He shrugged. "I have no idea, but it will be kind of obvious when we start sharing a room. I told Dad my virgin detection ability went away. He can draw his own conclusion as to why."

"What about Abby and Tony? Don't you want to set a good example?"

He snorted. "Tony? He's probably had sex more times than I did by his age. Abby? I don't know. She'll probably be fine with it. Maybe she'll see it as our relationship progressing."

"What about my grandmother?" She bit her lip. Her grandma already didn't like Jason because he descended from Proctors. Shauna didn't want to think about what would happen when she found out they were sleeping together.

"She's dead, Shauna."

"But she's visited me in your room. She'll see us together."

"Well, okay. She only visits while you're sleeping, so she won't be there while we're making love."

Her face heated. "Maybe she watches me until I fall asleep."

"More likely, she can only visit you once you've gone to sleep and slips into your dreams. Maybe she'll see us together, but she'll just have to get used it."

She closed her eyes and tipped her face to the ceiling,

shaking her head. It shouldn't bother her, but it was a huge step.

"Anything else?"

"What about me?"

His voice was softer. "Tell me about you." He touched her face and turned it toward him, studied her.

She didn't even know. It was too fast. She couldn't even tell if she was nervous, scared, or worried. Confused for sure.

"This is all new to me. You didn't ask me." She blinked back tears.

His eyes widened slightly. "I'm sorry. I didn't think. I love you, Shauna." He kissed her temple. "I want to make love to you as often as you'll let me. I want to hold you while we sleep. I want to wake up in the morning to your smile." He gazed into her eyes. "I would like your permission to move into your room with you."

She considered him. The love shown in his eyes. His concern for her feelings was there, too. His patience as he stilled, waiting for her answer.

He'd been hot and cold because of his worry about being turned into a monster—pushing her away when he was too afraid of the evil that plagued his family. Then he was wonderful and loving. He'd taken a leap of faith that his love would prevent the evil from overtaking him. Maybe she should take a leap of faith, too.

"Okay." She twisted, reached up, covered both his ears with her hands and kissed him. He chuckled and tumbled them back onto the mattress. She was breathless in minutes. His hand lightly skimmed her stomach as it worked its way under her shirt. He stilled and lifted his head.

"I left my bag in the hall."

"So?" She tried to pull his head back down to hers.

"That's where the condoms are."

"Oh. You don't have any more in the nightstand?"

"I only put one in there, just in case. You're the only woman I've ever entertained in here, so I didn't have a supply."

She giggled at his mock indignation. "But you had them in Jamie's room."

"That's because the dream took place in there. I knew I had to be prepared."

"The dream was far from accurate. We didn't make love in Jamie's room and didn't do half the things we did in the dream."

He chuckled and kissed her. "Feel like you're missing out on something? We'll get to all those things and more."

"More?" she squeaked.

He chuckled again. "When you're ready." He opened the door and she floated his bag inside. "Showoff."

Chapter 16

Shauna woke feeling unbelievably happy. Jason's arm rested on her waist and his face was only inches from hers. In sleep, his features were softer, and those long, dark lashes framed his beautiful, dark blue eyes.

It was miraculous the way she and Jason had found each other. If she hadn't overheard the conversation Nick had with that guy, she, most likely, would have married him. She grimaced at the thought. Even without meeting Jason, hopefully, those dreams would have saved her from committing to Nick. It certainly made her realize what was missing between them. She sighed.

Jason wrinkled his forehead as his eyes opened, and he ran his finger down her arm.

Shauna smiled and gave him a quick kiss. "Morning."

"I couldn't tell if that was a happy sigh or if something is bothering you."

"Oh, definitely happy. I was just thinking—" She nibbled her lip. "Oh, I probably shouldn't mention another guy while we're in bed."

He smirked. "I think I can take it. You can talk about anything."

Of course he could take it. She'd never had sex with anyone else. She kissed him and he tucked her closer. Shauna never felt so loved and safe.

She stared at his chest. Better than to watch his eyes. "I was thinking about how little I felt when Nick kissed me. I didn't think it was in me. And I was going to marry him anyway because I…I didn't know what else to do." She searched his eyes. "Sometimes, you just have to look at me and—" She dropped her eyes back to his chest, ran a finger over the chain of his replacement medallion. Maybe it gave him too much control over her by telling him this. He pretty much knew what he did to her.

He lifted her chin with a finger. The left corner of his mouth tipped up. "Go on. I'd love to hear the rest."

Shauna wet her lips. "Sometimes when you look at me, I can…hardly breathe, and I need to touch you." She put her hand on his cheek. He kissed her palm, and her breath hitched. Jason leaned closer and kissed her. Moaning, she wrapped her arm around his neck and pressed her body to his. He rolled onto his back, taking her with him.

***

Unlike Shauna's skip down the stairs, Jason made his way at a normal pace, enjoying her bubbly excitement. They showered together, once he'd convinced her they wouldn't be late.

Her elation helped ease his slight worry at becoming a homeowner. It hadn't hit him until that morning that he'd be responsible for maintaining a house, not just living in it like an apartment. His parents made it look easy. If anything needed fixing, they immediately knew who to call. Maybe he'd want to do some repairs himself, but he didn't have much in the way of tools or experience.

"Come on, Jason. You don't want to be late for the house closing." Shauna thrust her purse strap over her shoulder as she stood at the door, her eyes glowing, her grin the widest he'd seen it.

"Shauna." He caressed her shoulders. "You're more excited about this than I am. Calm down. It only takes fifteen minutes to get to the lawyer's office." Because he couldn't resist, he kissed her.

"That's not going to get me to calm down." She threw her arms around his neck and returned his kiss, her warm lips giving him a promise.

"Now, who's going to make us late?" He hugged her close.

"You. Definitely you."

Now that the virgin issue was gone, it was hard to keep his hands off her. Even after having made love twice that morning, Jason had to fight his desire to take Shauna back up to his room.

He laughed, too. "All right. Let's do this."

Two hours later, Jason walked out of the lawyer's office with his new house keys in his pocket, holding Shauna's hand. "So, you want to go to the house?" He was looking forward to getting her into his own place, not having to worry about a family member walking in when he kissed her or took it further.

Shauna grinned. "You even have to ask?"

After a stop at *The Black Kettle* to pick up a celebration lunch, they pulled into the driveway of his new home. Once inside, he set the bag of take-out on the kitchen island and leaned against the counter. "Do you want to eat or explore the house first?"

She glanced at the bag and then the living room, and back at him, biting her lip. "I don't know. You decide."

"Let's eat first." He pulled sodas, napkins, forks and two foam cartons out of the bag. If they didn't eat now, no telling how long it would be before they got back downstairs.

Jason slid into the seat beside Shauna. "I'm glad you requested they leave these chairs. It's more comfortable than sitting on the floor."

"Oh, I don't know. I like picnics."

He looked down at the floor. "I didn't think to bring a blanket."

He pushed the carton marked *turkey* in front of Shauna, opened the one labeled *roast beef*. He stuck a fork into the red potato salad as Shauna crunched into her pickle. Jason pulled his phone from his pocket and typed. "I need to get the locks changed and find a painter and flooring company. Mom can tell me who she uses. And then I'll need to update the security system."

"You're going to hire someone? Don't you want to paint your house yourself?"

Laughing, he said, "I haven't held a paint brush since I was in art class in eighth grade. I want to make sure it looks good when it's done."

"I painted all the rooms in my dad's house. I could do it."

"Shauna, this is a big house. They'll bring in a crew and have it done in a couple of days."

"I guess you're right." She looked crestfallen.

"But you're going to help me pick colors, aren't you?"

Her smile returned. "Yes, of course."

"Great. I'm not very good at that sort of thing." He tried to pick his sandwich up, but his hands bounced away from it.

Shauna giggled.

He raised his eyebrows. "You put a bubble around it? Are you mad that I'm hiring painters?"

"No. I'm just practicing. I should practice, right?" She grinned.

"Why don't you practice on your food?"

"But I'm hungry." She glared at his sandwich. "Bubble's gone."

Once they'd eaten their fill, they repacked the leftovers into the bag. "I haven't had such a fun lunch in…well never," Jason said.

Shauna winked at him and headed for the living room.

Jason came up behind her and nibbled her neck. "I think I'll steam clean the carpet in here. Just in case."

One side of Shauna's mouth lifted up, then Jason kissed her half-smile. "Okay, no more suggestive remarks in favor of getting things done. Come on." They made their way through the rooms as Jason entered notes on his phone of work to be done. He'd purposely left the master bedroom for last. It was a sunny room with windows on two walls. As with the other carpeted rooms, it had been vacuumed after the furniture was removed.

He pointed to the windows. "I'm glad they don't face east."

"I *have* noticed you're not a morning person." She smirked as she put her hand on his chest.

She was the only woman, besides his mother, who knew that. Wrapping an arm around Shauna's waist and pulling her close, he kissed her neck. "But have you noticed, I wake up much earlier with a little help?" So far, Shauna had been unsuccessful at pulling out of his arms in the mornings without waking him. And since she was squirming that morning, he couldn't let her go without making love to her.

He slipped two buttons open on her shirt. They were the only ones in the house, and he had no worries that someone might get home unexpectedly, a totally different feel from making love in his parents' house.

"Jason, what are you doing?"

He gave her that smile that she'd told him gave her butterflies. "I'm unbuttoning your shirt."

"Yeah, I got that. But why?" Her eyes darted around the room, to the windows, into the corners.

"This is my house now. This is my bedroom. I want to try it out."

"Um, there's no furniture."

He wasn't sure why she seemed a bit panicky, but he'd take it slow. "We don't need a bed. The floor is carpeted. It looks more cushioned where the bed sat." He led her toward that spot as he slid the shirt off her arms and unhooked her bra. "I'll even lie on the floor, so you don't get rug burns." As soon as he dropped her bra, he pulled off his shirt and wrapped his arms around her. "Hmm. You feel so good."

He kissed her neck, then trailed kisses across her jaw, and when she turned her head, he took advantage and kissed her lips. Usually, by the time they had half their clothes off, he couldn't slow Shauna down. This time she barely responded.

"What's wrong? Does the house make you uncomfortable?" It was the first time that she wasn't 'in the mood.'

Her forehead wrinkled. "I don't know. Something doesn't feel right."

"It's probably because you've been in a house with a protection spell for long enough that you feel the lack of it here." Now that she understood the reason for her worry, he should be able to get her past it. He kissed her neck and nibbled her ear, ran his hands up her back. She remained stiff. "This isn't going to work, is it?"

"I'm sorry." She bit her lip.

He kissed her. "It's all right. We'll get Mom and Dad in here tonight and do the spell. We can christen it another time." He wiggled his eyebrows at her, and she laughed. Her tension seemed to melt.

He pulled his shirt on, watching her closely as she fumbled getting dressed. Something more than an unprotected house bothered her.

Shauna followed him down the stairs. At the bottom, a flash of movement caught his eye. Someone stood in his foyer. He pushed Shauna behind him as he slowly made his way to the front door. His hand settled on the gun at his back. Maybe this was why Shauna was feeling off.

Vanessa stood inside his house and smiled at him.

Anger tightened his chest. "What are you doing in my house?" Maybe Shauna was right about Vanessa. He was beginning to feel stalked. Shauna kept telling him that Vanessa shot daggers at her. Maybe she really did want to hurt Shauna.

"Jason," Vanessa gushed. "I was so excited when Guy told me you'd bought his house. We're practically neighbors."

"What the hell are you doing inside my house?"

"Guy and Janet gave me a key so that I could water plants and take care of their cat when they were away." She peered over his shoulder and sneered at Shauna. As quickly, a smile appeared on her face as she spoke to Jason. "And it's no problem since I live so close by."

"Where do you live?"

Vanessa waved her right hand a bit behind her. "Across the street and three doors down, with my mother."

"I thought you lived on the other side of town." He couldn't believe he'd picked a house so close to hers. She was the last person he wanted to see frequently. It would be far easier for her to stalk him living in the same neighborhood. Bile rose up his esophagus, and he swallowed to force it back down.

"I don't want you in my house," he said more forcefully.

"Jason, don't be like that." Her voice wheedled.

He held out his hand. "Give me the key. I don't know why you'd think it was okay to walk into someone else's house." The thought made him angry.

"But you might need me to help out." She gripped the

key tightly to her chest.

"I don't think so." He waited, wiggled his fingers. He didn't want to fight her for them.

She stared at the key, then into his eyes, before finally dropping it in his hand.

"Now, I'd like you to leave."

"But, Jason."

"Now!"

"All right. I can see it's a bad time." She glared at Shauna, turned and left, slamming the door behind her.

Shauna stepped beside him, and he put his arm around her waist. "I definitely have to get the security system updated, and I'm changing the locks, just in case." Shauna appeared visibly shaken by the intrusion. "It's a good thing you had that bad feeling. God know what she would have done..." He drew her into his arms.

After a moment, he called his father.

"Hi, Jason. How's the new house?"

"Good, except I need a locksmith ASAP. Can you recommend one?"

Keyboard keys clicked. "Here we go." Reese recited the number.

Jason entered it in his list. "Thanks. I hope he can get the locks changed today."

"Why so soon?" Reese asked.

"We had an intruder with a key. I don't want to take a chance that she has more." That woman was never coming into his house again. It was bad enough she lived on the same block.

"She? Who?" Reese's tension came through the phone.

"Vanessa. She seems to have turned into a stalker. Can you and Mom come here tonight so we can do a protection spell?"

"Vanessa from the *Cozy Corner*?"

"Yeah. Long story, Dad. Can you come?"

"How about at dinner you tell us about Vanessa, and we'll come over after that?"

"That'll work. Thanks. See you later."

As soon as he hung up, Jason dialed the number his father had given him and arranged for the locksmith to arrive in an hour.

He wrapped his arms loosely around Shauna. "So, what do you want to do while we wait?" He tried one of his melting smiles.

"Not that." She tried to push out of his arms. "It would look like we just made love when the locksmith arrives."

"I wouldn't mind."

"Of course you wouldn't. It's probably some kind of macho guy thing."

He laughed and she crossed her arms. He'd think she was upset, except one corner of her mouth twitched up.

She tipped her head. "And I'm thinking, in my limited experience, that you'd want the first time here to not be rushed."

He set his hands on her arms. "You're right. I don't want any time restrictions. So, what should we do instead?"

"Maybe you should call the painter. He can bring some color samples when he's free. And call someone about the floors."

"Good idea." A quick call to his mother yielded the phone numbers her favorite painting crew and a flooring company.

"One of the paint crew will be here tomorrow afternoon, and the flooring guy the following afternoon." He checked the time. "We still have at least a half hour." Glancing around, the fireplace caught his eye. "Why don't I see if I can get the gas log fired up, and we can sit in front of the fireplace?"

"That sounds nice." She trailed behind him to the living room, sat on the floor and leaned on the hearth.

It took a few minutes to figure out how to light the gas log.

She stared into the flames. "The flames aren't as random as a fire with real logs."

"But it's a whole lot faster. Unless you're my mom, but then someone still needs to bring in wood."

Jason stretched out on his side, facing the fire with his head propped on his hand. Shauna settled in front of him, with her back against his chest.

Very soon, they'd be able to make love whenever they wanted, and wherever in the house they wanted. After the locks were changed and the protection spell was in place.

But outside, how safe was Shauna with Vanessa in the neighborhood?

Chapter 17

Something was up with Jason. She was pretty sure the painter, Miriam, knew he had other things on his mind besides paint colors, the way her eyes kept darting between Jason and Shauna. Nearly the whole time they studied the color samples, he touched Shauna—massaged her neck, placed a hand on her shoulder or at her hip, an arm around her waist. She almost laughed at the relief on his face when they finished choosing paint colors and the painter walked out the door. Shauna couldn't understand his impatience when he knew they had this appointment.

He leaned against the locked door and wrapped her in his arms. "I didn't expect it to take so long to pick out colors, but now I have you all to myself."

The doorbell rang, and Jason tipped his head back and groaned. "They're conspiring against me." He yanked the door open and an elderly man stood on the doorstep.

"Hi. I'm Howard." He pointed to the yellow house directly opposite. "I live across the street." The man stuck his hand out. "I saw the paint truck and figured you must be the new owner."

Jason shook the man's hand. "I'm Jason and this is my girlfriend Shauna."

Howard nodded. "Nice to meet you, ma'am. My wife, Mabel, is home most days. She'd love it if you came over and shared a cup of coffee with her."

Shauna smiled. "Thanks. I'll have to do that." Maybe the woman could be another grandma.

Howard nodded. "I'll be off. I'm sure you two have lots to do."

"Nice meeting you, sir," Jason said, and closed the door after Howard stepped away.

Jason wrapped his arms around her. "I'm glad that was short. Now, where were we?"

"Here." Shauna slid her hands up his chest and around his neck. She knew when they arrived at his new house today that they'd make love. It was the first time that it had been planned. It added a level of excitement and anticipation that she hadn't had before. "So, what's in the backpack?"

It sat beside the door, piquing her curiosity from the moment Jason carried it out to the car that morning. When she'd asked, he'd given her a too short kiss and told her she'd find out when the time was right.

He nibbled her lip. "There was champagne and glasses, but I snuck them into the fridge." He kissed her. "There's a blanket, so neither of us will get rug burns." He dropped kisses along her jaw until he reached her ear and she shivered. "There are a couple of towels and shower gel. I haven't decided if we should shower or use the Jacuzzi." When he sucked her earlobe, she moaned. She hadn't thought that far. How had he gotten together all those things for a wonderful, romantic afternoon?

He pushed away from the door and picked up his bag. Taking her hand, he led her into the kitchen. He opened the refrigerator and handed her the champagne then picked up the glasses.

"Can you feel a difference in the house?" he asked with a lifted eyebrow.

She nodded. With the new locks, Vanessa wouldn't get in again. "The house feels better today. I can sense the protection. After the protection spells on your medallions, I didn't expect the house protection to take so long." It had taken over an hour. Kathleen and Reese had stood in front of every window and door, each holding a white candle and the other's hand. They whispered a chant, held their candles together so the flames entwined and Kathleen only released Reese's hand long enough to dropped a pinch of something into the flame, causing a blue flame to flare for a moment.

Shauna wasn't sure exactly what Jason had planned, but every minute would be enjoyable. He held her hand as she followed him up the stairs and down the hall to the master bedroom. Once inside, she set the bottle on the fireplace hearth and unbuttoning her shirt. Jason put his bag on the floor and the glasses beside the champagne. His indrawn breath made her grin. Then that smile of his caused her insides to spin. His fingers beat hers to the front clasp on her bra and he unhooked it and slid it back with the shirt.

His gaze rested for a moment on her breasts before his lips skimmed her abdomen, between her breasts, up her neck to her lips. Her shirt and bra fluttered to the floor.

"I shouldn't be any more dressed than you are." He pulled his shirt off, let it fall beside hers, and took the blanket out of the pack.

Shauna touched it. "Wait. Let me do this." She stepped away from him and lifted her hand. The blanket opened on its own and straightened out, the four corners held taut. It settled to the floor, perfectly smoothed out.

He laughed. "Show off."

"I could levitate us or put us in a bubble, so we don't have to be on the hard floor."

He chuckled. "That's not going to happen. You'll get too distracted, and we'll plummet to the carpet."

"I could hold us just an inch or two off the floor."

"And then, you get wildly excited and float us up higher. Or, even without that, I wouldn't want to be dropped from two inches up when you lose it during an orgasm."

"Okay. I get your point."

He lit the gas fire, and picked up the glasses, filled them with champagne, then set them on the hearth. Reaching into his pocket, he pulled out two condoms and put them beside the glasses. There was one morning where they'd used two condoms, once in bed and then in the shower. The second time had been amazing. She'd been so sensitive, it seemed to take only seconds for her to peak higher than the first time and it turned out they weren't anywhere near finished. Her heart pounded just thinking about it.

His smile smoldered, and his hands lowered to his belt and unbuckled it. Her eyes flew up to his. He watched her. She still wasn't comfortable seeing him fully naked, which seemed kind of weird since she stood in front of him with bare breasts and it didn't bother her, at least not as much as the thought of him removing his jeans. In all those dreams, she'd never seen him naked below the waist. She'd felt his body against her, and felt him plunge into her, the thought quickened her breathing.

She'd been in museums, seen statues and paintings of naked men, so she couldn't figure out her hang up. Maybe she should try a quick peek. His zipper rasped down. Nope. Not happening this time. Maybe he hadn't noticed.

Each time before they made love, she'd either been in bed already, or Jason had removed her clothes. He'd kissed and touched her, so she hadn't had time to be nervous. Shauna was overcome by the desire to do it for him, to slowly remove her clothing and watch his eyes take her in.

Unbuttoning her pants, she drew the zipper down, so slowly she didn't hear it. He stilled as his eyes devoured her. She didn't feel confident enough to try some kind of striptease, but she could do a leisurely undressing. She slid the pants off her hips and they dropped around her ankles. She stepped out of them and as she pulled off her socks, her long hair fell over her shoulder. Some day she'd have to try long silk stockings. Now, those would be sexy coming off. Taking a step onto the blanket, she hooked her fingers in the sides of her panties and inch by inch, eased them down and off.

Jason took a deep breath and quick breaths followed. His arms had dropped to his sides, his hands fisted. Trying to restrain himself? Two more steps brought her inches from him. She rested her hands on his sides and slid them down. She reached his waistband and continued down, pushing the pants over his hips. The belt buckle clunked on the floor. Her eyes never left his, but she felt his erection press against her stomach.

He ran a finger down her jaw and over her lips. A corner of his mouth twitched up. "Afraid to look?"

She lifted a shoulder. So, he had noticed. "A little." It was less a fear than a feeling that she shouldn't look.

"We'll have to work on that." Pulling his feet out of his pants, he took her hand and walked backwards toward the blanket. They sat in the middle and Jason reached behind him for the two glasses, handing her one.

"A toast?" he asked.

"May you have many happy memories in your new home," she said and clinked his glass.

"Starting with this one." He kissed her and took a sip from his glass. She'd never had champagne before. The bubbles made it seem like soda, with a kick. After they'd drained their glasses, he set them back on the hearth. Putting his hand on her upper back, he leaned back, and she tumbled onto him.

"You feel so good." He ran his hands up her back and down, skimming them over her butt.

Tendrils of excitement flowed into her from everyplace their skin touched. Shauna wiggled and kissed him. He groaned and started to roll over, then fell back onto the blanket.

She smiled against his lips. He must have remembered his promise to let her be on top. She recalled the dream and let it guide her.

***

Jason flipped the blanket edge over them. Shauna sighed and snuggled back into him. Even after holding her for hours, he didn't want to let go. They'd made love in the Jacuzzi and in front of three fireplaces. He'd lit the fire in each one and these were the only flames he'd looked at. Shauna picked up her glass, took a sip and grimaced. Hours of sitting in front of one fire or another had warmed the champagne. He should have left it in the last room.

"I can hardly believe we made love in four different rooms," she said.

His arm tightened around her. He'd never used so many condoms in one day before. Thankfully, he still had a few more in his bag. Definitely needed to buy more. "We're not done yet."

"For today, we are. I don't know if I can walk."

He chuckled, kissed behind her ear. "I think we'll have to head back to my parents' house soon. I've enjoyed getting to know more of you and my house." He trailed his hand over her stomach, along her hip, down her leg and back again. He'd explored every inch of her, but Shauna hadn't gotten below his waist yet, except she did seem to like his butt. He'd have to figure out something to make her more comfortable another time they came to the house. He was still surprised at her nervousness. She'd had an x-rated movie in her dreams, starring them, and he didn't understand this hang up.

***

The next day Jason and Shauna pulled into his driveway, and spotted Vanessa in a yard across the street and three doors down. She picked up a cat, and turned toward them, glaring.

Shauna groaned. "Of course, she has a black cat, the witch."

Jason chuckled. "Half the people in town are considered witches, including you and me. You'll have to come up with something else to call her."

"Well, how about a word that rhymes with that? I can't believe she lives so close to you."

He squeezed her hand. "I wish I'd known. Pretend she's not there."

"Easy for you to say. You don't get that dagger glare."

He retrieved a small, black plastic bag from the door pocket and met her in front of the car. He tangled his hand in her hair and kissed her. He didn't stop until she was breathing hard. "That should make her realize she doesn't have a chance with me."

Her mouth dropped open. "You were just putting on a show?"

"I enjoyed it, too. Does that count?" He nipped her lip.

A van with *Millet Flooring* painted on the side pulled in behind them before she could answer.

They shook hands with Bob, the gray haired floor guy, and went inside. The voice over the phone made him expect a younger man, and his quick, no nonsense movements didn't betray his age. They trailed behind Bob as he entered each room, made suggestions and took notes in a small notepad. He'd polish all hardwood floors and carpets would be replaced in three bedrooms. Bob retrieved samples from the truck and they chose carpet and colors. In less than an hour he was gone, leaving them alone.

"I've got something special in mind." Jason retrieved the folded blanket from the dining room hearth and the bag he'd dropped on it earlier and led her upstairs to the master bedroom. He flipped the blanket open in front of the fireplace and lit the fire. After kissing her, he pulled her shirt over her head, then kissed her before removing each piece of clothing. "Now lie on your stomach on the blanket."

She scrunched her eyebrows and nose, but he pointed and she lay down, resting her head on her hands. He quickly stripped off his clothes, straddled her and sunk to his knees.

He massaged her head and ran his fingers through her hair, then pulled a bottle from the plastic bag and squirted a liquid into his hand. With the oil distributed, he rubbed his fingers on her neck, circling his thumbs into tight muscles in her shoulders. Her moan made him smile. Replenishing the oil, he worked his way down one arm and then the other, until he reached her fingers.

He scooted down and slid his palms over her back, pushing the heels of his hands into tight areas. His fingers skimmed the sides of her breasts and she sucked in a breath. He smirked at his intentional tease. Farther down, he skimmed her butt, then massaged it. More effort than he expected had to be expended to not turn her over and ravish her, but he needed to follow the plan. Each leg got special attention, followed by her feet, finishing by nibbling her toes.

With her eyes still closed, she said, "Mmm. That felt so good. I've never had a massage before."

He lay down beside her and kissed her nose. "Now it's your turn," he said quietly.

***

"My turn?" she squeaked. He wanted her to touch him all over the way he'd done her? Well, it wasn't all over. "Um, okay." Encouraged by his smile, she sat up.

She'd never given a massage before. Maybe she'd do it wrong and he wouldn't like it or she'd hurt him. She wanted to make it feel as good for him as it had her.

Straddling him, she started with his head, running her fingers from his neck to the top. She tipped her fingers so her nails skimmed his scalp. Then she used the pads of her fingers and more pressure, making slow circles. At his neck, she added oil to her hands, and tried to work the muscles the way he'd done it. His response made it sound like she was doing it right. She decided to make a change to what he'd done and kissed his neck, her breasts skimming his back.

"I like that." His eyes were closed, and the corner of his mouth ticked up.

After massaging his shoulders, she kissed each one then massaged her way down his arms, leaning forward to kiss his hands. He lifted his head and skimmed his lips across the side of her breast.

"Hey! No touching." She had to concentrate on what her hands were doing. That kind of distraction could derail her.

Scooting down, she worked over his shoulder blades. Her thumbs pushed and circled on each side of his spine, slid down an inch then circled again. He moaned when her nails raked up his back, so she could massage his ribs from the top. Muscles flexed as her freshly oiled palms pushed into his ribs. She kissed several spots along his spine as she moved down. She hadn't thought about the oil. At least, it wasn't an unpleasant taste on her lips.

Her hands skimmed over his butt several times before she felt ready to massage him there. He seemed to like that, too, as he tensed his tight buns. When she'd decided to kiss the places where she massaged him, she didn't think about this spot. She massaged him longer, working up the courage to kiss him. Finally, she scooted down and kissed each cheek then started massaging his legs. Her hands were smaller than his and his legs so muscular. She used both hands on one leg and worked her way to his foot, stopping to kiss the back of his knee and then the bottom of his foot. Then she repeated the same on the other leg.

She lay down beside him and kissed his nose like he'd done to her. "How did I do?"

He opened his eyes and gave her the sexy smile that caused feathers to tickle her stomach. "It was perfect. Now, shall we massage fronts?"

"Fronts? Uh, no." She shook her head. Her face heated up.

He dragged his pants over, reached into a pocket and pulled out two handkerchiefs with a flourish. "How about if we're both blindfolded?" He twisted his upper body toward her and waved them back and forth.

He dropped one over her hands. She studied him then stared at the handkerchief. Could she do it? She gazed into his eyes. "I…I'll try. I won't promise. If you massage first and I can't do it, will it be okay?" She bit her lip.

He touched her face. "All I ask is that you try. You tie me and then I'll tie you." He turned his back to her.

She shook out the handkerchief, refolded it and saw he was doing the same. She covered his eyes and tied it, then turned her back to him.

His hand brushed her upper back, traveled to her neck, then to the top of her head. The cloth covered her eyes. He joined the ends in back and skimmed a hand over her face, shifting the handkerchief down a bit, and tied the ends of the handkerchief together.

She lay back down and waited, wondering if he'd pushed up the mask to stare at her, but it didn't matter. He'd already seen her. A hand touched the top of her head, brushed across her forehead, over the cloth, down her jaw and across her lips. His lips lightly touched hers and were gone. His hands rubbed together. He must have oiled them. Fingers glided down her neck and a hand went to each shoulder. He massaged until her muscles relaxed. Again, he worked down her arms.

Anticipation quickened her breath. This was so much more intimate than when he'd massaged her back. She wanted to see his face as he touched her, know where he was going next.

His fingers skimmed across her collar bones and barely touched her breasts. She took a breath as he massaged them and it felt wonderful, but didn't seem sexual. His touch was different than when they made love. He didn't touch her nipples, but kissed each before moving lower. Her ribs and stomach received gentle circles with his fingertips. Her breathing became erratic as she wondered what he would caress next.

His fingers skimmed the hair between her legs and stayed there only long enough to make her want them to never leave. A kiss showed he was moving on. He massaged both legs and down to her feet, placing a kiss on each big toe. He moved up beside her and startled her with a kiss on her lips, then settled down beside her.

"Your turn."

Shauna sat up and tried to slow her breathing. Her body still tingled where his fingers had touched her so intimately. She swung her leg over him and sat at hip level. Her bottom sat atop his semi-erect penis warm against her skin, but she couldn't afford to think about that right now.

There was a job to do. Stretching her fingers out, she skimmed his chest, chin and nose, blindfold, until she'd reached his hair. Bending her fingers, she raked her nails over his scalp, smiling at his groan. She then touched his forehead, cheeks and chin. Her lips met his for only a moment before she fumbled for the oil and coated her hands, ran them over his shoulders and massaged, working gently up his neck.

She thoroughly squeezed and rubbed each arm then brought her hands to his chest. His indrawn breath when she skimmed over his nipples brought her tentative touch to them again.

She startled when his hands skimmed the sides of her breasts. "Hey, it's my turn for touching."

His hands dropped away. "Sorry."

She pushed against his ribs and wondered if he was ticklish, but after a quick squeeze to his side, he didn't flinch or wiggle.

Scooting down, her hands molded around his hips, pushing her thumbs beside his hip bones. Curly hair tickled her fingers and she froze as she realized how close her hands were to *that* part of him. She skimmed her fingers down his thighs and calves and massaged his feet. She'd work her way up and hopefully her courage, too. Each muscular calf received her touch and then his thick thighs.

Too soon, the ultimate goal was within reach. Could she touch him there—on his penis? Jason wanted her to. It was the whole purpose of this massage experience. He'd touched her and it felt good even after his fingers had moved on. She moved her fingers closer and closer again. Smooth skin moved under one finger. Her other hand closed in and touched the side of his full erection. He gasped and his breathing changed. Did it feel the same as when he touched her in her feminine counterpart? She slipped the first hand up his length—smooth and soft. Only his lips were softer. She tentatively gave two gentle squeezes and his breath hitched.

Then suddenly, memories flooded her mind. It was too much like another time. Touching, not seeing. "No! No! I won't look!" She jerked away from him and bumped into the hearth. Shauna ripped the blindfold off and dropped her forehead onto her raised knees and wrapped her hands over her head. She took great gulping breaths between sobs.

"Shauna! Honey. What is it?" He ripped off his scarf and lifted her head.

She blinked away tears. "Jason! I remember." She threw her arms around his neck. He pulled her trembling body onto his lap and she snuggled into his embrace.

He rocked her. "Honey, what do you remember?"

"Grandma did something to make me forget, but now I remember."

He stiffened for a moment, then kissed her forehead and pressed his cheek to her. "Forget what? Can you talk about it?"

She quivered. It was so fresh in her mind now. "When we were eleven, Kristy and I used to go to the library every Thursday after school. We walked home. When we reached our street, Kristy turned right to walk the block to her house and I went left for the three blocks to my house." Jason remained quiet, but tightened is arms around her as she took two deep breaths. "I had to pass a small wooded lot between two houses, but when I got to the edge of trees this time, I got a creepy feeling. I stopped and thought about running to Kristy's house, but convinced myself it was fine. I wish I'd gone with the feeling." Even without remembering, she never doubted her inner voice again. Shauna pressed her lips together.

Jason kissed her cheek. "You don't have to say any more."

"No. I think I need to." She pulled his arm from around her and held his hand in both of hers. "I only took a few steps when a man stepped out from behind a tree and dragged me into the woods."

Jason's hand tightened almost painfully on hers before he relaxed it. "Oh, honey, no."

She shook and fresh tears rolled down her cheeks. "He pulled down his sweat pants, grabbed my hand and wrapped it around his—penis. He squeezed my hand and yelled—no—whispered loud to open my eyes and watch what I did to him. I refused to look. Someone shouted behind me. It was Dad." She exhaled, still relieved after so many years that her father drove by the vacant lot right when she needed him most.

"The man released me, and Dad punched him in the face so hard he almost fell. The man ran away. Dad carried me to the car. I wouldn't let go of him so he could put me in, so he left the car there and carried me home."

Jason wiped tears off her cheeks with his handkerchief. "I'm so sorry."

"Even then, I knew it could have been worse." She shivered at the remembered nightmares, always imagining what if her father hadn't shown up.

"How did your dad find you?"

"Grandma called him at work. She told him he needed to find me in the woods near our house or someone would hurt me."

"She had a premonition. Thank God for that."

"Dad knew to trust what Grandma said."

"And then your grandmother made you forget."

She nodded. "I had nightmares every night for two weeks. Grandma asked me if I wanted to forget it. I said yes, and she did something, then I didn't remember it anymore."

Jason embraced Shauna. "I am so sorry I made you remember."

"I had to. It was affecting me without my knowing

why." She snuggled her head against his shoulder.

"Do you want to get dressed?"

"No. I want to shower off this oil and get in the Jacuzzi. Maybe I can relax again."

"If that's what you want."

She touched his cheek, concern and worry in his eyes. "It seems that knowing the reason for my aversion has taken away most of my hesitation. I mean, I understand it wasn't you forcing me to do something I didn't want." Shauna gazed into his eyes. "I want you, Jason. In every way."

He smiled. "C'mon. Let's get this oil off."

"Mmm. And then, I want to check you out."

Chapter 18

Shauna bolted up in bed and squinted into the corner of the room. "What?"

The light her grandmother always turned on was lit and she sat in the rocker. Shauna fumbled to pull the blanket back up, the sheet cool against her bare skin, and drew her knees to her chin. She should have put her nightshirt on after she and Jason made love.

"Shauna. What in the world are you doing with that boy? He holds darkness." Her grandmother couldn't have sounded more shocked.

She knew her grandmother would find out, but it was still embarrassing to be caught by her, naked in bed with a man who wasn't her husband. And a man her grandmother didn't like.

"Grandma, he's not evil. I can feel it."

The old woman flicked her head at the sleeping form beside Shauna. "All you're feeling is lust."

"Grandma!" Shauna shook her head. "That isn't true." *This is not happening*. She caressed Jason's arm, warm with tickly hair. He cared for her. It wasn't lust, but an indescribably close connection.

She spoke firmly to her grandmother. "We care for each other. He's protected me." She couldn't tell her how Jason had fought the spell so that he didn't hurt her. Grandma would latch onto that and not believe it was only a spell. "Are you sure you sense evil in Jason or are you basing your opinion on the family you once knew?"

Her grandmother sighed and didn't answer. "Have you been practicing your abilities?"

Shauna relaxed. At least she could talk about this without enduring her grandmother's displeasure. "Yes. Abby suggested I try to levitate myself, and I found I could. That could come in handy if I ever break my leg. I've been practicing bubbles so much that when Tony dropped a plate, I suspended it in a bubble before it hit the floor."

"That's good, dear. You need to be able to do these things without thinking about how to do them."

"They've gotten so easy, that I have to remember not to do them in public. Are you going to teach me something else?"

"No. I came because there's been a disturbance." Her grandmother leaned forward. "You're in danger. I don't know what it is, but I sense that it will come from within Rawlins and from outside. Two evils will join forces against you."

"Two?" A cold finger slithered up her spine. "How am I going to fight two?"

"Keep practicing, Shauna." Her eyes flicked over to Jason. "Be careful with that one. Maybe he's the evil from Rawlins."

"He's not!" Her hand tightened around Jason's arm. "But I'll be more careful." It had to be Vanessa. No one else seemed to hate her.

"I must leave now. I love you, dear."

"I love you, too, Grandma."

Shauna snuggled into Jason's side. That exchange with her grandmother could have been worse.

***

She woke on her back with his body pressed against the

side of hers, the weight of Jason's arm settled under her breasts and she blinked against the sunlight. A strange smile graced his face. Not the sexy one. Not the making-a-joke one.

"Um, what does that look mean?"

His smile grew bigger. "I had this dream."

"Was it that dream?" She grinned. "Do you have something new to show me?"

He slowly shook his head. "No. Your grandma was there."

"What?" she squeaked. "You were in my dream with Grandma?"

"I woke with your hand on my arm. Maybe that's what pulled me into it."

She covered her eyes. "Why didn't you say something? What did you hear?" She couldn't remember at what point she touched him. Wasn't it seconds after Grandma woke her? When he didn't answer right away, she squinted at him.

"I didn't want to interrupt." His serious face made her nervous. "She knows you're in danger from people inside and outside of Rawlins. Maybe Nick has figured out where you are." He kissed her. "And I'm not going to harm you, so we have to figure out who in Rawlins would."

"Vanessa." The dagger woman made perfect sense. She didn't know how the two could meet up, but they'd make the perfect evil team.

"Vanessa doesn't want us together, but I find it hard to believe she'd do something to hurt you."

"Why can't you believe that of her? You didn't date her very long, so there was something about her you obviously didn't like."

"She was too possessive, too soon. I didn't like how clingy she was."

"Well, she's still clingy, which is probably why she

gives me those killer looks. So, if it's not her then who would team up with Nick? No one else in Rawlins seems to have an interest in me."

He shook his head. "Maybe he's going to hire someone here to help him."

"So, we're pretty much in the dark still. I wish Grandma would have had more information. I feel like a noose is closing around my throat."

***

Jason could barely keep up as Shauna ran barefoot from room to room in his new home. She practically glowed. He had more fun watching her than seeing the results of the new paint and flooring. They'd picked warm tans for the walls in the public areas and barely-there blues, grays and creams for the bedrooms. The new carpets in the bedrooms were plush and beautiful. The buffed hardwood floors looked new.

The last room she entered was their bedroom. After inspecting it, she threw her arms around him. "I love it. When can you start moving in?"

He wrapped his arms around her. "We have to wait for the finish on the hardwood floors to harden before putting furniture on it, so two days. I've already set up the furniture delivery for the day after that. The pod is arriving tomorrow, and then I'll have my heirlooms delivered from storage." He gave her a quick kiss. "If you help with unpacking boxes, we can be in here that much sooner. Maybe four or five days."

"We?"

"Shauna, you keep talking about the house as if it's just mine."

"It—"

He covered her mouth with his fingers. "It's our house. We picked it out together. We bought furniture together. I can't imagine living here without you." He kissed her again. "I thought you understood. I took a huge risk the first time we made love. I wouldn't have done it for anyone else."

She blinked several times, tears shimmered in her eyes. She wrapped her arms around his waist and snuggled her head against his neck. "I thought when this was over, you'd send me away."

He gave her a squeeze and kissed the top of her head. "I couldn't do that. I'd be tearing out a piece of my heart."

"But I'm a job to you."

"I'm glad you were a job. Otherwise, we might never have met. But you stopped being a job when I fell in love with you." He pushed her back, staring her in the eye. "I refused anymore pay because you're the most important person in the world to me."

Her smile grew wide.

He wrapped his arms around her and buried his face in her hair.

His phone rang, and he swore. Someone had the poorest timing ever. He plucked his phone from his jeans, and checked the ID before answering.

"Hi, Dad."

"Jason. There's trouble." He stiffened and Shauna lifted her head from his chest. "I took your Mom to lunch at *The Village,* and we saw Nick there." Jason tightened his hold on Shauna. "After he left, I talked to Amy. She said he showed her a picture of Rachel and asked if she'd seen her. Amy told him she hadn't. She said the guy gave her the creeps."

Nick might check with realtors, in case Shauna had tried to find an apartment. "Can you call Allen, just in case Nick thinks to talk to a realtor?" Shauna stiffened against him at Nick's name. "Ask him to not to share anything about Rachel, and let Allen know that Nick might refer to her by a different name."

"All right, I'll call Allen right now."

"Thanks for the heads up, Dad." He disconnected.

Shauna pushed away from Jason and stared at him. She'd paled and her bottom lip trembled. "Your dad saw Nick? Here?"

He wrapped his arms around her. "In Amherst. Mark emailed me a couple days ago. They found out that Kristy's phones had been tapped."

"I thought there was a chance he'd give up, but if he's come this far, he won't stop until he finds me." She started to shake and Jason pulled her close. "You know, I thought we were overreacting when I told Kristy about what I overheard Nick say. Then her father whisked me away before I could think about it." She lifted her head. "What does he want with me?"

"Maybe he's simply angry that you left him."

"I'm scared, Jason. He's too close."

"I won't let anything happen to you. The security system is being upgraded this afternoon."

Her eyes widened. "What about your family? If he finds out I'm staying there, he may hurt them to find me. Maybe I should run."

"Do you want to run for the rest of your life?"

She shook her head.

He'd already thought about his family. "We'll move in here today and camp out until the furniture arrives. This is my home territory. Trust me." He held her chin. "I'm going to keep you safe, Shauna. I promise." He kissed her, soft and tender, and felt Shauna relax in his arms.

Now he had to make good on that promise.

Chapter 19

Sun streamed through the sliding glass door in the empty dining area. The sunlight warmed Jason's back as he flipped a pancake then turned the hickory bacon. He touched his gun in its holster clipped to his belt. Shauna shifted and groaned as she sat on the other side of the island. Her elbows rested on the counter with her chin on her hands.

"Are you okay?"

"My hip's a little sore. The sleeping bag wasn't thick enough." She gave him what he was coming to recognize as her sexy smile. "One more night, and we'll have your—our—new bed."

He stared at her, seeing an image of her naked body on their new bed.

"You're going to burn that pancake." She lifted her chin toward the pan on the stove.

He spun around, scooped the perfectly golden pancake out of the pan and dropped it onto the plate, then poured more batter. He turned back to her. "Actually, I meant, how are you holding up with Nick so near?"

He added a pancake to his plate, rounded the island, and set both plates in front of her. He kissed her forehead.

She shrugged. "I'm okay if I don't think about him."

He sat next to her, and picked up the maple syrup, smothering his pancakes. "It's more important than ever that you stay close to me. Mom can bring groceries if we run low. We can't chance you being seen in town right now."

She paled. "Do you think he'll come to Rawlins?"

He squeezed her hand. "He started where Kristy's phone call caught us. He'll most likely search surrounding towns."

As they cleared away dishes, there was a knock on the door. Jason looked out the window. "The moving pod is here." He jogged outside to show the driver where to set the storage unit. It lowered to the ground at the edge of the driveway, then Jason signed a paper, and the movers left. Shauna leaned against the doorway. Jason walked quickly to the front door and nudged her inside. "Why don't I bring boxes inside, and you can move them to the rooms marked? That way you won't be seen by anyone passing by."

"But it'll go faster if I help you bring them in. You're on a side street. Why would Nick go up and down every street?"

Jason sighed, and ran a hand through his hair. "No, Shauna. You're staying inside."

She glared at him. He wouldn't give in on this.

She crossed her arms. "Fine."

"And stay out of sight of the doorway." Jason strode to the container and unlocked the door. He stared inside. He probably should have gotten rid of more stuff.

He lifted two boxes from a stack, carried them into the house, and set them to the left of the door.

Shauna motioned, and the top box lifted. She leaned around it. "Both go upstairs." She waived her hand and the boxes floated, one behind the other up the stairs.

He kissed her temple. "See. Your skills are better used in here."

He headed back outside. After several trips, he decided to get some water. Since Shauna was no longer at the door, she must have gone upstairs to direct the boxes into the appropriate rooms. He snagged two bottles from the refrigerator and stepped into the living room. "Shauna? Let's take a water break."

Silence. No response from Shauna. No boxes bumped upstairs.

She was probably in the bathroom. A glance down the hall showed the door was open.

"Shauna!" He dropped the bottles and raced up the stairs. All the boxes sat in the hallway. "Shauna!" He checked every room and didn't find her, then galloped down the stairs and out the front door.

"Shauna!" A black car about two blocks down, raced away. A chill ran through him. Nick must have found her. Still, he ran back into the house. There was a chance she was still there.

"Shauna!" The house felt empty. That's when he noticed the kitchen door to the deck was slightly open. He ran back outside, and rounded his car that he'd parked in the street and found the flat tire. "No!" He'd let the most important person in the world to him be kidnapped, and he couldn't follow them.

A perky voice startled him. "Jason, who's Shauna?"

He spun around. "Vanessa, did you see a guy here a few minutes ago?"

"Yeah. He had his arm wrapped around that friend of yours. Walked her right to his car and they left."

He grabbed her shoulders and knew he held them too tight. He should have trusted Shauna's instincts about Vanessa all along. "Did you have anything to do with this?"

She glanced at each hand on her shoulders and smiled. "With what?"

"With that man kidnapping her."

"It didn't look like kidnapping to me."

"Did you tell him where to find her?" He controlled his rage. Vanessa might not have been responsible.

She shrugged slightly under his hands. "That man came

into *Cozy Corner* last night and was showing people a picture. He said his fiancée was missing. Imagine my surprise when he said her name was Shauna and not Rachel. So I told him she was hanging out with you." Vanessa grinned. "I like the way your hands feel on me, Jason."

He pushed her back. He couldn't touch her any longer. He wouldn't touch her again. "Vanessa, if you were a man, I'd beat the crap out of you. Get off my property." He turned his back to her, pulled out his phone and dialed.

"Hi, Jason."

"Dad." His voice cracked.

"What's wrong?"

"He took her. Nick's got Shauna." It was a stab to his heart. He'd failed her. She could be hurt. Nick might be torturing her. He didn't want to even think that he might have plans to kill her and dump her body. He ran a hand through his hair, took deep breaths.

"Easy, son. Push away the pain and think of it like a mission. Have you called the police?"

"They'll just waste my time when I should be searching." He glanced up as Vanessa entered a house down the street.

"What do you want me to do?" His steady voice calmed Jason.

"Can you get Mom and bring her over here? Maybe she can pick up something." There wasn't much of a chance. He didn't even know how far his Mom could hear thoughts, but right now it was the only thing he had.

He opened the back of the SUV and pulled out the spare tire. It was a good thing it was a regular tire and not a donut, because it was going to get a workout. By the time the tire was changed, his parents had pulled into the driveway.

His mom jumped out and wrapped her arms around him. "Jason, I'm so sorry. I'll do anything I can."

"I have to make a call first." He'd been so panicked, he hadn't even thought clearly. It was hard to be professional when the woman he loved was in danger. He dialed and waited for the pickup. Before there was a response, he said. "Mark, Nick got her."

Mark swore. "Jack and Kristy are not going to be happy with you."

"Yeah, well, you can thank Kristy and her phone calls for getting him on track, so I'm not happy with either of you. I need to find out if Nick flew in here, and if so, I need his rental car information., I also need the make, model, and plate number of his own car if he drove up."

"All right. I'm on it."

Jason pocketed his phone and touched his mother's arm. "Mom, can you ride with me and try to pick anything up from Shauna? I'll assume Nick is staying in Amherst since that was where he was first spotted, but he may head back home. Why don't you two get in my car? Dad, can you look up hotels and motels in the Amherst area, and we'll cruise past them?"

Kathleen bit her lip. "Honey, just so you know—if she's unconscious, I won't get anything." Worry strained her voice.

Jason closed his eyes for a second. "We'll hope for the best. He better not have hurt her." He clenched his fists.

They scrambled into the car, and Jason headed down the road. After they'd driven silently for twenty minutes, Jason pulled into a small motel's cracked parking lot. He slowly drove down the length of the building. "Anything, Mom?"

She shook her head. "No. Not from Shauna and not from anyone thinking about her."

He pulled back onto the road and sped up.

"Jason, next left there's another small motel," his dad said.

Jason turned at the next street, drove two more blocks and pulled into the parking lot. He cruised down the length of the building like before and looked at his mother. She shook her head. His father directed him to a larger hotel and then the next.

Chapter 20

Shauna stared out the car window. She'd calmed down enough to think, but it wasn't helping. She should have screamed the instant Nick grabbed her in the kitchen, but she'd been paralyzed by fear. It didn't help that he'd pushed a gun into her ribs. She shouldn't have been surprised that he had a gun. There'd been no time to put a bubble around herself. The snarling, angry face didn't look at all like the man she thought she'd known. She blinked back tears because it would probably make Nick angrier. She couldn't believe she'd ever thought she could have a relationship with him.

He hadn't said much yet. She didn't know what he intended to do with her. She looked down at her zip tied hands, wrists already reddened from her struggles. A second zip tie looped to the seatbelt. She couldn't even try to jump out of the car. There was no way she could escape. A glance at the speedometer showed he was driving exactly the speed limit. He wasn't taking chances of getting pulled over.

She didn't dare ask him how he found her at Jason's house. She worried about Jason. He would feel like he'd failed because Nick took her, but it wasn't his fault. If she died, she couldn't imagine how that would affect him. She knew how she'd feel if he died, filled with heart wrenching despair. She hoped this pain wouldn't push him over the edge into evil. She had to get away from Nick and back to Jason.

"Where are we going?" She tried to make the question

sound meek, maybe only mildly curious. She'd almost always done what he asked her to do. But then, she thought he'd done what was best for her.

He sneered at her. "So, why did you leave me like that, Shauna?" He pulled the engagement ring from his shirt pocket. "Do you know how I felt when I found this?" A lot of hurt filled the question. He slipped the ring back into his pocket. "And then you take off with some guy you just met."

Shauna had gone to Kristy's before leaving with some guy, but she definitely wouldn't elaborate on that.

Nick snarled like an animal. "I bided my time. I knew you were hurting after your father died. I held back. I should have screwed you." He squeezed her shoulder and she winced. "Maybe that's what you really needed."

Did he mean that he should have raped her? He couldn't still want her after she'd left him. Maybe he'd take his anger out on her and then kill her.

She shivered. Maybe she should she tell him the real reason she left. *It wasn't that I didn't care for you, I was afraid that you'd had someone murdered.* He had her anyway. She needed to know. "I worked late one night."

He glanced at her, his eyebrows raised.

"I heard a guy tell you that he'd disposed of a package in the river. Two days later, on the news, they said that a body was found floating in the river. I put it together and got scared."

His eyebrows rose and the car slowed. "You think I did that?"

She couldn't tell if it was real surprise or if he was a good liar.

"It seemed like too much of a coincidence."

"Well, it was a coincidence. That guy disposed of—contraband when the Feds got too close. I'm not a murderer, Shauna. Is that why you took off?"

"Yes. What contraband? Drug? Guns? Did you think I'd find that acceptable?" If the news was anything to go by, most people who were involved in that kind of thing ended up having to kill people to keep their secrets. He didn't want her to think he was a murderer. How far would he go to get her back?

"You kidnapped me. Don't you think it would have worked better to talk to me?"

He glanced at her and back to the road. "You wouldn't have given me a chance to talk back there at that guy's house." His anger seemed barely suppressed.

"A friend of a friend arranged for him to be my bodyguard."

"And now this bodyguard knows every square inch of your body."

"Why do you say that?" He was only guessing. She was afraid that he would hurt her or force her to have sex. Maybe he wanted her to think he still cared until he could find a place to kill her. No. He wasn't going to kill her, at least not until after he raped her.

It was so different with Jason. She'd trusted him before he trusted himself with her. He cared so much that he didn't want to hurt her or become evil and hurt anyone else. At first, she'd been nervous around Jason because of the dreams, but it was nothing like the revulsion she now felt for Nick. It was amazing how she felt it now and not before.

"That waitress saw you around town with him. She said he wouldn't give her the time of day because of you."

So, Vanessa told him where to find her. "He was doing his job."

He smirked. "Not very good at it, is he?"

He'd told her that he hadn't killed anyone. She wasn't sure if she believed him, but she could act like she did. Or maybe she should convince him that she didn't love him.

"Nick." This was harder than she thought it would be. "I really believed I cared for you at one time, but those feelings ended a while ago. I don't love you, Nick. I can't be with you. Please, let me go."

His hands tightened on the steering wheel, his eyes on the road. "You used to love me. You will again."

"No. I was grateful for how you helped me. But that's not enough."

He glared at her. "You loved me. You'll move into my house. You'll sleep in my bed. You'll love me again."

"But—"

"Enough. Why don't you take a nap? You'll feel better."

She turned away and sighed. He hadn't tried to find her because of a murder, but because he was obsessed with her. At least she had a better chance at staying alive.

They'd been driving for almost three hours, getting farther and farther from Jason. An *Entering New Jersey* sign flashed past. Shauna tipped her seat back and closed her eyes. He really thought she could sleep? He turned the radio louder.

***

Jason feathered kisses across her forehead and she snuggled deeper into his safe arms. She came up through the layers of sleep. The hum of the road, an occasional bump, the purr of another car passing, reminded her she was with Nick. It was so not a good time to wake feeling sated from lovemaking while she sat next to a man who frightened her. Hopefully, the dream meant that she and Jason would be together again. She hadn't had one since they'd made love. She ached for him.

During the dreams before, she'd been focused on the

sex. It was all new to her, and it was amazing. This time was different. Even though they'd done all those things, the feelings were more intense. She felt his love flow through her, warming her like a hug. It was better than the lovemaking.

She cracked her eyes open. The sky was starting to darken. She had no idea how long she'd slept. They could be hundreds of miles away from Rawlins. From Jason.

"*Shauna?*" She stiffened, and then forced her body to relax. It sounded like Kathleen's voice in her head. She hoped Nick hadn't noticed her response.

"Kathleen?"

"Oh, thank God. Are you okay?"

"So far. Where are you?"

"Fairly close since you can hear me."

It was hard to hide her excitement. Jason and Kathleen were going to try to rescue her. "*I'm pretending to be asleep. What should I do?*"

"Wake up and tell him you need to use the bathroom."

"Okay. How did you find me?"

"Mark got the GPS coordinates of Nick's rental. Jason's been speeding ever since."

Shauna forced a yawn, tipped her seat back up and looked around.

"Um. Is there a rest stop nearby?" She actually could use one. Looking at the clock on the dash, she calculated they'd been on the road about five hours. She was hungry, too.

Nick studied her for a couple of seconds before turning back to the road. "I don't trust you to go into the ladies room and keep quiet."

"Most of these places have a family bathroom. I could use it, and you can stand right outside. No one else will be in there." Once inside the building, she could run and scream for help.

"I still don't like it. We'll stop on the side of the road."

"I don't want to pee in the bushes." Obviously, he didn't think it through. Wouldn't he be afraid she'd run away? Maybe he expected to stand right beside her. That wasn't happening.

"Shauna, does Nick have a gun?"

The gun. If she ran, he wouldn't have to be close to stop her. *"Yeah, he used it to get me in the car. I haven't seen it since, so I don't know where it is."*

There was silence for several minutes.

"We're going to pull off the road when I think it's clear," Nick said.

"And then what? I need some privacy." Shauna didn't want to make Nick angry, but she wanted details to pass on to Kathleen.

"Kathleen, we may be stopping on the side of the road. He's afraid I'll talk to someone at a rest stop. He's right. I'd scream bloody murder. He's trying to pick a spot."

***

Jason glanced at his mother. She still had a blank stare on her face. She'd tried a few times to reach Shauna with no luck. She had to concentrate harder than usual because they were farther apart than she was used to. She could reach his dad from a few miles away, but that was because they had a connection.

Kathleen blinked. Jason returned his gaze to the road. Traffic was light after making it through rush hour and they were making better time.

"I reached her. She's all right. Nick has a gun. He wants to pull over on the side of the highway for the pit stop."

He relaxed a little. She was still alive and apparently

unharmed. He studied his mother. "I can tell there's more. What is it?"

She took a breath and let it out. "I looked into Nick, too."

Jason's hands tensed on the steering wheel.

"He doesn't want to hurt her. He's got her engagement ring in his pocket, and he's planning on forcing her to wear it when they get to his house. He's going to hold her in his bed until she's ready to—"

"The hell he will!" Jason's knuckles turned white on the wheel, and he took deep, controlled breaths.

Kathleen touched his arm. "There's more."

"I don't want to hear more," he growled.

She rushed on. "He killed her father so he could get close to her."

Jason slammed a palm against the steering wheel. "He destroyed her life so he could pick up the pieces? He's more of a monster than I thought."

Reese's hand squeezed his shoulder from the backseat. "Son, Shauna's going to get hurt if you don't calm down and plan this out."

Jason slowed his breathing, tried to get in a mission headset. "You're right, Dad."

"Shauna told me that when she gets behind the bushes, she would put herself in a bubble."

Jason relaxed a little. He'd planned on asking his mom to tell her to use the bubble, but was glad she'd thought of it herself. He hoped she could get far enough away to use it.

"When she's away from Nick, I'm going to strike him with lightning."

Kathleen gasped. "Jason, you can't. It would kill him and you don't want that on your conscience. You can protect Shauna without killing him."

Jason relaxed his grip on the wheel.

Kathleen touched her son's arm. "Maybe you can just strike near him. Scare him into giving her up."

He'd forgotten that his grandfather-by-blood had used lightning to kill her mother and brother. "All right, Mom. I'll strike near him. That should knock him out and we can tie him up for the police. But if it doesn't, I'm giving him a full on strike."

"They're pulling over," Kathleen said.

Jason doused his lights and pulled into the emergency lane, about three hundred yards behind the other car. He flipped a dial on the dash that turned off the interior lights.

"Dad, call the police." He pointed at a small green sign. "There's the mile marker."

Jason used his infrared vision, watched Nick get out of the car and circle the hood. When he opened the passenger door, Jason saw a flash of metal. A knife. He hoped Nick was just freeing her hands with it. Then he stood up, pulled Shauna out of the car and spoke to her. She nodded and started walking toward the trees, holding her hands awkwardly in front of her. He was surprised that Nick hadn't followed her, but he did see him pull a gun from his jacket. When Shauna got about ten feet from Nick, a purple bubble surrounded her.

"Mom, Dad, can you see Shauna's bubble?"

"I can barely see Shauna," Kathleen said.

"I can't, either."

"Good. She's got it around her." He waited until Shauna was behind a tree. "All right. Stay in the car until after the lightning strike."

Jason got out and gently pushed the door until it clicked. He stepped behind the car, crouched down and crept into the ditch. He started lifting his arms to call for lightning when Nick's body rose into the air. Two shots rang out. Jason ran.

Nick kept rising, his screams filling the air as he flailed

his arms. Then he paused and his body dropped, his scream turning to a shriek. Jason stopped and watched. It only took a couple of seconds for Nick to drop twenty feet and hit the ground with a thud and groan. Bones had to have broken. The man deserved that and more. There was only the swish of a car passing.

Jason called out. "Shauna, I'm here, but stay in your bubble just in case."

He walked toward the unconscious man, one leg twisted and bleeding. The gun sat a foot from Nick's hand. Jason kicked it farther away, and searched Nick's pockets. He found zip ties, which he used on Nick's wrists.

He stood and a gentle, cushion bumped him. Shauna's bubble dissolved, and she wrapped her arms around him, pressing into his back. He returned his vision to normal, spun around and wrapped his arms around her, kissing the top of her head.

"Shauna, I'm so sorry I let him take you."

"It wasn't your fault. How could you know he'd break into the house?"

His arms tightened around her for a second. He tipped her head up and drank her in. He'd been so afraid he'd never see her again. "It looks like you didn't need me to rescue you."

"I'm glad you're here. Nick took me by surprise and I couldn't use my abilities when I was so close to him. When Kathleen suggested the bathroom stop, I was able to use them."

Jason kissed her, glad she was safe.

"Shauna, I'm glad you're all right," Kathleen said from behind Jason.

"Mom, you didn't wait."

"Shauna said it was safe."

Stepping out of Jason's arms, Shauna gave Kathleen a

hug. "Thank you. You don't know how much better I felt when I heard your voice."

Sirens blared before the blue, flashing lights were visible. Jason wrapped his arm around Shauna's shoulders. It was going to be a tough few hours. She'd have to talk to the local police as well as the FBI since the kidnapping crossed state lines.

He warned his parents. "You didn't hear or see anything from my car." He whispered into Shauna's ear, "Tell them Nick stopped to let you relieve yourself, and you were in the trees when you heard Nick scream. You don't know what happened to him."

Chapter 21

Shauna was left exhausted after having been kidnapped by Nick and all the repeated questions from the police and FBI. She'd told them about overhearing the conversation between Nick and the man who dropped a package in the river, and reading about a body of a man found in the river the next day. She repeated every detail of how she'd run from Nick, Jason watching out for her, and Nick kidnapping her at gunpoint.

After the police released them, they found a hotel to rest for the remainder of the night. Jason had insisted on holding her through the night, but didn't make love to her. Shauna felt safe in his arms, but it seemed like something was missing.

They got on the road after breakfast. Although Jason had put his arm around her as they walked to the car, he seemed distant. She hoped the old Jason wasn't back. He drove, and his dad sat beside him. She sat behind Reese in the backseat with Kathleen. If she had wanted to, she could have reached forward and touched Jason's arm, like Kathleen had done with Reese, but she was afraid he'd shrug her off.

The men were deep into a conversation, so Shauna leaned toward Kathleen. "How did Mark get the GPS info to find me?"

"It must not have been easy, because he took nearly a half-hour to call back after Jason called him. He had to find out if Nick drove up or flew in. Mark must have called most of the rental companies to find where Nick rented his car, then he had to convince them to give him the GPS information. He called Jason and gave him a description of the car and where it was located."

Shauna squeezed Kathleen's hand. "You must have exhausted yourself, trying for hours to reach me."

Kathleen turned her hand over and clasped Shauna's. "It was worth the headache."

Their conversation turned to talk of Rawlins, the people living there and their ancestors. It was still a long five hour drive back, but she enjoyed the company, unlike the terror of the day before.

They pulled into the driveway of Jason's house. Shauna had only slept there two nights in a sleeping bag. A nearly empty house shouldn't feel like home, but wherever Jason was felt like home.

She was out of the car before she noticed Tony's car in the driveway. She had expected Kathleen and Reese would leave right away, but with Jason's brother there, they all went inside.

The boxes they'd set by the door had been moved, some in the kitchen and some in the living room. The furniture had arrived. That was probably why Tony was there. The family room looked good with the pieces they'd picked out.

Footsteps clattered down the stairs. Tony and Abby reached the bottom.

"Hi, guys," Tony said, then looked at Shauna. "I'm glad they got you back safely, Rachel."

"Actually, it's Shauna. We changed my name when I was in hiding." She'd grown to care for them and hated what they might think of her lying to them about her name, maybe speculating that she could have lied to them about other things.

"So, you're not really related—"

"Oh, I am. Marie Williams was my grandmother."

"That's cool." Abby gave her a hug. "I'm glad you're back, too, but it may take a while to get used to calling you Shauna."

Jason wrapped an arm around Abby. "Hey, you two, thanks for coming for the furniture delivery."

Reese dropped a hand on Jason's shoulder. "It's been a tough couple of day. Why don't we let Jason and Shauna get some rest?"

"Thanks, Dad." He put an arm around each parent and hugged them. "I couldn't have done it without both of you."

Kathleen kissed his cheek. "I'm glad we could help." She patted Shauna's arm and headed for the door.

Shauna stood next to Jason but didn't want to risk rejection if she reached for his hand and he pulled away. They watched his family file out then he led her to the living room. "Shauna, I need to tell you something."

They sat, facing each other. He was more serious than she'd ever seen him, maybe even nervous. He ran a hand through his hair and looked away from her. She had no idea what could be so bad after what they'd already been through, but his grave expression told her it was probably something she didn't want to hear, and she steeled herself for the worse—being without him.

***

Jason took Shauna's hands in his, staring at them. "Shauna, I have something to tell you that I know is going to hurt you. I don't want to have to say it."

"I think I know what you're going to say, Jason." She tried to tug her hands out of his, but he didn't let go.

His eyebrows rose. "You do?"

She nodded. "I sensed something was wrong all day,

and I figured that you didn't want to talk about it in front of your family."

"You're right. I didn't want them to see your pain. Shauna, I'm so sorry. How could you know what I wanted to say?"

She shrugged. "It was the way you kept your distance, as if you didn't want me to know the truth."

"Of course I didn't want you to know the truth. If it's too painful for me to speak about it, how could you bear hearing it?"

Shauna sighed. "I just wish you'd told me sooner."

"I only found out yesterday."

She furrowed her brows. "Wait. What?"

"I didn't know before then."

She squinted. "You didn't know how you felt?"

"Well, no. I had no idea it would bother me this much, but I figured I had to be the one to tell you." Jason still held her hands but leaned back to get a better look at Shauna. "What are you talking about?"

"About you not wanting to be with me anymore, now that the case is over. I figured you got caught up in protecting me and now that you don't have to—"

Jason covered her mouth with his hand. "Stop right there. How can you even think that? I love you, Shauna. You mean more to me than anyone. I can't let you go."

Shauna exhaled, her shoulders sagged. Jason stroked her hair and kissed her. He leaned his forehead against hers. "Honey, believe me, I love you."

She hugged him. "But I don't understand. If you didn't want to break up with me, what's so painful that it's hard to tell me?"

For a few moments, he'd thought she'd made it easier for him, but he still had to tell Shauna about her father. He'd do everything he could to prove Nick murdered him. It practically killed Jason to have to tell her, but she needed to know.

"Shauna." He waited for her to pull back a look at him. "When Mom was communicating with you, she decided to probe Nick, too, to see his intentions. She found something else."

Her eyebrows scrunched together. "What did she find?"

He closed his eyes. He didn't want to hurt her more than she'd already been hurt. Pulling her hand from his, she palmed his cheek. He turned his head and kissed it, taking her hand back in his.

"This is so hard."

She squeezed his hands. "Jason. You're scaring me."

He took a deep breath and let it out slowly. "Nick killed your father to get close to you."

Wide eyes stared at him, then tears filled them, and she shook her head vehemently. "No! It was an accident. It had to have been an accident!"

He shook his head.

The tears spilled down her cheeks. "Nick took my father from me?" She covered her mouth, but a sob escaped. "He comforted me after he killed my father? He arranged the funeral. Helped with all the forms. Let me cry on him. And it was all his fault?"

Jason pulled her onto his lap, wrapped his arms around her and tucked her head into his neck. "I'm so sorry." He hadn't wanted to tell her such devastating news. "I wanted to tell the police, but who's going to believe someone read his mind?"

She sniffled. "I can't believe I didn't realize it. Yesterday he told me he wasn't a murderer. He sounded so believable."

"People who lie all the time are good at it."

She kissed his neck. "So this is this why you were

distant this morning?"

He held her tighter. "Was I? I'm sorry. I dreaded having to tell you."

He kissed her, saddened that she needed to be consoled. Shauna cried for a while, telling Jason all the things that had made her father so special. He wished he could have met such the man who'd raised such an amazing daughter.

She wiped her eyes and smoothed down her hair. "I must look a mess." She sniffled.

Jason pushed a strand of hair behind her ears. "You are always beautiful, Shauna. "I love you." He kissed her, hoping it told her how much he loved her.

Shauna sighed. "Jason. I don't know how I doubted you."

Jason stood up with her in his arms and headed for the stairs. The door to his bedroom was partially closed and he kicked it all the way open. They spied the bed at the same time. It had been set up and made with the linens from the closet. A skimpy negligee lay on top of the bed. His siblings must have had fun with that.

Shauna looked up at him. "Tony and Abby did that? How embarrassing!"

"I guess I should have hidden it, instead of putting the bag beside the sheets."

"Oh, you bought it?" She smiled, and he gave her a boyish grin.

Jason set her down beside the bed and threw back the covers. He pulled her shirt over her head. Shauna unbuckled his belt, and she smiled up at him.

***

Two hours later, Jason groaned when Shauna stretched, purposely rubbing against him.

She dropped her hand on his hip. "Let's eat and bring in more of your stuff from the storage container."

Jason kissed her shoulder and trailed kisses to her ear. "You don't want to stay here longer? I'm hurt."

She laughed. "I wouldn't want to hurt your feelings. But after that workout, you're feeding me."

They rushed downstairs and prepared sandwiches together. He dabbed mayonnaise on her chin and grinned.

"Jason!"

She snatched a napkin from the counter and he grabbed her wrist. "Wait. Let me." He took her napkin and wiped her chin, then kissed the spot and moved to her mouth.

"I'm hungry," she mumbled against his lips.

"Yeah, me, too." He deepened the kiss.

She gave in for a minute then pulled back. "Food. I need food."

"If you insist." He hugged her tightly before releasing her. "I came so close to losing you."

"You have Grandma to thank for teaching me how to make bubbles and levitate."

"Thank you, Grandma!" he shouted up to the ceiling.

Shauna giggled.

They rushed through the meal and headed outside to the storage unit. They carried in several boxes each. Shauna picked up a small end table, and Jason grabbed a lamp. He followed her inside. She set the table beside the couch and headed back outside. He set the lamp on the table, and plugged it in.

Once he went back outside, he found Vanessa standing in the driveway, talking to Shauna. He raced to Shauna's side, not wanting Vanessa anywhere near her.

"Vanessa, I told you I didn't want you on my property."

"Oh, Jason. I was telling Shauna I was glad to see she was back. I thought she'd left for good with her fiancé." Her voice was filled with sarcastic cheerfulness.

Shauna's shoulders were stiff, her mouth a straight line.

"Good-bye, Vanessa."

"But I'm not done yet, Jason. You need to know something about Kathleen."

"I'm not interested." He clasped Shauna's hand and took a step back.

"Did you know that your mother," she used air quotes around the word, "is a killer?"

He let go of Shauna and fisted his hands at his sides. It had taken him too long to realize how hateful Vanessa was. She'd say anything to get what she wanted.

"I said get off my property. I don't want to hear your lies."

She lifted her chin and glared at him. "She murdered your real parents and my father. Do you think she did it so she could have you and Jamie for her children?"

"Leave here now," he roared. He'd always known that he and Jamie were adopted because their parents had died, but Kathleen would not have killed to get them. He took a step toward her but Shauna restrained him.

Shauna set a hand on his chest, over his heart. "Don't believe her, Jason. She's trying to hurt you."

He covered her hand, let her love calm him.

Vanessa's cold eyes chilled him. "Henry Goodwin was my father. I remember how he used to visit my mom and me. He'd give her money. Then Kathleen took it all away. We had nothing after that! And Kathleen never had to pay for murdering five people. If the sitter hadn't backed out at the last minute, my mother would have made it six."

Vanessa pointed at him. "You were supposed to be mine," she screamed. "My mother said that we were destined to be together. Our children were supposed to be more powerful than any of our ancestors. But, no—"

She reached for Shauna, and he twisted to keep Vanessa's hands off her. The moment Vanessa's skin touched his, he felt soiled.

"You wanted this . . . this outsider when you could have had me!" Vanessa spun and stalked away.

Shauna shivered. "I think she's gone over the edge."

He tightened his hold on her and stared at Vanessa's retreating back. His loving mother couldn't be a killer. "I don't believe her."

"Vanessa wants you to push the people who love you out of your life. She wants you miserable and then maybe she'll have a chance with you."

"She doesn't deserve any of our attention. Let's bring in more boxes." He picked one up and followed Shauna to the house.

He couldn't think of anyone who cared more for people than his mother. She wouldn't hurt anyone, let alone kill them. She'd begged him not to kill that scum, Nick. When he was a kid, she bandaged scraped knees, kissed them all better. Read him bedtime stories. Someone like that was not a killer.

Only a few items remained in the storage unit when his phone rang. He set his box down and checked the display. "Hi, Mom."

"Hi, Jason. I know you probably decided to finish unloading that storage box and didn't think about dinner. Why don't you two come over here when you're done?"

"Thanks, Mom. We're almost done. We'll be there in a little while."

Shauna came out of the house. "Dinner with your family?"

"You don't mind, do you?"

She kissed his cheek. "Of course not. I like your family."

He hugged Shauna but sensed the same horrible feeling in his spine as when Vanessa touched him. He glanced down the street and saw her glaring at him, and regretted all those times he hadn't believed Shauna about Vanessa's daggers.

Chapter 22

Jason and Shauna arrived in time to set the table. Abby was at a girlfriend's house for dinner, so they'd be joining his parents and Tony for dinner. His brother plied them with questions about Shauna's kidnapping, recovery and police questioning. He must not have been able to get anything out of their parents. Jason glanced at Shauna. She seemed to be taking it all right.

Tony laughed when he told him how Shauna had levitated Nick, but Shauna turned her head away. Jason hoped she didn't have nightmares about hurting Nick. "It was self-defense," he said to Tony. "Totally justified." He reached under the table and took her hand.

"Hey, Shauna, you should join the super heroes."

"Bro', you do know they're not real, don't you?"

"Of course. It just would be really great."

"Speaking of super heroes—Mom, Vanessa thinks you're some kind of avenging angel. Today, she accused you of killing Nathan and those others. Can she be any more crazy?"

Shauna and Jason exchanged a split-second glance.

Reese cleared his throat. "Jason, what are your plans now that you're not Shauna's bodyguard?"

"I still have to put a sign on the office building, and I have to create some advertising."

The remaining dinner discussion centered on Jason's business.

At the end of the meal, Tony stood, and Kathleen

touched his arm. “Tony, can you clear the table?”

“Sure, Mom.”

“Jason, come sit in the library.”

“Um, okay.” He grabbed Shauna’s hand. He sensed something weird was going on, and he didn’t think he could do it without her.

The four of them entered the library, and Reese closed the doors. Almost the only times that they were shut was when he was in trouble, and his parents didn’t want the other kids to hear their discussion. Sleet entered his chest and he squeezed Shauna’s hand. He didn’t want to hear whatever they had to say.

Reese and Kathleen sat on the couch in front of the fireplace, their joined hands tightly clenched. She bit her lip and stared at his dad, and he rubbed the back of his neck.

Jason needed Shauna’s strength, so he angled the closest chair to his parents, sat down and pulled Shauna onto his lap, one hand around her waist. This wasn’t going to be good.

Kathleen glanced between him and Shauna. “Honey, maybe Shauna should go out with Tony.”

Shauna started to get up, but he held her down. “No. She stays here.”

Kathleen glanced at Reese, and he nodded. Kathleen pulled in a shaky breath. “Vanessa wasn’t wrong.”

Jason leaned into Shauna. “Mom, you’re saying you killed those people?”

Kathleen nodded, and tears glistened in her eyes.

Reese wrapped an arm around Kathleen. “We did and it needed to be done. Let us explain.”

After several seconds, Kathleen regained control, and wiped her cheeks. “I’d hoped you’d never find out.”

“All right. Explain.” He couldn’t help the hard edge to his voice. The parents he thought he knew had become strangers. He’d had a better, more loving life with Kathleen and Reese as his parents than he would have had with Nathan and Elise. But to find out that they'd killed people just like Nathan had?

Kathleen sat up straighter. "The second night I was in Rawlins, I had a dream about a girl tied to a stone table. It was in a basement room with candles in sconces on the walls and on stands. I could tell she was going to be sacrificed. I rushed up to her to try to free her, but as soon as I touched her, I woke up. A couple of days later, the police found her body, stabbed through the heart."

She looked down at her hand entwined with Reese's and shivered. "Uncle Gerald left a journal that Reese and I started reading. Gerald had a suspect list, but he died before he could narrow down who was involved in the murders occurring at each solstice and equinox. Nathan was at the top of the list. It turned out he was the ring leader and his disciples were his wife, my housekeeper, Mary Beth, Jonathan Walker, and Henry Goodwin. While we were trying to figure all that out, Hannah was teaching me how to use my abilities."

His mom took a couple of breaths and closed her eyes for several seconds. "There was a door in the basement that used to lead to the sacrificial chamber."

Shauna gasped. "I felt evil coming through that door."

Jason's heart pounded. "That chamber's in our basement?"

Kathleen shook her head. "There was a long tunnel that led to it, and also one from Nathan's basement. It was probably half way between the two houses. After the…incident ended, we filled it in and sealed the doors."

Kathleen blinked quickly several times, but tears slipped down her cheeks.

"Another girl disappeared just before the solstice, so I was shocked when Mary Beth let Nathan and Jonathan

Walker into my house. They took me into the basement and…that room and tied me to the sacrificial table."

Jason gasped. "Mom." He hadn't known that his mother was going to be sacrificed. He held Shauna tighter. He couldn't imagine life without his mom.

"I wasn't only a virginal sacrifice. My powers would have made those present very powerful and given Nathan my abilities. He may have been unstoppable."

The pain in Reese's face was almost overwhelming. Jason knew that heartsick feeling from almost losing Shauna.

Reese ran a hand over his eyes. "Hannah came to me in a dream and told me that Kat had been taken. I raced here and put together a potion to make me appear invisible, then another one to turn anyone who breathed it catatonic. I went into the sacrificial room and put the four people watching the sacrifice to sleep, but then Nathan had his knife over Kat. I tackled him and knocked him out before I freed her." He gazed with adoring eyes at his wife. "She begged me to look for the missing girl." Reese glanced back to Jason. "We looked in some of the rooms down there, but we had to leave. The invisibility potion I'd taken had a side effect of temporary blindness, so we couldn't stay long. We barely made it here before I lost my eyesight."

Kathleen resumed telling the story. "After Reese could see again, we went back down to the ritual room. The missing girl was on the table, and Nathan was chanting over the knife. I put a bubble around the girl to protect her, then a larger one to enclose everybody. Then I started throwing fireballs into the bubble. We saved that girl, and there were no more deaths."

Standing, Kathleen took her son's hand in both of hers. Her sad, fearful eyes beseeched him. "Jason, I've always been saddened that I had to take lives, but I don't regret what

I did. Nathan was too powerful to be contained any other way. It was the only way to stop him." She looked at Reese then back at Jason. "It was Reese's idea to adopt you and Jamie. I took your parents from you, I needed to make up for it." She blinked back tears. "I love the two of you just as much as Tony and Abby. You couldn't be any more my son than if I'd given birth to you."

He stared at her for several seconds. He could see the love, and knew she was being honest, but he still couldn't see her as someone who had killed other people. The loving woman he'd called Mom had killed five people. And he found out because Vanessa had wanted to taunt him. They should have told him before now.

He placed gentle hands on Shauna's waist and pushed upward. She stepped aside and he stood. "You should have told me before now." Kathleen gasped and put her hand over her mouth. Jason ignored his mother and touched Shauna's cheek. "I need to go. Alone. I need time to deal with this."

Tears shimmered in her eyes. She kissed his cheek. "Just remember, I love you."

He stomped to the front door, and slammed it behind him. Not as satisfying as he'd hoped.

***

Shauna stared after him, wishing he'd let her come with him. She would have stayed quiet and let her love seep into him. Maybe he needed to rage and throw things. She had no idea what she would have done in the same situation.

His world had been turned upside down. How must he feel to learn that the mother he thought of as loving and sweet had killed his parents? She remembered how devastated she had been at eight, when her mother left her. This had to be far worse.

Kathleen squeezed her hand. “He needs to fit all the pieces together to make his world right again.”

Shauna’s tears blurred her vision and she blinked rapidly. “He’s hurting so much. I wish he’d taken me with him.”

Maybe Jason’s world would never be right again. His mother wasn’t just the woman who’d adopted two orphans, she’d made them orphans. She hoped Vanessa hadn’t accomplished part of what she’d wanted—alienating Jason from his loving family.

Chapter 23

Jason pulled into his driveway, and felt so alone without Shauna by his side. He scraped his hand down his face. What must she think of him? He'd practically rejected his parents and left her there.

His head knew that his mother had taken lives because it was the only way, but his heart pained him because he never would have believed she was capable of killing. Sure, he'd had to kill twice, but those had been kill or be killed situations. But that was the same for his mother. That girl would have been dead if not for his mother's actions. And if she hadn't killed Nathan, he might have come after her again. A war seemed to tug inside him.

Jason headed for the house, feeling exhausted. He'd never wanted Nathan for a father, but to find that the deaths weren't an accident, that the woman he thought of as his mother, had actually killed his parents was more than he could handle. He knew all the reasons were valid, but still, his mother had murdered five people. No. It was self-defense and defense of another. He grabbed his hair and screamed.

He stopped in the kitchen and grabbed a bottle of scotch and a glass before trudging up the stairs to his bedroom. He lit the fire, sat in the chair in front of the fireplace, and poured a drink. It went down smooth, and he poured another and gulped it, filled his glass again. He stared into the fake flames of his fireplace. Shauna was right, the flames weren't random enough, not like a real fire with burning logs. It was hard to contemplate life, staring into flames that didn't change like life. No surprises like he was hit with by his parents. He tipped his head back and closed his eyes. He didn't want to think at all.

He emptied the glass, capped the bottle and set both on the mantel. Maybe he could lose himself in sleep. He stripped and got into bed and stared at a nearly dark ceiling.

He hadn't known that his mother had almost died that night. He'd known that a girl had been rescued, but not that his parents had done it. That should be what was important. His brain told him it had to be done to save his mother and that girl, but his heart couldn't wrap around the fact that she'd killed. He wondered if it could have been done a different way.

If Nathan had lived, the woman he loved and called Mom would have died. His life would have been so much different, but not better.

Sleep finally dragged him down.

"Jason, we must talk."

He opened his eyes and looked around the dark room. He didn't recognize the voice. "Who's there?" Shauna was the only other person with a key. She wouldn't give it to someone he didn't know.

"Jason, come down to your family room."

Nothing to do but check it out. He pulled on pants and shirt. He didn't know who was down there, so he shoved his gun into the back of his pants.

He frowned at an older woman dressed in gray pilgrim-like clothing. "Who are you?"

"I am Hannah Rawlins."

"No way!" When he'd gotten pulled into Shauna's dream with her grandmother, he'd kept his eyes closed, so he didn't know how alive a dead person would look. "If you're Hannah, why would you appear to me? I'm not related to you." If she was Hannah, she was no threat.

"Please be seated."

He sat close enough to easily talk, but far enough to take action, if needed.

"Kathleen is so very worried about you. I have come to ease your mind."

"I don't know if that's possible." He leaned back, feeling somewhat more comfortable.

"In my time, I knew the evil I killed was only a temporary suspension. I could only stop it for a short time. There have been waves of evil through these centuries, temporarily suppressed by a Rawlins each time. I sensed there would come one Rawlins who would use her great power to kill the evil, but also her wonderful love to end it entirely. There will be no more evil of this kind in Rawlins. Kathleen's love for you and your sister has changed your souls. You are no longer ensnared by the power of evil."

"But she killed people."

"Kathleen destroyed evil the only way it could be done. She did better than I. She also saved the life of an innocent woman. I have always regretted that I could not do so."

Hannah leaned forward and took Jason's hand. It was cool, but surprisingly solid. "There was no choice. Evil had taken over those lives. I will show you what your life would have been if Nathan had lived."

"Is this like the Ghost of Christmas Past?"

Her eyebrows rose. "I know not of what you speak."

Visions filled Jason's mind.

The knife came down. Kathleen's scream was cut short as the blade entered her chest and blood flooded the front of the white gown. A golden wind swirled and entered each of the five participants of the sacrifice. Nathan smiled. "So much power!" Reese entered the room but was too late to save her. Nathan flicked his wrist, and the knife he'd been holding flew into Reese's chest and he fell.

"No!" Jason screamed. His heart twisted at the sight of his mother and father dying at the hands of that evil man.

"Jason, there was no choice for Kathleen."

He was plunged into another scene

Jason saw himself, maybe seventeen or eighteen, walking into Nathan's house. He'd never seen his own eyes so cold. No! Amy. They'd been friends in high school, had worked in his father's restaurant together. But in this vision, there was no restaurant, no Reese as his father.

They stopped in the living room. Nathan had been seated in front of a fire. He stood. Jason felt a slight tingle. Nathan's power?

"No one saw?"

Amy looked puzzled.

"Of course not, Father."

"Good, good. Let's get downstairs."

Jason took her hand. "This way, Amy."

She resisted. "Where are we going?"

"Downstairs, so you can meet my mother."

She let him lead her through the room and down some stairs. "What's she doing down here?"

"Preparing for my birthday." They reached a very old, wood plank door with an iron doorknob.

"I didn't know. I would have gotten you something."

He opened it and pulled her through. His father closed and locked the door behind them.

He snaked his arm around her, dragging her through a tunnel. "Oh, but, you're my present. You get to be my first sacrifice. I'm very excited about it."

Jason cringed at the evil in that voice. Not sweet Amy. He'd gotten to know her so well while working with her. She shouldn't have any interest in this Jason. Where was Dave? Ah, Jason was the one who'd introduced her to her future husband.

Amy tried to pull away from him. "What do you mean, sacrifice? You invited me to dinner with your family."

He shrugged. "I lied. You wouldn't have come otherwise." He tugged her to a stone table, picked up a white gown and shoved it into her hands. "You can go in that room to change." He pointed to a door.

She dropped it on the floor and wrapped her arms around herself. "I'm not putting that on."

His father crossed his arms and watched. "It's too bad you didn't inherit my ability to compel."

Jason gave Amy an evil smile. "I hoped you'd say that."

She tried to run, but Jason hit her, and she collapsed on the floor. He laughed and looked at his father. "See, I've got it."

"No! Enough." Jason's breath sawed in and out. To see himself hit Amy and enjoy it, and know he'd brought her there to kill her, sickened him.

Hannah removed her hand from his. "I am sorry I had to show you what could have been."

He trembled and concentrated on slowing his breathing. He put his elbows on his thighs and dropped his head into his hands. "I so wish I hadn't seen that." He couldn't imagine being that boy.

"Jason." Hannah's voice soothed. "The love of a powerful mother is what saved you from that life."

He looked at her and shook his head. "I never thought about it like that. I thought I was different because I wasn't trained to do evil things. I never even thought that Mom's love changed who I am."

"I will let you sleep now. You have much to think about."

***

"Shauna, dear, wake up."

Shauna rubbed her eyes. "Grandma? You sound upset."

"You must go to him."

Shauna sat up and stared at her grandmother. "Go to Jason?"

"Your young man needs you. He had a conversation with Hannah and is feeling despair over what he might have become."

"Jason? He had a conversation with Hannah? Am I really awake?"

Her grandmother smiled. "As much as you can be with me."

"But I thought you didn't like him."

"I thought he was evil like his father and ancestors, but he isn't. Kathleen saved him. Now it's your turn to save your young man."

"He needs me? I should go now?"

"Yes, now." Her voice was pleading, but strong.

"All right. I'll go."

"And I expect an invitation to the wedding."

Shauna's heart skipped a beat. "Um, okay. Sure, Grandma."

Shauna woke up and looked around. Wedding? What was Grandma talking about? She got up and dressed. She should wake somebody to drive her to Jason's house, but it was so late. No. It was only two blocks away. She scribbled a note, rushed down the stairs and dropped it on the kitchen table, so they'd know she'd left.

Before stepping out the door, she made sure she had the key Jason had given her. The street was quiet and peaceful. No cars passed. To be safe, she put herself in a bubble and jogged. The street lights were spaced close enough that she wasn't in total darkness at any point. Jason's car sat in his driveway.

She marched up the steps, pulled out her key and dissolved her bubble. Her hand trembled as she slipped the key in the lock. Maybe Jason wasn't ready for her to be back. Well, she could sleep in a guest room. Grandma thought he needed her, and in this case, she knew Grandma was right.

He'd been hurt and needed her. The door opened silently, and she locked it behind her. The room was bright enough from the streetlight shining through the front window that she could make her way up the stairs. Jason's open door beckoned, and she took a deep breath inside the room. She hoped this was the right thing to do. At the side of the bed, she stripped off her clothes and crawled in beside him. She lightly kissed his cheek, smelling alcohol. She put her head on his chest, wrapped a leg around his and settled in. It felt perfect.

Jason's arm came across her back and he sighed. "Shauna, you came." He feathered kisses across her cheek. "I can't believe what a fool I was. I left you. I treated Mom so badly." He kissed her hungrily. "I need you."

***

The morning light poured into the room, waking Jason. He needed to get curtains or blinds on the windows. Fortunately, they didn't face east. With a pounding headache, even this light was too much. He looked down at Shauna. He'd gotten so used to waking beside her that he'd forgotten momentarily that she shouldn't have been there. He'd abandoned her at his parents' house. She'd been exactly what he needed last night. Her caring, her giving, her love, were what had gotten him through. His brave woman had no idea what she'd be walking into when she got here, but she came for him. He didn't think he could love her more, but that simple act expanded his heart. She was beautiful inside and out. He ran a hand up and down her back, hoping to wake her gradually.

"Mmm." She lifted her head and her warm eyes took him in. "Jason, are you all right?" She touched his cheek.

He took her hand and kissed her fingertips. "I'm fine. I had an interesting visitor. Kind of like the Ghost of Christmas Past or maybe future or alternate life." He chuckled.

She frowned. "What does that mean?"

"Hannah came to visit me. She showed me what my life would have been like if Mom had died when Nathan took her. It wasn't pretty."

"You…you would have been evil?"

"The evilest."

She shivered.

He kissed her forehead. "Hannah said that Mom changed me with her love. Jamie, too."

"I knew that." Shauna kissed his chest. "When you had that other medallion on, it was a hint of what you would have been."

He shook his head. "Not even close. The evil coming off Nathan and that Jason…" He shuddered.

She kissed his chin. "I know what can take your mind off that."

"Exactly what took my mind off it last night?" He twisted so she was under him and she shrieked.

"So, after we finish here," he said and looked down her body, "and in the shower, I'll make you breakfast."

She pushed herself higher and kissed him.

He returned her kiss, hungry for her but pulled back. He sat up, taking her with him. Jason hoped he was doing this right. Everything depended on it. "I love you. I can't imagine living in this house without you. That's why I wanted your help to pick out the house and furnishings. Will you marry me?" The words flowed out easier than he'd expected. He meant every single one, even though they hadn't known each other very long.

Her eyes widened, and her mouth dropped open. He leaned back to study her reaction. For a space of three seconds, he thought his heart was going to be crushed.

She shoved him back on the bed and kissed him more aggressively than she ever had before. With greater strength than he thought he'd need, he pushed her off. "Does that mean yes?"

"Yes, it means yes." She pressed into his arms, but he continued to hold her back.

"Next week?" If he had the power to fly, he'd take her to the clouds.

She frowned. "What next week?"

"A wedding next week." His smile seemed stuck in place.

"Next week? So soon?" She raised her eyebrows.

"I don't want a big wedding," he said. "Do you? Why wait? I want us to belong to each other every way possible."

"All right, next week. Now will you let me have my way with you?"

"Any way you want."

She covered his face in kisses and nibbled her way to his neck.

"I love you, Shauna." Jason finally felt like he was home.

Chapter 24

They walked up the steps of Jason's parents' house and Shauna stopped him. "I forgot. Grandma wants an invitation."

He tilted his head and wrinkled his eyebrows. "Invitation?"

"A wedding invitation."

He chuckled. "You do remember she's dead, right? How do you propose to give her an invitation? And how do you expect her to attend? In spirit?"

"Well, of course in spirit. I don't know how to give her an invitation, but we could have the wedding here, so it's likely she could attend in spirit."

"That suits me as long as my parents agree." He pushed the door open, and they entered the house.

They found Kathleen in the kitchen. He snuck up on her and startled her as his arms wrapped around her. "I love you, Mom, and thank you for saving me."

She turned, hugged him and kissed his cheek. "I love you, too, Jason. What do you mean 'saving' you?"

"Hannah visited me last night."

Kathleen gasped. "I didn't think we'd ever hear from her again."

He chuckled. "I didn't think I'd hear from her since she's not my ancestor. She was worried about you and how I reacted to—what you told me last night."

Shauna came up behind him, put her head against his arm and hugged him.

"She showed me what my life would have been like without you," Jason said. "Your love changed me, chased away the evil. So, thank you."

Both women blinked back tears. He glanced between them. "That wasn't supposed to make you cry. How about some good news? Shauna has agreed to marry me."

Kathleen hugged Jason and Shauna together. Tears slid down her face. "Shauna is special. That's wonderful, but not unexpected."

Shauna's eyes widened. "You're not surprised?"

"Well, between your shared dreams and the way you two look at each other, I'm not surprised."

Shauna squeezed his waist. "Really? I was surprised."

Jason chuckled and pulled her close. "Shauna, you just don't know this town yet. We were bound to be together after we'd had the same dream." He kissed her cheek.

He looked at his mother. "So, Mom, can we have the wedding here next week?"

Her mouth dropped open, stunned speechless for several seconds. "Next week? That's not enough time."

"It's only going to be family," he said.

"And Kristy," Shauna added.

"I supposed we could persuade Pastor Collins to officiate," Kathleen said. "And Jamie will be done with exams halfway through the week."

***

Jason pulled the car up behind the shipping container and turned it off. The street was quiet, no traffic. Kids were still in school.

Shauna placed her hand on his thigh and he covered it with his, gazing at her.

"Can we finish unloading today?"

"Yes, but I'll have to call Tony for the big stuff."

She slowly shook her head and smiled. "We can do it. I can levitate anything that's too heavy."

He waved his hand around. "People can't see you use your ability."

"I still don't understand why I can't openly use it in a town full of people with abilities."

He shrugged. "Not everyone has abilities now. Some newcomers don't even know it exists."

She wiggled her fingers. "I can pretend that I'm carrying things but levitate instead. Any spying neighbors would just think I'm really strong."

He chuckled. "All right, all right. We'll give it a try."

He picked up a box and propped it on his hip. Shauna used her power to lift a large box that would have required two men. They returned outside for more boxes. Jason stepped inside the storage unit and froze when he heard Vanessa's voice behind him. No! Vanessa was not going to hurt Shauna. He rushed onto the driveway and moved Shauna behind him.

"Vanessa, I told you to leave us alone."

"But, Jason, I know you need comforting today. You had such a lot thrown at you. It must be hard to suddenly lose your family."

He seethed. "How can you still think you have a chance with me, especially when you had no chance to begin with?" Shauna's hand touched his back, and her warmth flowed into him. "I still have my family and the woman I love. Give it up. Even if I'd come back home alone, I wouldn't have dated you, so go find someone else to harass."

Vanessa glared. "That medallion was starting to work, but then she probably messed it up."

He reached behind him and took Shauna's hand. "That's right. Shauna's love destroyed your spell."

Hands fisted at her sides, Vanessa snapped at them. "She doesn't deserve you. My mother's premonition showed that you'd marry someone descended from a founding family and have powerful children. That would be me. I can give you those children."

"Nice of your mother to recognize that Shauna is descended from a founding family. She happens to be a Williams." Maybe that revelation would be enough to make her see how hopeless it was for her.

"No!" Vanessa gasped and stepped back. "That's not possible. She's not from here." Vanessa was a beautiful woman, but her features, distorted with rage, had become ugly.

"But her grandmother was. Vanessa, just go home."

Her high pitched shriek hurt his ears. She raised her arms, and he stepped back and to the side, taking Shauna with him. Vanessa snapped her hands toward them, and jagged blue lightning streaked from her fingers, one grazing Jason's arm. Damn, that hurt. He couldn't take his eyes off Vanessa to see what damage she'd done. He wiggled his fingers. It couldn't be that bad.

A breeze passed him. He frowned, and whispered. "Shauna, did you just do something?"

"I put her in a bubble. She hurt you."

Vanessa glared. "If I can't have you, neither can she. Protect her all you want, but I'll still kill her after you're gone."

Jason didn't know how well Shauna's bubble would hold, but if Vanessa's lightning made it through, he would physically take her down and knock her out. There was no way he'd let Vanessa harm Shauna.

Again, Vanessa raised her arms and whipped her hands forward. Lightning flew from her fingers, hit the bubble and bounced off the inside walls. Her body stiffened and glowed.

Her fingers curled as her scream echoed throughout the street. Electricity popped. He squinted at the bright ball, not able to see inside. Then the lightning disappeared and all that remained was a pile of gray ash cradled in the bottom.

Shauna quivered behind him. He turned and enclosed her in his arms. "Jason, I didn't mean to do that."

He pulled her closer, rubbing his hands up and down her back. Her tears soaked through his shirt. He rested his cheek on her head. "You didn't. Vanessa did. That would have been us, except for your bubble." His sweet Shauna had protected them and now had to deal with causing a death. She hadn't intentionally killed Vanessa, but had saved lives, just as his mother had.

He jumped at a gravelly voice. "Hey, there. Good riddance!"

Jason's head snapped up, and he stared at Howard, a neighbor who had introduced himself a few days before. "You saw that?"

"Yep. She's deserved that for years. Hard to believe she did it to herself." He waved his hand at the remains. "You might want to undo whatever it is that's holding the ashes like that."

Shauna twisted in Jason's arms and put her back against him. The ashes fell to the ground.

"Wish I could have done something like that, for all those times she zapped my cat, made my wife drop groceries, tripped me. Who knows what else she's done. But me, all I can do is warm a cup of coffee."

"So, now what?" Shauna asked. "Should we call the police?"

The man shrugged. "We could just let the ashes blow away and be done with it. You did nothing wrong. Eventually, her mother will report her missing, and not even she will miss Vanessa. They hated each other."

Shauna squeezed Jason's arm. "I almost feel sorry for her. Didn't she have anyone?"

Howard shook his head. "Not that I ever noticed." He seemed to study Jason. "So, how about we walk away from this?" He nodded toward the pile of ash.

Jason raised his eyebrows at Shauna, and she shrugged. He turned to Howard. "Like you said, we did nothing wrong. Let's just try to forget it." He felt sorry for Vanessa. Her mother must have been feeding her those lines about him for years. If Vanessa could have ignored it, maybe she would have been lucky enough to find someone to love her like he'd found Shauna.

***

Shauna ran to the door when the doorbell rang, and threw it open. "Kristy!" She wrapped her friend in a tight hug. It felt more like years instead of a couple of months since she'd last seen her. So much had happened.

It was three days before the wedding. Kristy had insisted on renting a car and driving herself to Shauna's house. Her excuse being that she'd have to go back to the airport the night before the wedding to pick up her parents.

Shauna dragged her inside. Jason came up behind Shauna and wrapped an arm around her waist. He pointed a finger at Kristy. "I have words for you."

Shauna glanced over her shoulder at him. "Jason…"

"No. She needs to hear this."

"Ja—"

He clapped a hand over Shauna's mouth and glared at Kristy. "You jeopardized Shauna's life by breaking protocol making those phone calls to her."

Kristy bit her lip. "I know. If I could take it back, I would. It's just that, we were used to calling each other a couple times a week."

Jason's chest expanded at Shauna's back. "If you'd said something to Mark about it, we could have come up with a way for the two of you to talk."

Kristy crossed her arms. "I asked him. He just said it wasn't possible. So, I took things into my own hands. I'm sorry."

Jason still had his hand over her mouth, so Shauna licked his fingers. He chuckled and dropped his hand.

Shauna took Kristy's hand. "Well, I forgive you. I should have asked, but things were so stressed here, I didn't even think of it."

Kristy smirked and glanced at Jason. "Yeah, I can tell how stressed." Kristy picked up her bag. "So, where am I staying?"

"Follow me." Shauna climbed the stairs with Kristy behind her. "Jason insisted I put you in one of the rooms farthest from ours."

Jason's voice reached her from the bottom of the stairs. "Hey, you weren't supposed to tell her that."

The women laughed. "Jason, you have no idea what girls talk about," Kristy said.

"Now, you're scaring me," he grumbled.

Shauna stepped into the first room on the left and closed the door after Kristy entered. She sat on the bed and her friend joined her. "I have a weird question."

Kristy lifted her eyebrows. "Yeah?"

"Do you remember that day we walked home from the library and a man attacked me?"

Kristy grabbed her arm. "You remember? A couple weeks after it happened, your grandma called and said she'd hypnotized you into forgetting, and told me not to talk about it anymore."

Shauna bit her lip. "Even though I couldn't remember, it

was kind of messing with me."

Kristy tipped her head. "Is that why you never had sex, despite my trying so hard to get you to?"

Shauna shrugged. "Maybe. I don't know." She grinned. "But I can't say never anymore."

Kristy pushed Shauna's shoulder. "I knew he'd be the one after you had those crazy sex dreams about him."

"It took a while because he had his own sex hang-ups."

"What? A guy like that does not have sex hang-ups."

"He did. But it was only with me." She waved her hand. "And that's all I'm saying about it. Now, what's up with Mark?"

Kristy's shoulders slumped. "Oh, him. Nothing's up with him. Absolutely nothing. And I don't want to talk about it."

***

Shauna and Kristy spent two day dress shopping, and picked out flowers. They talked non-stop about everything that had happened since they were last together.

On the morning of the wedding, Shauna and Kristy had gone to the Ballard's house and taken over Jamie's room to prepare. Kristy pinned up Shauna's hair and curled the ends, artfully leaving a few ringlets to frame her face. They helped each other with their dresses. Shauna wore a knee length white dress, the wide straps resting on the edges of her shoulders. The lacey bodice was just low enough to nicely display the necklace Kathleen had given her, and the back plunged nearly to her waist. Kristy's dress was similar, but a pale yellow.

Classical music drifted up from the library, one of her father's favorites. No wedding march for her. Shauna clasped her hands. "It's time!"

Kristy hugged her. "You're a beautiful bride." She tipped back, with her hands on Shauna's shoulders. "Let's get this done, girl."

They snatched up their flowers and Kristy led the way to the top of the stairs. She paused, and Shauna pulled in a deep breath. Kristy trailed one hand on the banister and held her roses in the other, a darker yellow than her dress. Shauna followed, carrying her fragrant bouquet of white roses.

The groom and best man stood at the library door, Jason a couple of inches taller than Tony. Shauna smiled at Jason, handsome in a black suit. It was the first time she'd seen him in anything but casual clothing and his appearance took her breath away. She paused for a second to drink him in. He was hers. Who would have thought that a dream could lead to her finding the perfect man?

Her heart fluttered and swelled with love. He'd made love to her so tenderly that morning and reminded her that the next time would be after they wed. They'd make love later that night and then they were set to fly somewhere in the morning for a honeymoon. He wouldn't tell her where but had enjoyed helping her buy two swimsuits and summery clothes before Kristy arrived.

It took everything in her to not urge Kristy to walk faster. When they reached the doorway, Kristy wrapped her hand around Tony's elbow and they walked toward the fireplace, where Pastor Collins stood.

Shauna put her arm through Jason's, and he kissed her cheek, his love glowing in his eyes. His warmth filled her, and she couldn't resist kissing his jaw.

She scanned the room. Her new family was there, including Jamie, who she'd briefly met, and Kristy's parents, all with smiling faces. The furniture had been pushed back to make room for everyone. She saw a shimmer in the sunlight behind Jason's family and could feel her grandmother's presence.

She whispered to Jason, "Grandma's here." She gave his arm a squeeze.

He whispered back. "Hannah is, too." They finished the walk and stood in front of Pastor Collins.

They glazed at the Pastor, but once he started to speak, they turned toward each other. Jason took her hands in his and gave them a squeeze. Everyone around them faded into the background as they stared into each other's eyes and recited the age-old words that would bind their love together forever.

THE END

Next book in the series: **Rawlins 3: Jamie's Trials**

It's hard to keep a deadly secret when your life depends on revealing it…

Theron overhears two men discussing kidnapping his best friend, Jamie, the woman he's been in love with for over a year. He races to her home in Rawlins, to protect her.

Jamie's sexy dream, starring Theron, makes her realize he's more than her best friend. Then he shows up at her parents' door, ready to do anything to keep her safe. Despite their best efforts, Jamie is kidnapped.

Jamie's kidnaper wants her to use the special powers that she's vowed to never use. If she doesn't, he may kill the man she's imprisoned with, but if she helps the kidnapper reach his goals, others may die. Her only hope is that she can stay alive long enough for Theron to find her.

Books by Deborah Wallace

Rawlins Series (Paranormal romance)
Kathleen's Legacy
Jason's Forbidden Woman
Jamie's Trials
Adam's Redemption
Kristy's Puzzle
Tony's to Protect – *Fall 2022*

Wounded Warrior Hearts Series (Clean romance)
Wounded Warrior Hearts: Steven
Wounded Warrior Hearts: Amy
Wounded Warrior Hearts: Russ

Choice Series (Romantic suspense)
Second Choice
Third Choice
No Choice
Her Choice
Series complete

Unknown Series (Romantic suspense)
Father Unknown
Killer Unknown – *Summer 2022*

Other Books (Romantic suspense)
I Shot the Sheriff
New Memories
Your Love Belongs to Me
Summer Love

Check out my website for details on these books and where to find them. You can also sign up to receive emails when I have a new book. www.DeborahWallaceBooks.com.

If you can take the time, I'd love if you left a review of my book on your favorite Book sites. Thank you.

About Deborah Wallace

Someone suggested I try writing, and stories started populating my brain, begging to be put on paper (or my computer screen).

I have been called a Jane-of-all-trades, from seamstress to house and furniture designer/builder to computer programmer to technical writer and bookkeeper. I even do car maintenance. I've also guided a team of 'Future Problem Solvers'.

I grew up in Michigan, but Massachusetts has been my home for more years than I care to think about. I love the history here, the museums and antique houses, the seacoast and hiking trails.

My three children have grown and scattered, but my husband is by my side, encouraging my writing.

www.ingramcontent.com/pod-product-compliance
Lightning Source LLC
Chambersburg PA
CBHW022000170626
46808CB00001B/232

9781951457020